W9-BUC-331

In My Bedroom

Also by Donna Hill
in Large Print:

If I Could

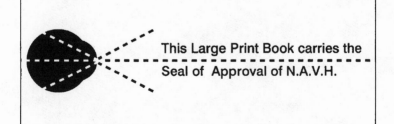

This Large Print Book carries the
Seal of Approval of N.A.V.H.

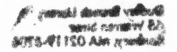

In My Bedroom

DONNA HILL

Thorndike Press • Waterville, Maine

Copyright © 2004 by Donna Hill.

Published in 2004 by arrangement with
St. Martin's Press, LLC.

Thorndike Press® Large Print African-American.

The tree indicium is a trademark of Thorndike Press.

The text of this Large Print edition is unabridged.
Other aspects of the book may vary from the original edition.

Set in 16 pt. Plantin by Ramona Watson.

Printed in the United States on permanent paper.

Library of Congress Cataloging-in-Publication Data

Hill, Donna (Donna O.)
    In my bedroom / Donna Hill.
      p. cm.
    ISBN 0-7862-6945-6 (lg. print : hc : alk. paper)
    1. Women motion picture producers and directors —
Fiction.   2. Adult child sexual abuse victims — Fiction.
3. African American women — Fiction.   4. Female
friendship — Fiction.   5. Savannah (Ga.) — Fiction.
6. Married women — Fiction.   7. Large type books.
I. Title.
PS3558.I386415 2004
813'.54—dc22   2004053018

This novel is dedicated to my mom,
Dorothy Hill,
for making me strong,
for always believing in me,
and making me believe in myself.

As the Founder/CEO of NAVH, the only national health agency solely devoted to those who, although not totally blind, have an eye disease which could lead to serious visual impairment, I am pleased to recognize Thorndike Press★ as one of the leading publishers in the large print field.

Founded in 1954 in San Francisco to prepare large print textbooks for partially seeing children, NAVH became the pioneer and standard setting agency in the preparation of large type.

Today, those publishers who meet our standards carry the prestigious "Seal of Approval" indicating high quality large print. We are delighted that Thorndike Press is one of the publishers whose titles meet these standards. We are also pleased to recognize the significant contribution Thorndike Press is making in this important and growing field.

Lorraine H. Marchi, L.H.D.
Founder/CEO
NAVH

★ Thorndike Press encompasses the following imprints: Thorndike, Wheeler, Walker and Large Print Press.

Acknowledgments

Many thanks go to Debra Uffer, psychotherapist, of Brooklyn, New York, and Michelle Paynter, psychologist, specializing in psychological trauma of women, Kansas City, Missouri, for their help and insight with everything from hospitalization procedures to treatment protocol. I deeply appreciate your time and your expertise.

Many thanks to Cecelia (cece) Falls for allowing me to share her beautiful and poignant words with the world.

Thank you to the incredible readers who through the years have shown their support of my work and have shared their reading experience with others.

Thanks to my editor, Monique Patterson, for getting excited about this book and believing in it. To my agent, Pattie Steele Perkins, for being the best agent a girl could want.

Most of all, my thanks to God for allowing me to do what I love, for giving me the gift of words and the power to use them.

7:11

not just numbers
not just
a date
a time
a place
a memory

not just the pleasant things —

not the heat from hot concrete
burning my bare feet
while i jumped from
foot to foot
balancing

not the sound of sirens
breaking through hot stillness
heard from blocks and blocks and blocks away

not the rush of neighbors
or the booming bass voices of paramedics
sent to rescue mommie
from the gift
of being a woman

not the baby
born on the stairs

while white men stared
and i
waited for the first cry

not today

no
today
i remember
the stench of alcohol

today
i still feel unwanted touch on my neck,
the falling of fabric from my shoulder
the tearing of skin
in dark places

today
i remember the sheets
and night heat
and floating

today i remember
closing
my eyes
and learning how
to be in 2 places at the same time
while he was inside   me

i was even further in

and out

i was out too
out a
and away
and there
too

today
i remember flying
and imagining
— no knowing
that THIS
is not what love feels like
and THIS
is not what reconciliation
looks like
that THIS
is not what it IS

today i remember
the birth
of new shame
and secret keeping
and the hard part about telling the truth

i remember without being taught
that THIS is something
no one wants to hear
and so they don't

and so they didn't hear me
and they stopped seeing me
and I stopped seeing myself

and maybe it was me
who let my dreams die
inside while i was flying
floating, escaping being there

today i am remembering
today 23 years ago
and i am not remembering
summertime
or laps in sparkling blue, chlorinated cool,
    water
no
today
i am remembering death
and resurrection
and i am flying

i am in two places
i am there
i am here
and i am remembering

cece falls ©8/2002

Prologue

The screening room was dark. Empty save for Rayne Holland, who sat alone among the fifty-plus red velvet seats. The only illumination came from the sliver of light emanating from the projection booth above her head. By degrees the wide screen filled with the stark black-and-white images of the documentary she'd worked for nearly two years to bring to life.

Back When We Were Free, her fourth such effort, was based on case studies of incest survivors. The film recently garnered her an Independent Film Critics Award, the Black Filmmakers Award, and a Sundance Award. There was Oscar buzz in the air, but Rayne didn't hold out much hope for that, not with the wealth of powerful documentaries coming from foreign countries this year.

The pain-filled voices and haunted eyes of the women emerged one by one, their graphic accounts played out for all those who dared to listen. It was both horrific and emancipating to hear their tales of physical and emotional recovery from society's dirtiest secret.

How many times had she listened to these women, watched their expressions as she recorded their terror, and captured on film their sense of ultimate violation that had dominated most of their lives?

A thin sheen of perspiration began to coat her body, beginning at her belly, rising upward to her face then down between her thighs. Her heart suddenly raced as an unknown sense of dread crawled along her flesh, raising the fine hair on her honey brown arms. A strong male hand clasped her shoulder.

I won't scream. I'll be good.

"Great piece of work, Rayne," Kevin Simms, one of the directors, whispered in her ear.

Her body shuddered. The sudden touch of a thick masculine hand sent a chill through her, ripples of a nameless fear that was all too familiar.

"You okay? You're shaking like a leaf." His hand slid down her clammy arm.

The images began to merge, disappear into the background. Rayne blinked, tried to clear her vision, and turned toward the direction of the voice. She tugged in a shallow breath and forced herself to smile — laughing lightly.

"Sorry, Kevin. You scared the hell outta me." She adjusted her white blouse and buttoned the top button, keeping her hands close to her throat. "I . . . thought I was alone."

Kevin chuckled. "Figured only little kids were afraid of the dark."

Things happen in the dark. Rayne's insides constricted as the eerie words she had not spoken came alive in her mind, shouting at her, clawing at her body. She sprang up from her seat, dropping the stack of papers onto the carpeted floor. It was all reflex.

"Here, let me help."

Panic rose. "I'm fine! Forget it. It was my fault." She could hardly breathe.

Kevin reached down and when his hand brushed against hers, she screamed and ran toward the door.

"Rayne! Rayne. What the hell is wrong with you?" Kevin bellowed, his voice bouncing off the emptiness, becoming one with the dark.

Rayne pushed through the swinging doors and out into the sudden blinding light of the corridor. Bumping and pushing past her coworkers, she sprinted toward the exit, not hearing the startled comments or seeing the quizzical expressions.

Things happen in the dark, was all she could hear coming from somewhere deep inside of her.

Sunlight pierced through the gloom that had enveloped her as she gulped in the outdoor air and headed for the parking lot. By rote she located her vintage 1965 red Mustang convertible, gunned the engine, and raced all the way home.

"Mommy . . . Mommy."

A tiny hand shook Rayne's shoulder. She gazed into the brandy-toned eyes of her five-year-old daughter, Desiree. A calm settled over her. She looked around and realized that she was sitting in her kitchen. *When had she come into the kitchen?*

"Mommy, aren't you going to take me to school?"

"School?" Rayne asked, confusion muddying her thoughts.

"It's Monday. You always take me to school on Monday."

Monday? How could that be? The last thing she remembered . . . was . . . getting into her car and driving home from work. That was . . . two days ago?

She blinked, then hugged her daughter as much for assurance as to show her love.

Where had the two days gone? Fear gripped her. She searched her mind, tried to replay all the images and she couldn't remember. Couldn't remember.

"Mommy, you're squeezing me."

Rayne kissed her forehead and slowly relinquished her hold. "Sorry, sweetie. Mommy just needed some extra loving this morning."

Desiree grinned. "You're funny, Mommy."

"Desi, you're going to be late for school."

Rayne and Desiree turned toward the kitchen entryway. Paul Holland's usually warm and inviting brown eyes and ready smile were absent this morning, replaced by hovering shadows beneath his lids like smeared mascara, and tight lines bracketing his mouth, giving his dark features an almost menacing look. He appeared tired and worn to Rayne and she wondered why.

Desiree dashed into the sturdy arms of her father who scooped her up and balanced her sixty pounds on his hip. He kissed the top of her head, then put her down. "Go on and get your things, pumpkin. I'll take you to school this morning."

"But today is Monday," she protested. "Mommy takes me on Monday."

"What did I say, Desi? Mommy . . . isn't

feeling well. I'll take you to school."

Desiree's wide eyes darted between her mother and father before she marched off to her room.

Paul Holland came fully into the kitchen. His imposing form, chiseled by his regular workout regime, seemed to suck the air out of the room, Rayne thought.

He went to the counter and poured a mug of coffee from the pot, then turned to his wife. "This can't go on, Rayne," he said quietly.

For a man of his size, Paul Holland was a soft-spoken man who possessed a gentleness that belied his physical attributes. Most people who met him were immediately intimidated until they actually got to know him. It was the gentleness of his voice that had drawn Rayne to him. There was a soothing, almost mesmerizing quality to his tone. It could almost make her believe that it was safe in the dark.

"I don't know how much of this you think I'm supposed to take. How much any man is supposed to take. I want us to have a real marriage where I don't feel as if I'm either making love to a corpse or raping some tearful virgin."

Rayne flinched.

"I have needs, Rayne. Needs that should

18

be filled by my wife." He pulled out a chair and took a seat opposite her at the table. "Don't you love me anymore?"

The question was asked with such heart-breaking sincerity, that Rayne felt the sting of it fill her eyes. "Of course I love you. Why would you ask me something like that?"

"Why? You can sit there and ask me why? Where have you been for the past two years? It certainly hasn't been in this marriage. Every time I try to touch you, you practically crawl inside yourself. How do you think that makes me feel? This weekend was the last straw. You actually fought me like I was some stranger on the street."

This weekend? Fought him? Oh, God, I don't remember. I don't remember.

"Aren't you going to say anything?"

"I . . . I'm sorry, Paul. I'll do better. I promise. It's just . . ." She didn't know what it was.

Paul stood and looked down into her imploring eyes and tried to remember all the reasons why he fell in love with her, why he stayed in this frigid union.

"I can't keep this up, Rayne," he said, a sadness in his voice so heavy the words barely rose from his throat. "It's got to change."

Rayne clutched his hand. "It will. I promise. I love you, Paul. I don't want to lose you. I'll do better."

Paul stared at her for a long moment, then turned and left the room.

"Hey, Kevin," Rayne greeted, entering the editing room.

Kevin looked up, grunted something unintelligible and moved past her, careful not to get too close.

"Kevin?"

He spun toward her, pointing a finger in her direction. "Look, I don't know what your game is, but we've been friends a long time and I have no intention of ruining my career and my reputation on some trumped-up sexual harassment suit. I'd just as soon not be alone with you — if you don't mind." He walked out, slamming the door behind him.

Rayne stared at the closed door and tried to piece together what Kevin was saying. What had happened between the two of them? Why couldn't she remember? She sat down heavily on the cushioned stool at the console and covered her face with her hands. What was happening to her? Her head snapped up at the sound of someone opening the door.

"Rayne, there you are. I was wondering if you were coming in today," Cynthia Dixon, one of the executive producers, said. She eased alongside of Rayne and sat down. "Kevin mentioned you weren't feeling well on Friday and left early. You okay?"

"Yeah . . . I'm fine. Thanks. Just . . . felt a little queasy."

"Hmm, another member of the family on the way?" she teased.

Rayne laughed. "No, I don't think so. Desiree is already a handful. I don't know if I could keep up with two little ones, a husband, and a career."

"Well, Ms. Lady, with three major awards under your belt, I'd say the career part is well on its way. It's only up from here. Everyone in this business respects your work, your dedication to the craft."

"I think I do okay."

Cynthia dropped her arm around Rayne's shoulder. "Wait until the awards dinner Friday night and you'll see how much you're loved."

Rayne drove through the streets of Savannah, Georgia, inhaling the fresh scent of spring, the pungent aroma of glistening green grass and fragrant blooms. It was a beautiful city, filled with history and old-world charm. It had inspired her first professional film effort seven years earlier, shortly before her marriage to Paul.

Paul had entered her life as unexpectedly as a sudden summer shower. Truthfully, at the time she thought that the real attraction was between Paul and her best friend, Gayle. They'd been friends first, having met at a banking conference. And although Gayle had been engaged to James Davis for more than a year, she'd always complained that the relationship was moving along at about the speed of a slow drip. But when she returned from that business trip, all she could talk about was this great guy she'd met named Paul Holland.

Guilt and a sense of betrayal often plagued Rayne during the early days of Paul's courting of her. Gayle insisted that she was being silly, of course there was nothing between her and Paul. They were just friends. She had James. Gayle seemed to work extra hard to get Rayne to let Paul into her life, from arranging dinner parties to giving them "extra" theater tickets. So Rayne went along and married Paul. It seemed right. It felt as if it should be right as well.

She made the turn onto Dupont Lane

and pulled to a stop in front of Gayle's home. Gayle had the perfect dress, she'd said, and insisted that Rayne would look like royalty in it at the awards dinner.

As always Gayle's home was immaculate, everything in its place. And Gayle looked as radiant and as well put together as if she'd just stepped off a magazine cover. A part of Rayne envied that ability in Gayle, her aptitude to put herself out there on display, to have heads turn in her direction and not feel vulnerable and naked where Rayne would rather remain invisible. Perhaps that was why she'd chosen filmmaking as her profession. It allowed her to see the world, but not have to play a role in its turning.

"Where's my darling goddaughter?" Rayne asked after plopping down on Gayle's imported Italian leather couch. The maroon leather furnishing and spit polished maple accessories stood in sharp contrast to the white carpeting and stark white walls.

"Her dad took her to the park. Some kind of puppet show."

"Oh, I wish I would have known. I would have brought Desi."

"Maybe next time. But this gives us big girls a chance to chat. Plus I'm dying to see you in the dress. You're going to love it."

"I'm really not looking forward to Friday," Rayne muttered, all enthusiasm gone.

"Why in the world not? It's your night. You worked for it."

"You know I don't go in for all this high glamour, smiling and grinning. I'd rather just do my work and go home."

Gayle shook her head. "Well, it's time for you to come out from behind the camera and get your due."

"I'll just be glad when it's over."

"How's Paul these days? He must be excited for you even if you're not."

Rayne looked away, staring sightlessly out of the bay window. "Fine."

"Really? It doesn't sound fine by your tone. Is . . . everything okay between you two?"

Rayne glanced at her friend. How could she explain what she was uncertain of, talk about what happened in her bedroom? How could she reveal such an intimate part of her marriage to anyone? Gayle would never understand.

Rayne blew out a breath and smiled. "Things are better than good. Paul is the best. He's been so patient with me while I worked on this last project. Any other man may have walked out with all the time I spent at the studio and in the field. I think he may have felt left out, but he never said a word. I have every intention of making it up to him." She smiled brightly.

"Maybe you should plan on getting away, just the two of you. Desi could stay with us. I know she would love it, and so would we."

"You know, I think you're right. We haven't been away since our honeymoon."

"Then do it, girl." She grinned. "I have friends in the travel business. I know I can get you a great deal."

"Sure. Sounds fine. I know I have some time coming to me. I'll check with Paul."

"Consider it done on my end. Just give me some dates. Now . . . let's go check out 'the dress.' " She took Rayne by the hand and pulled her upstairs.

"You look pretty, Mommy," Desiree said, looking at her mother put the finishing touches on her hair.

Rayne turned on the dressing table stool and clasped her daughter around the waist. "So do you, sugah. Just like a princess."

"You're the queen and Daddy is the king."

"That's right. Now we're going to get ready to leave as soon as Daddy brings the car around. And you promised to be a big girl for me tonight."

"Yes." Desiree nodded vigorously.

"Okay, run and get your shoes."

Alone again in the room, Rayne pulled open the dressing table drawer and took out the note she'd found earlier in Paul's suit pocket. She folded it in half and pushed it into her purse. She inhaled a deep breath. Tonight was her night. She'd talk to Paul about the letter when the evening was over.

"Rayne! Desi! Let's go, ladies. The car is out front," Paul called out from the bottom of the stairs.

Rayne took one last look at her reflection. "Coming," she replied.

The next thing Rayne remembered was the blinding glare of oncoming headlights and the piglike squeal of tires. It was a clear night, a vast horizon of stars gently tossed across a velvet black sky. Who was driving? Maybe she was, or him. It happened so fast. Headlights coming at them with almost unlawful speed, circles of white light on the windshield, someone

26

fighting with the steering wheel. The brakes cried out in an almost human voice, and then the car lurched to the right and spun around in a complete revolution. A crashing sound on the passenger's side was followed by something massive striking them head-on, and the entire vehicle raised up, lifted by an invisible hand and thrown against a rail, sending off a spray of sparks. Horrifying, bloodcurdling screams rang in her ears.

Then strong hands lifted her up out of the crumbled steel and shattered glass. *Blood everywhere.* She tried to speak but the words were trapped in her throat. A face leaned over her as she clutched desperately at a white sleeve. *Was everybody all right? My baby! Paul!* Her lips formed the words, the broken sentences gurgled in her bloody mouth. *No one could hear her.* An oxygen mask was placed over her face, just as she went limp on the gurney. And then nothing . . .

One

June. A Savannah June. Hot. Lush. Rich. Damp, like a satisfied woman. Even in this place of unreality where the trio held court, that fact could not be denied.

It was an odd assemblage they made, yet commonplace, at least here at Cedar Grove, where fractured minds were prodded and patched. One walked tall, cloaked in a posture of importance, willowy flame-red hair brushing swaying shoulders. The other, a birch brown and catlike in grace, appeared cover-girl stylish, pushing the third, silent bronze-toned beauty in a wheelchair. Yet the trio appeared to move almost seamlessly across the lush green grounds of the Savannah, Georgia, facility — embraced by rose bushes, towering magnolia trees, and jasmine vines — wrapped up, it seemed, in the tranquillity of their surroundings. In truth, that was a lie.

A closer look revealed two pairs of eyes, one brown set, one green, both intent and serious, their dual voices barely carried by the feeble breath of the afternoon breeze. It was the third who was their concern, the focus of their hushed conversation. From time to time, they ceased speaking to look mournfully upon Rayne Holland as she sat motionless in the chair, her gaze fixed and unseeing. So they believed.

I know why I'm here, Rayne thought, listening to her doctor and her best friend discuss her "illness" as if she were invisible. *They think I'm crazy because I cut my wrists, because I won't talk. I don't talk because they can't hear me. They won't hear me, they never have. I'm just tired, that's all. Tired of all the talk, the emptiness, the betrayals by people who claim to love you. That doesn't make me crazy, just fed up*, she concluded, beginning to unfasten the buttons of her pale peach cotton blouse, the tiny white buttons taunting her nut brown fingers with slippery elusiveness. She knew Dr. Dennis would stop her, because for some reason she couldn't stop herself.

"We've discussed this, Rayne," Pauline Dennis said, speaking with a calmness that chilled Rayne, stilling her shaky fingers. "Button your blouse, Rayne."

Rayne released a long, deep sigh, heavy

enough to drop to the ground, hitting it like a rubber ball and bouncing back into her chest, until next time. She did what she was told, as she'd always done.

Periodically, as the trio meandered down the paved pathways that ran the circumference of Cedar Grove Medical Center, Gayle Davis, Rayne's lifelong friend, would stroke Rayne's mane of black, crinkly hair with a slender brown hand, almost as you would a pet or a small child who'd wandered into your space in the midst of an adult conversation. Absently.

Rayne hated when Gayle did that. Hated it. It infuriated her so much that she'd almost shouted the words: *Stop it, dammit! I'm not that stinking cat of yours, or your neglected daughter.* But she didn't. She'd never been able to express her feelings, the emotions that swirled within her. So instead, she screamed the words — in her head — where they bounced around, echoing over and over: *Stop, stop, stop* . . .

Inside her head was as far as she could go these days — most days, actually. Lately, though, she'd wanted to crawl out, back into the world again. But thought better of it. It was safer just where she was. She gathered her hair in her hands and dragged it in front of her makeupless face, effectively escaping.

"Why does she do that?" Gayle whispered harshly, moving to brush the hair out of Rayne's face.

Dr. Dennis stopped her. "Fix your hair, Rayne," she instructed in a cool monotone.

Rayne emitted another baleful sigh and did as she was told.

"These are all manifestations of Rayne's trauma, Mrs. Davis, her unspoken need to hide, to disappear, get away from whatever is haunting her. They'll slowly stop when we get to the core of her problem."

Gayle shuddered despite the warmth. "What *is* her problem? It's been two months, Dr. Dennis," she complained, her voice taking on that clipped tone that often grated on Rayne's nerves. Rayne never told her about that, either. "I don't see any improvement." She adjusted her fitted gray linen jacket over her round hips. "Paul and Desi have been gone for almost six months. She was coming to terms with it. And then . . . this. You came highly recommended — as the best." Gayle's voice hitched a notch as if she no longer believed in the laundry list of recommendations attached to Dr. Pauline Dennis's name, Rayne mused, as Gayle patted her head again and continued to push the chair.

Stop, stop, stop . . .

Pauline nodded in doctorlike agreement. "I appreciate your concerns, Mrs. Davis. But you must understand that recovery from a mental breakdown is not like a broken limb where the doctors can give you a timetable for healing. At this point, I'm not quite sure what triggered Rayne's break. She won't talk. I do believe, however, that Rayne's problem dates prior to the deaths of her husband and daughter. Something that was never dealt with. The car accident was only a trigger for her suicide attempt at her father's house."

Gayle stopped short, jerking the chair to a halt. "I've known Rayne almost all my life, Doctor. If there had been some . . . some underlying problem, something wrong, I would have known. She's always been well adjusted, hardworking. Everyone loves Rayne. You've got to do something to help her. We're closer than most sisters."

We were until I found out you were sleeping with my husband, Rayne reflected absently. *But it doesn't matter much now — since Paul's dead.* She blinked and her thoughts snapped to other things, their voices fading into the scenery.

What was worse than being patted on the

32

head? Rayne wondered. *Oh, yes — being spoken about as if you weren't there,* she thought, and heard her laughter as the realization chimed in her head. *They think I don't hear, I don't feel, don't think. It's not true. It isn't. I write it all down in my journal, every night when everyone is asleep and the nurses are busy skulking in the corners with the doctors . . . whispering, always whispering. Giggles . . . sometimes.*

The soothing tones of Dr. Dennis drifted to her, scattering her disjointed thoughts. "Unfortunately, in cases like these we usually discover that the patient, over time, has developed the ability to function quite normally in society, developing a barrier against the world to hinder discovery of what is truly going on with them or often to protect themselves emotionally from further harm." *Much as I have done,* Dr. Dennis thought as she gazed across the landscape of the mentally ill.

"I just don't understand it. If something had been going on in Rayne's life, some secret or whatever, she would have told me. I know she would." She breathed heavily. "Has her father been here to see her?" Gayle asked as they rounded another curve.

Rayne sighed again.

Pauline stuck her hands into the pockets of her starched white smock, so stiff it barely moved. "No. He's called several times to check on her progress."

They came to the end of the path, the wrought-iron gates, like swirling black storm clouds, the cutoff point for insanity.

Gayle turned to Pauline, the honey brown of her eyes shimmering in the sunlight. "Please, Dr. Dennis, whatever you need to do to make Rayne better, just do it. You don't know the Rayne that I know, that the world was beginning to know. She's a wonderful, caring person with a brilliant filmmaking career ahead of her." Her voice faltered momentarily with emotion, like the sound of a stereo losing an instant of power.

Emotion, real or imagined — Rayne couldn't tell.

"Please help her," Gayle pleaded.

Pauline, reading her assurance cue from the watery look in Gayle's eyes, placed a gentle hand on her shoulder. "We're going to do everything we can for Rayne, believe me. Time and patience are the great healers," she said, the line memorized from more than a decade of practiced repetition. "Give Rayne that," she added, the solemnity of her tone calming the jangles in Gayle's stomach.

Rayne almost believed the words. *Time* and *patience*. Almost.

Gayle blew out a breath, her bangs responding with a slight flutter. "I suppose none of us have a choice," she said. She came around to the front of the chair and bent down, placing her newly manicured hands on each side of Rayne's face.

"Rayne, honey, it's me, Gayle. Just say something, Rayne. Let me know you hear me."

You hurt me, Gayle, she screamed in her head. *You were supposed to be my friend. I trusted you with my secrets, my fears. And you used them to screw my husband! You bitch. Did you hear that?*

"We all love you, Rayne, and want you to get better. Your goddaughter, Tracy, misses you terribly."

I had a daughter once, Rayne recalled. *Her name was Desiree. My baby.* She *loved me. But she's gone, too.*

As Gayle leaned forward to kiss Rayne's cheek, she frantically raked her fingers through her hair from the nape of her neck, bringing the thick bush forward to shut out Gayle's face. But not before that instant of clarity beamed in her eyes. That instant of pure hatred and pain that reached down with cold fingers deep into

Gayle's soul and squeezed, sending shockwaves of ice coursing through her veins. Gayle shuddered, rocking back on her haunches. A feeling of physical violation permeated her.

On shaky limbs she stood, forcing a smile.

"Fix your hair, Rayne," Pauline instructed.

Rayne did as she was told.

"Uh, I'll be back . . . next week," Gayle muttered. "If you need anything, you have my number."

Pauline studied her for a moment. "Are you all right?"

"Yes, fine." She wanted to run. "I've got to go." She turned and hurried down the last few yards toward escape.

Pauline gripped the handles of the chair, turned it around, and headed back toward the facility. "Gayle's a good friend, Rayne," she said in that cool voice. "She loves you a great deal. And she's very worried about you."

Rayne sighed heavily.

Pauline learned from the weeks of working with Rayne that her sighs were an indication that she was tuning out a comment or situation. It was the only outward sign that she understood, or had any feelings about what was going on around her. At least it was a start. Although this case was difficult, Pauline was intrigued by Rayne Holland, intrigued in a way she was not with her other patients. She knew Rayne heard and understood, was aware of the world. Why wouldn't she speak? What had so traumatized her that she'd rather be silent, shrink into a tiny dark corner of her mind to hide? From what? Who? There was something about Rayne, a familiarity of spirit that drew Pauline to her, a part of her that understood the torment and fear. It was as if they were joined in some intangible way. Pauline shrugged off her moment of frustration and continued down the path, even as her resolve to uncover what lay beneath Rayne's veil of self-protection grew.

By degrees the natural light, the sounds of nature, the scent of flora and sweet rich earth began to diminish to a trickle, like a hose almost shut off but not quite. If Rayne squeezed her eyes shut and thought really hard, she could hold on to her piece of serenity for a few moments more. A few moments before the baby blue walls and the rustling of white stockings brushing against thick thighs, the metallic clang of medicine carts and food trays, the irritating sounds of Muzak pumped in from some unseen source and the cloying scent of disinfectant — a few moments before they overwhelmed her with the weight of their existence.

The moment was gone.

"I'll see you tomorrow, Rayne, for our regular session," Pauline said, pushing the chair back into Rayne's private room. Her haven.

Her room was located on the sixth floor of the *facility* — as it was called — a corner room that overlooked the garden below. Spacious, and painted in a soft peach — her favorite color — the perimeters at the top and bottom of the smooth walls were covered in a riotous fabric of bursting flowers that matched the short curtains, camouflaging the protective mesh that pressed erotically against the window.

In the morning, when the sun first rose above the trees, the light filtered through the mesh, casting shadows of boxes and diamonds across the walls. Sometimes Rayne would imagine that they were small, secret passageways. Passageways to freedom.

An oversized chintz chair, hugged by several throw pillows, sat on the gleaming wood floor. There was nothing in the room that was personal. No photos or mementos from her life. It was almost as if Rayne Holland's existence began when she entered Cedar Grove. But of course that was not true. She had a life, or at least she thought she did, until it came apart.

Rayne moved languorously across the room toward the window where a row of potted plants sat on the sill. Picking up the water jug, she meticulously watered each one.

Pauline watched, her hands hidden in the deep patch pockets of her smock. Sighing, she turned and quietly closed the door behind her.

Rayne heard the click of the metal against metal. She lowered her head.

I know you're trying to help, Dr. Dennis, she thought, looking up to stare out across the sea of green below. *I want you to help. I want to feel again, rise above the dark clouds that push me down, smothering me in nothingness. I'm tired of being tired.*

Two

The drive back to the center of Savannah took less than twenty minutes. To Gayle it felt like forever. Each visit to Rayne depleted her in ways she could never explain or understand.

Some days it took all she had to walk through those gates, face her friend, and see her . . . that way. *Oh, God.* Her throat burned and tightened, her eyes filled as she drew closer to her home.

They'd been so close once, sharing everything, Gayle reminisced, a sad smile shadowing her coral-tinted lips. They'd met in fifth grade in Ms. Hubert's English class. They were both ten years old. Gayle hated English. Rayne was the brightest one in the class. Outside of class she was so quiet, hardly said a word to anyone. But there was something about Rayne that drew Gayle. Everyone said Rayne Mercer was weird, at least when she was younger. Gayle didn't think so. She just needed a friend.

One day at lunch in the school cafeteria, Gayle spotted Rayne sitting alone. As usual, the cafeteria was in a state of bedlam with the student body of three hundred making good use of their free time. The cacophony of raised voices, banging, slamming utensils and trays competed for superiority. Yet Rayne seemed oblivious to it all as she nibbled on her peanut butter and jelly sandwich and sipped her milk right from the carton, peering sporadically over its red-and-white top to the sea of faces that swirled around her. She reminded Gayle of someone sitting back watching a movie, there but not really a part of it all, just an observer.

Gayle took her tray, loaded it with meat loaf and mashed potatoes, and boldly marched over to Rayne's table.

"Hi. My name is Gayle."

Rayne slowly looked up, her wide brown eyes staring, her bushy black hair fanning about her head like a halo. "Hi," she finally mumbled over a mouth full of her sandwich.

Gayle took an empty seat opposite Rayne. "You wanna be friends?"

Rayne shrugged. "Guess so."

And they'd been inseparable ever since. Gayle thought she'd simply die when

Rayne's father suddenly sent her to live with her Aunt Mae in Stone Mountain, Georgia. Rayne's mother Carol had been dead for ten years when Edith became the second Mrs. Mercer. Gayle always believed, until this day, that it was Edith who was behind Rayne's banishment. She was sure that Edith was jealous of Rayne and her father's closeness. Maybe she was, too, at times. Not so much about that, but the fact that as they grew older Rayne was the one the boys always looked at first, tried to talk to. It was Rayne's aloofness that seemed to attract them, like dust bunnies under the couch. The aloofness and the sultry, erotic beauty. Gayle struggled to look average, fought daily battles with her weight. Rayne never seemed to gain a pound. Makeup and designer clothes were the furthest things from her mind. Rayne Mercer had it all. Gayle could only hope some of it would rub off on her. Still, she could never forgive him for sending Rayne away, no matter what Edith may have wanted.

When Rayne's aunt became ill and could no longer care for her, Rayne returned to Savannah just in time to celebrate her seventeenth birthday and their last year of high school.

"It's so great to have you back, Rayne,"

Gayle enthused as they'd sat together downing cans of Coke and bags of chips on Gayle's canopy bed. "It hasn't been the same around here without you. You know how bitchy some of these girls are around here. They all think you're trying to steal their man or something."

Rayne pushed her hair away from the sides of her face. "You still seeing Rick?"

Gayle shrugged. "Yeah, off and on. He can be such a pain in the ass sometimes. All he ever thinks about is football."

They both laughed. But Gayle wondered just how long it would be before Rick and every other boy in Savannah was drawn to Rayne. She didn't want to think about that. Rayne was her friend.

"So." Gayle stretched out across the bed. "How does it feel being back home? How's the wicked witch treating you?"

Rayne appeared to stiffen, her gaze veered off across the room, but not before her eyes sparked with something that momentarily chilled Gayle. Rayne's smile fluttered, like blades of grass against the wind. "Fine," she mumbled into the can of soda.

Gayle frowned. "What's wrong? Aren't they glad to have you home?"

"Sure. I guess . . . it's just different, that's all, after being away for so long. I have to get . . . adjusted . . . to being back. Anyway, I don't want to talk about that. Catch me up on what's been going on."

Gayle looked at her friend's averted face for a long moment, trying to pinpoint the unsettled feeling that bubbled in her stomach. She couldn't, at least not then. As the days turned into weeks, rolling into the holiday season, Gayle and Rayne rekindled the embers of their friendship. That fractured moment in Gayle's bedroom was forgotten.

Why had she remembered that particular day? Gayle wondered, pulling the Lincoln Town Car into her winding driveway. She turned off the ignition and her heart slammed against her chest as recognition flooded her. The look that had darkened Rayne's eyes that day in her bedroom so many years ago was the same look she'd seen earlier at the facility. A look of pure unadulterated hatred that almost possessed a life of its own in its raw power.

Gayle wrapped her arms around herself to ward off the chill that rippled in waves up and down her body. What had she done, then and now, to evoke that kind of response from Rayne?

She may never know, she thought, shutting off the car's engine. Perhaps she should have mentioned to the doctor the truth about Rayne, the little things she'd noticed over the years: the days of silence, her irrational fear of the dark, being touched, and . . . sometimes it was almost as if the Rayne she thought she knew . . . was someone else entirely. But that was silly, a long time ago, she reasoned. When Rayne locked herself away in that silent world, it felt as if a part of her had shut down as well, and there was nothing she could do to help. Simply watch and wait for it to pass, like now. Rayne's illness was spilling over into her own private life, her life with her husband, James, and their daughter, Tracy. As much as she loved Rayne and wanted her well, she knew she couldn't continue to let what was happening with Rayne stain her own life as well. But what else could she do? Rayne was her friend.

Gathering her purse from the cream-colored leather passenger seat, Gayle entered the house from the kitchen.

Pristine as always, the Davises' black-and-white kitchen, as well as the rest of the two-story, four-bedroom home, was photographically perfect. Every utensil, towel, item of clothing, piece of furniture was in its place. To the casual observer it would appear that all was right with Gayle Davis's world.

Gayle checked the rectangular clock that hung on the eggshell-white wall above the refrigerator. The house was quiet. James and Tracy must still be out, she concluded. He'd promised to take their six-year-old daughter to the movies and to pick up a new pair of sneakers.

Visions of her daughter made her smile. Tracy was her joy and she couldn't begin to imagine what life would be like without her daughter in it — a fact that made her ache all the more for Rayne. To lose your child and your husband was more than anyone should have to withstand.

Gayle walked upstairs to her bedroom, stepped out of her dove-gray pumps, putting them, by rote, into the clear plastic shoe bag that hung on the inside of the cedar walk-in closet.

Just as she slipped out of her suit and hung it on the padded hanger, she heard the front door open, then close, followed by the sound of muffled voices.

Her heartbeat accelerated just a bit, and she drew a shaky breath to ease the sudden flutter in her belly.

"Gayle!"

Her pulse quickened. "Up here."

Footsteps on the staircase thumped like

tribal drums in her ears. She turned toward the open door, putting on her best smile.

"Hi," she murmured as James entered the room, his broad shoulders and six-foot-plus height taking up much of the doorway. There was a time when the sight of James Davis made her heart race with joyous anticipation. Now, it only thundered with apprehension. Where had things gone so wrong?

James tossed his jacket across the pearly white bedspread. Gayle cringed, but held her tongue.

"How was your visit with Rayne?" He sat on the side of the bed and pulled off his Nike sneakers.

"Same as usual." Then the image of Rayne's final look at her jumped in front of her eyes like someone leaping out of the closet to startle you. She felt her body vibrate before blinking the vision away. She swallowed. "I talked. She was silent."

James looked over his shoulder at his wife, seeing the dejection cloud her face. He blew out a short breath of frustration. "I don't know why you keep putting yourself through this, Gayle, week after week." He tossed his sneakers into the corner. "You know how upset you get and she doesn't even know you're there. And look what it's doing to Tracy and me."

"She's my friend, James. I don't expect Tracy to understand but I'd think you would." She slammed the closet door shut.

James snapped his head in her direction. "Seems I don't understand a lot of things, Gayle. Maybe if you were as concerned with what's happening in your own home as you are in trying to put your friend back together, we'd have a marriage instead of an arrangement."

He sprang up from the bed and stormed out. Seconds later, Gayle jumped at the sound of the door to the den slamming shut. She knew he'd be in there for hours, sealed away, shutting her out, just like Rayne. But what scared her most was that sometimes she found a macabre relief in his isolation. It kept them from facing whatever it was that was wrong with themselves.

Gayle squeezed her eyes closed, maybe hoping for a miracle to turn the clock back to when their world was good. When she opened them, Tracy was standing in front of her.

"What's wrong, Mommy?" Tracy's round, dark eyes, so much like her father's, stared intently at her.

48

Gayle forced a smile and walked toward her daughter. "Nothing, sweetie. Mommy's just a little tired, that's all." She knelt down in front of her and kissed the tip of her caramel-toned nose. "Did Daddy get your new sneakers?" She tucked two wayward braids behind Tracy's pierced ears and noticed that one of the pair of tiny pearls was missing. *Third pair,* Gayle mused.

Tracy grinned, exposing a gap in her top row of teeth. "Yep. Daddy got my sneakers. Just what I wanted. Wanna see?"

"Sure."

Tracy darted off down the wide carpeted hallway toward her bedroom while Gayle pulled on a pair of sweatpants and a T-shirt. Was James right? Was she sacrificing her family, her stability, for Rayne? She looked at her reflection in the mirror. No. The truth was that what was wrong between her and James started long before Rayne became ill. Whether the trouble in her marriage was real or manufactured, Gayle was no longer sure. What she was certain of was that she wanted more. Her home, her career, her husband and daughter weren't enough, they didn't fill that empty space inside of her. She had ambition, dreams that reached beyond hearth and home. James knew that when he married her. So why, then, couldn't he understand when she told him she wanted more than this? "If you truly loved me, you would support me," she'd told him. She'd come to believe that James's complaints, his demands on her time were simply smothering and controlling, not coming from any true need of his. Rayne understood. She understood Gayle's drive, her desire to carve a place for herself in the world. She listened, when James wouldn't.

So what else could she do when Rayne became ill? She couldn't abandon her friend, she concluded, sliding her feet into her slippers. Rayne had no one. Unless you really wanted to count her father, William Mercer, and her stepmother, Edith — neither of whom had been to see her since she'd been at Cedar Grove. If *she* had her way, they'd never see Rayne. Rayne had no love for either one of them.

Funny, though, one would think that Rayne's breakdown would have occurred right after the accident that killed Paul and Desiree. But it didn't. She tried to kill herself nearly six months later in her father's house. And no one knew why.

"See, Mommy," Tracy sang, running back into the room with her new sneakers on the wrong feet, jarring Gayle from her thoughts.

Gayle laughed, her first real laugh of the day. "Come here, sweetie, and let's fix those sneakers."

Pauline sat behind her desk entering some notes into Rayne's folder. She'd been working with Rayne for six weeks and knew little more about her now than she did when Rayne was admitted. Looking over her notes, she hoped to find some clue, some tiny seed she'd missed that would help her to heal her patient.

Her eyes glided over the pages: *Rayne Holland — age thirty-five, professional filmmaker. Married for eight years to Paul Holland, age thirty-six, with one child, Desiree Holland, age seven, both killed in a car accident after returning from awards ceremony honoring Rayne's latest movie, which she'd written and directed. Marriage — solid, daughter in second grade. Next of kin — William Mercer and stepmother, Edith. Natural mother died of heart failure when Rayne was six.*

Her own mother died when she was ten. She was the only female in a house of men. Pauline looked at her notes again, beyond the handwritten lines to something that glimmered just beyond the surface. *No mother in the home. Father distraught. New marriage. How long was the father solely re-*

sponsible for his daughter? How long had the two lived alone under the shroud of the mother's death?

Rayne presented no history of psychiatric problems, although being the sole survivor of a tragic car accident was enough to send anyone teetering on the brink.

Yet Pauline didn't believe the accident was the single cause of Rayne's break, and neither did her colleagues. After conferring with them over the case, they'd agreed that Rayne's family needed to be consulted.

Pauline had only spoken to Rayne's father three or four times, one of which was when Rayne was admitted, the others brief, perfunctory. He seemed nice enough, genuinely concerned and distraught over his daughter, but he hadn't been back since. Pauline found it peculiar that he'd never come to visit. But perhaps it was the nature of Rayne's and his father-daughter relationship. She'd seen worse.

Maybe it was time that changed. She flipped through the case folder until she found the number of the Mercer home in Atlanta.

"Bill," Edith called from the kitchen. "Telephone. It's Dr. Dennis from the hospital."

William Mercer turned off the faucet in the bathroom sink, snatched an off-white towel from the ringed hook anchored to the wall, and dried his barely wrinkled face. He peered into the medicine cabinet mirror. Empty, shadow-rimmed eyes gazed back at him from skin the color of lightly sautéed butter. A full cap of wavy black hair, streaked with pencil-thin strands of gray, covered his head. He ran a mittlike hand — knuckles oversized and imposing from years of grueling construction labor — across his hard square jaw. The corner of his mouth curved slightly upward. "Not a stubble. Smooth as a baby's ass. Yessir."

"Bill!" Edith shouted this time. "Telephone."

"Comin', sugah."

William trotted down the stairs into the kitchen, briefly pecking Edith's cheek and patting her behind before taking the phone. He could have answered the phone in the upstairs bedroom, but whatever the doctor had to say he wanted Edith to be part of it. They shared everything.

"Yes, Dr. Dennis. Everything all right with my daughter?" His eyes narrowed ever so slightly.

"Mr. Mercer, I'll get right to the point. We are concerned about the lack of

53

progress that Rayne is making."

"Concerned? I don't understand. Thought you docs got together and said it might take a while. Ain't that right?"

Pauline pressed her lips together, gathering her thoughts before she spoke. "Mr. Mercer, what we indicated was that a full recovery would take time. Rayne has made no significant progress toward recovery at all. The most I've been able to do is reduce her dosage of medication."

"Then you doctors ain't doing yo' damned jobs," he bellowed.

Edith clasped his rock-hard arm and he tossed off her embrace as you would an annoying fly, sending her bouncing against the kitchen counter.

"Maybe we just need to take her out of there and put her someplace where she can get some real help."

Pauline flinched. She had a sudden, surreal sensation run the course of her body, as if she'd experienced this all before, the calm cajoling ushering in the storm. Something dark hovered in the back of her mind. She pulled in a deep breath, willing the images to retreat to the recesses of her consciousness, where she'd kept them buried for decades. Back where they belonged.

"We're trying to help her, Mr. Mercer. Moving Rayne at this stage, I believe, will do her more harm than good."

There was a stretch of silence, a long, empty desert road. The only sound was the faint hum of the phone circuitry.

"Is that right," he finally said in his customary manner, his tone having returned to warm and engaging in the blink of an eye. "What can me and my wife do to help?" He put his arm around Edith's narrow shoulders and pulled her tight against the hard lines of his body.

"I'd like both you and your wife to come in. I want to speak with you, ask some more questions, and hopefully fill in some gaps."

William's right cheek twitched. "Is that right," he said again.

But this time, to Pauline, it sounded more like an accusation than a banal response. Like the accusations that used to come from her father. *You call this clean?* he would state more than ask, running his hand across the kitchen counter. *When I get back, I won't have to ask again. Your mother wouldn't leave a kitchen looking like this. Isn't that right, Pauline?*

"Yes, Daddy," she would murmur.

"I work too hard to come home to a filthy house." And then her uncle Thomas would

appear, put his arm around her, and tell her it would be all right. William Mercer's voice became her father's, scolding her, warning her. She rubbed her hands up and down her arms to get rid of the chill that ran through her.

"I work hard, Doctor, to keep a roof over our heads and food on the table. Don't seem like it makes much sense to hike all the way to Savannah just to run our jaws."

Pauline blinked hard and forced herself to focus. "I perfectly understand about your job, Mr. Mercer," she said, almost apologetically. "You could drive down on a Saturday, spend the day, and we could talk. You could get to see Rayne. Maybe it would help her." Why did she suddenly feel like a small child begging to stay up past curfew, the vulnerable little girl who could not stand up to the men in her life?

William's jaw clenched. "I'll have to get back to you on that, Doc. I'd need to work a few things out."

"Of course. But I must impress upon you, the sooner the better."

"Is that right."

Another chill scurried up Pauline's spine. "I'll be looking forward to hearing from you soon."

"I'll be sure to get back to ya."

"Thank you."

"You have a good day now, Doctor, and thanks for calling about Rayne. Tell her . . . her daddy asked about her."

The dial tone buzzed.

Pauline slowly returned the receiver to its base and realized that her hands were sweating.

Three

Outside in the long, blue corridor, there were people, people. Rayne knew they were there. She could hear their whispers, the moans, the slow shuffle of slippered feet. But here in this room behind locked doors she wasn't one of them. She was safe from their madness.

Aimlessly, she walked toward the window and stubbed her toe. On the floor, at her feet, was the brush, the stiff brush that she had run across her thick black hair. When had she dropped it? Had she combed her hair today? She couldn't be sure. They didn't allow mirrors in the rooms of the facility. She giggled at their stupidity. Didn't they know that she didn't need a mirror to see herself, to peer at this new stranger, to view what remained after everyone had stolen the essence from her? She picked up the brush and ran it again and again through her thick, tangled hair.

No. She didn't need a mirror. Her mind was the mirror. *Memories.* It was as if she saw that morning all over again in a dingy repeat, a black-and-white repeat of the incident. The incident. The illness. She had a mirror that day. What she saw in that mirror frightened her, the furrows in her brow, the dark cavernous circles around her eyes, the gray pallor of someone who was no longer inside herself. A shell of flesh with the soul removed. It was a stranger staring back at her that day with the hollow eyes and zombie face. For two hours she'd stared at this dead version of herself in the mirror, frozen by the terror of what was concealed in the agony, evident in the glass before her. When the pain became too much, she shattered the mirror with the brush, its shards sparkling as they cascaded down around her bare feet to the tiled floor. She retrieved one long sliver, glanced at her wrists, thought of that sweet release. Oh, yes. Peaceful release.

She wanted to scream now, to yell, to shout — to tell — but nothing was there. Nothing escaped her lips. Mute. Not one sound in her closed throat. Sometimes it could persuade anyone, even her father at times, but now it could do nothing. It no longer possessed any power.

Traitor. Her fingers felt the tendons in

her neck quake at her touch, but still nothing.

Pressing her face close to the mesh-covered window she studied the hazy reflection, shivering slightly. Today wasn't one of those scary days. A wayward finger tentatively stroked the reflection in the glass, then touched her face, caressed her cheek.

"I am real," came a whisper, scruffy like the sound of sandpaper against wood. She blinked, looked rapidly around the room, the foreign sound startling to her ears. Was the voice in her head — had she spoken those words? Was she truly becoming like those shuffling feet, connected to detached bodies, in the corridor? Terror swirled in her belly. *I used to have a sweet voice, didn't I?* she thought, struggling to get the image in the window into focus. It had to be sweet to beg and plead, to make it stop.

Memories. There were so many things she wanted to forget and other things she prayed would not fade. Paul and his face, his brown handsome face with those eyes that seemed to know everything in just a single glance.

But after two months, it was his eyes that caused me to dress in the locked bathroom or in the hallway if they were just getting up. I didn't want him to read my body. If he saw me naked, he would know, would know everything. The secrets. *The truth was there in the folds, on the surfaces of my smooth skin.*

Rayne's eyes suddenly darted around the room.

They won't hear you if I tell them to stay out. The whispered idea came to life in her head. *No one can hear you. You have to keep them out. They can't see you naked. Not them, too. You know you don't like it.*

Yes, Paul always ridiculed me about that, she mused, her thoughts shimmying like heat snakes rising from the ground. She backed away from the now barricaded door, the memories as fresh as an open wound.

He said I acted like a naïve, puritanical virgin, always hiding my body, making rare love in the dark. He taunted me about my need for privacy, my obsession with hiding my body, the urge to stay clean — pure.

She frowned. Yet there was so much that she could not remember about her marriage to Paul. Like the times when she would come home from work and the next thing she would remember would be the feel of Paul between her legs, his large hands covering her body, the feel of him inside her, pounding away at her, telling

61

her how good it was, thanking her, and then nothing. It was as if during those times of marital intimacy, she simply disappeared, not knowing how her clothes had been stripped from her body or the feelings and words that were shared between her and her husband. Sometimes she wouldn't remember anything at all until she felt a dull ache between her thighs while she worked at the film studio. It was then that she knew that something had happened.

But there were things that she did remember — didn't want to remember, but she couldn't stop the images and the sound of Paul's harsh, chastising voice . . .

"You're sick, Rayne! You need help," Paul had shouted one night when he insisted she get undressed in front of him — in the light.

"Don't do this, Paul. Please." She begged him in that voice that was sweet, pleading. "I can't."

"You can and you will."

He stormed across the room, his eyes blazing with an almost irrational passion. She watched herself, outside herself as she had done with the stranger in the mirror that day. This Rayne, this stranger who sometimes said and did things *she* would never do.

She backed up into the corner, choking on her own air. Her head spun.

Paul grabbed her then, shook her until her teeth snapped against one another.

"Take off your fucking clothes. Be a woman for once in your pitiful life."

Paul snatched the collar of her blouse and tugged until the buttons erupted into tiny white projectiles across the floor.

She screamed at him, screamed something that made him stop. At least she thought she did, or maybe it was the look on her face. She tried to cover herself, disappear into the wall.

Paul suddenly went for her bra then, as if snapped from a trance, tugging it until the clasp popped and her breasts burst free, exposed and vulnerable.

Terror, deep and pervasive, filled her. Her body prepared itself. Hot, salty tears streamed down her face, mercifully clouding her vision, down into her mouth, between the valley of her breasts. Oh, God, she felt so helpless, helpless to defend herself, weak and inconsequential. Her cries didn't matter. Her pleas fell on deaf ears. Her struggle was futile as it had always been. It was easier to let go.

And then nothing. A part of her seemed to turn off and shut down, disappear to some safe place where there was no pain, no violation. The place to which she'd always escaped since she was six years old and the shadows came in the night — when it all began.

Somehow she knew if she hid there, turned off her mind and body, Paul couldn't really hurt her. No one could. Not really. Because it wasn't Rayne whose body he was pushing into, tearing into, filling until he flooded her. It was an empty vessel, some other self, devoid of sensation and emotion. That's all she was. Empty.

Yes. It was safe there.

Desiree was conceived that night. Her baby. The only one who ever loved her — truly loved her for who she was. Her mommy.

Desi was gone now, wasn't she? Rayne had no one to love her. She tried to clear her head as she looked around, her room slowly coming back into focus.

Rayne saw her reflection in the window and wondered when she'd taken off her clothes. Who was this who stood in front of the window now? Naked. Distant. Defenseless. In her body but outside of her flesh. Exiled. A fugitive spirit. Untouchable.

It's all right, the soothing voice whispered, willing her mind not to panic. *You're just tired, not paying attention. That's all. That's all.*

Walking on unsteady legs, Rayne crossed the small space to the closet and slid the pine-wood doors open. She smiled and took out her favorite peach-colored cotton knit dress and slid it over her head, over her nude body.

The dress provocatively hugged her curves, defined her jutting breasts, narrow waist, and full, round bottom. Rayne touched her body in a way she only vaguely remembered experiencing, as if from afar, feeling the dips and curves of her frame with a mastery that surprised and aroused her. What had happened to her inside Paul never understood, and neither did Daddy.

Rayne peered at her blurred image in the window and smiled, stepping into her low-heeled sandals. She pushed the chair away from the door, momentarily perplexed, wondering when it had gotten there as she stepped out into the corridor.

No one really noticed her, she thought, walking slowly down the hall. Besides, there was no escape. She saw the nurses, doctors, and guards using magnetic cards to access the doors and elevators. They had no fear that she would get out into the world, she mused, passing several mixed couples of doctors and nurses, their heads almost touching as they whispered and gestured. *They're too busy with their own lives, their own secrets to even see me.* But she had secrets, too, she thought, images of shadows in the night hovering over her as she slept, touching her, wetting her, creeping through her mind, opening closed doors, as she rounded the corner, blurring her vision.

Soft moans could be heard just below the levels of natural hospital noises. So low that one might think it was only imagined. But it wasn't.

It was *her* moans, Rayne's, struggling against the powerful human shadow that weighed her body down, smothering her screams with big, sweaty hands and a penetrating tongue, its weight slamming against her body again and again, grunting, whispering, her head snapping back and forth. And then there was nothing. She vanished and the moans stopped and the dark shadow slithered away making room for her in the blue corridor. She was safe. She'd gotten away.

Breathing deeply, Rayne walked a bit farther down the hall. There he was, sitting in the same spot he always sat in every evening this time — at the foot of the bed, watching the old man. There was a quiet strength about him. Not because of his size. It was dignity and self-respect that widened his shoulders, held his head high — even in this place where many are beaten back and down by the weight of their circumstances.

Silently watching, just outside the doorway, she willed Robert to turn around and see her, really see her, in her dress — as a woman. Not some object, but worthy to be cared about, truly cared for.

Sometimes he did notice her, and he would smile or say hello, ask her how she was doing. But never once did she feel that he saw her as a woman. Today he would. Today she would finally answer him when he spoke, and she wouldn't feel dirty or shamed by her need to feel needed. She'd promised herself that she would. The *other* Rayne was weak. *She* was strong. The *other* Rayne would never talk to him. Rayne didn't talk to anyone. That's why *she* was there. *She* smiled.

The old man sat military-style straight in the guard-railed bed. Dark, luminous eyes stared at some distant point in time — maybe to some old war or forgotten story.

His features were dark, the color of tree bark, unlined, making the marking of his age difficult. Cutting-edge cheekbones dominated the almost aristocratic face, covered by a skullcap of silver hair that appeared painted on his narrow head. The lines of his mouth were singular, with no particular definition — thin on top, the bottom fuller. He had been quite handsome once, and still was in some eyes.

Occasionally, the old man would turn to his son who sat stoically in the chair beside the bed and speak in a voice so low it could only be heard between the two of them — father and son. *Whispers.*

Then the old man's voice suddenly rang strong and clear: "Did you get your report card, Bobby? Don't want to have to go back up to that school behind you, boy." He shook his head, feeling his way through his memories. "You gon' worry your mama to death."

The man in the chair didn't move, didn't respond, accepting what was.

Rayne knew the man in the chair was the son — Robert — the gardener. She'd heard his preacherlike voice, emotion-filled, heavy, persuasive, tell Dr. Dennis about his visits to his father. The good doctor would always respond in a soft lilt, the consoling, understanding tone that she sometimes used, putting a hand on his shoulder. Touching him.

Rayne stared at the man in the chair — Robert — with the heavy, persuasive voice and a face and body that only vaguely resembled the old man in the bed. His face was fuller, smoother, the color of brandy. His shoulders were broader, more powerful. But it was his eyes that drew her. Black, wide, laced with silk, filled with something kind. She could tell.

Maybe he would turn and look at her today in her favorite peach dress. She needed to see kindness today from someone who had nothing to gain by giving it.

Turn around and look at me in my peach dress. Please, she silently screamed.

Robert felt her presence before he was fully conscious that she was there — almost in the room. He wanted to turn, look at her face. But he knew if he did, she would run off as she always did. Run like a frightened doe.

He smiled. That's what the stunning girl-woman reminded him of, a frightened doe, trapped for an instant in the light of someone's eyes. He'd tried to find out from

Dr. Dennis why she was there, what circumstances had brought her to Cedar. "Very tragic," Dr. Dennis had confided to him one day on the grounds. "Her husband and daughter were killed in a car accident several months ago. She was the only survivor," she'd added, unwilling to divulge anything further, nothing more to mar that ethics code, and telling him no more than he already knew.

Robert understood that kind of pain, that kind of loss that could hurt you so deeply all you wanted was nothingness, because you'd gone beyond the ability to feel — anything.

Maybe if he turned slowly, so as not to startle her, she wouldn't run and he could catch that almost-there smile and the brief light of response in her eyes that told him she knew well what went on around her — at least most of the time.

Robert wasn't certain what it was about the girl-woman that drew his attention, evoked the rusty shield of protectiveness in him. Maybe it was because she vaguely reminded him of his sister, Nicole. His eternally lost and searching sister. Nicole had worn her neediness like a gossamer veil, faint and floating around her like mist. It made you want to get closer to see if it was real, push it aside, and touch what was beneath. Protect it. Yes, there was a need floating around Rayne Holland, too, and he wondered if it had ever been filled — touched. A budding flower, delicate, one that needed tender care. That's what she was. But why had she singled him out? Didn't she know he couldn't help her?

He looked at the old man. His eyes were closed. *What are you dreaming about, old man, huh? Do you ever dream about what you did to us? To Mom, Nicole, to me? Do you ever see us in your dreams?*

Slowly he turned toward the door, his expression hardened by emotions that rose up like bile into his throat, burning.

Rayne's breath caught. Her heart began to hammer as images of that very same expression engulfed her, terrified her, held her immobile with dread. But then the eyes softened. The brackets around the full lips eased into an inviting smile.

"Hi."

It was almost a whisper, but not quite. It was more like a rumble, distant thunder, the warning before the storm.

Say something, girl. That's what you're here for, the whispered voice in her head scolded. *"Act like a woman for once in your miserable life,"* Paul shouted, and a cold

71

sweat crawled along her body, trickled down between her breasts, slid down her spine.

The muscles in her throat contracted and released, squeezing the life out of the air that struggled to push the words into the world.

"Hel-lo." She wanted to run, but her feet sank into the quicksand — at least she thought it was quicksand.

Robert angled his head to the right, his smile crinkling his eyes. "How are you today?"

Her throat closed and she saw the simple words she wanted to say scurry down the corridor like startled mice. She must catch them, bring them back. She spun away and hurried after them, the squishing sound of the quicksand echoing with each step.

Robert sighed, staring at the empty doorway.

Four

Robert felt an urge to go after her, but caught himself and stopped in the threshold. He thought of his sister, Nicole, and his inability to stop her. What made him think he could do any more for this woman, this stranger? He turned away from where Rayne had been only moments before, returning to stand by the chair next to the bed. He looked down at the old man who had not stirred in his sleep. He reached for the newspaper on the nightstand and left the room, his duty done.

As he moved down the corridor — a nod of his head or a bare smile to acknowledge recognized faces — he saw her.

The peach dress flowed over her body like the stroke of an artist's brush on canvas, the lines of her form outlined in a soft haze of muted color and sensuous movement. He could almost hear the gentle swish of her body as it moved beneath the dress, undulating in languorous waves. Then she turned the corner and was gone.

Robert's thigh slammed into the metal edge of a linen cart. The sharp jolt shot up his body and erupted in his head, bringing reality into focus.

What in the hell was wrong with him? He tenderly rubbed the injured spot on his thigh. For a few disjointed moments, he'd actually reacted to Rayne Holland as if she were a "normal" woman. But the facts were obvious. Rayne Holland was anything but normal. She was hospitalized in the psychiatric ward of Cedar Grove. She was not mentally well. To what degree, he was uncertain. But to any degree, good sense dictated that he stay away, not be taken in by the haunted look in her eyes, the aura of vulnerability that awakened a buried part of him, reached out to him and begged him to protect her. Something he'd been unable to do for his own family and was unwilling to do now.

"Robert. Still here?"

Robert turned to see Pauline stepping out of her office. She locked the door behind her. Smiled.

"How was your father today?"

He shoved his hands into his jean pockets, wishing he could shove away the image of Rayne's face in that brief instant that he'd glimpsed the turmoil.

74

"Robert. Are you all right?"

"Oh. Yes. Sorry, I guess I was lost in thought — thinking about my visit."

Pauline looked at his profile as they walked down the corridor. Firm. Determined. Distant. "I was asking about your father. How is he today?"

"Pretty much the same. Some days he's aware I'm in the room. Other times he thinks I'm one of his partners from the old neighborhood, or still six years old."

"Alzheimer's is a very difficult disease. It's just as hard on the family as on the patient. Scientists are working day and night to come up with a treatment to alleviate the symptoms. There's a new study that has detected the gene that makes some people predisposed to the disease . . ." she was saying, but Robert wasn't really listening.

A part of him ached seeing his father the way he was, especially when he could remember how he had once been a whole and vibrant man, before he left and abandoned them all. Then there was that other part, the dark hurting part of him that somehow felt vindicated of his hatred for his father, believing that this was his due for what the man had done to his family.

"Are you on your way home?" Pauline

75

asked, severing his twisting thoughts.

He turned, seeming to notice her presence for the first time. "Yes. Can I give you a ride somewhere?"

"No. I have my car. I was . . . wondering, if you're not in a hurry, maybe we could stop off for a drink." She hesitated when he didn't respond. "I can tell you have a lot on your mind. Maybe you'd like to talk about it. Talking helps, you know."

"Is that the doctor I'm hearing or Pauline Dennis?" He gave her a questioning smile.

"Probably both. To tell you the truth, I'm not too sure there's any difference."

"There should be, you know. A difference. A dividing line that separates who we are from what we do."

"Perhaps we are what we do."

"Touché, Doctor." He looked momentarily down at the pale blue tiled floor. "A drink sounds real good about now."

Pauline smiled. "I know a great little place. It's about fifteen minutes from here."

"Lead the way."

Rayne took off the peach dress that felt like warm hands along her flesh. She stood in front of the window gazing out onto the rolling lawn below. Her eyes trailed the

76

pair as they moved toward the gate. Together. Smiling. Whispering.

The next thing she remembered was that
somehow the sun had vanished after being
there only moments ago. A shaky hand
pressed against the mesh-covered window.
A single tear slid down her cheek.

How long have I stood here? Rayne wondered in confusion, the waning light of
evening having departed, leaving the
grounds below illuminated in bands of artificial brightness from the spotlights that
sat in huge rotating barrels. Daytime had
eluded her somehow, slipped between the
crevices of her mind, and escaped. Night
took its place, covering everything in its
path in a cloak of false security. It was at
night that it came. The hurt. The shadows.
When they couldn't be seen, couldn't be
heard. Only by her.

Her body glistened with sweat. She
trembled. Frantic eyes darted around the
near empty room, listening, waiting for the
footsteps. All she could hear was the ham-
mering of her heart, thudding like a drum
out of control.

Rayne backed into the corner, her eyes
wide, trying to see through the darkness.
The cool wall shocked her as her bare flesh
pressed against it, then she slid down its

crack into a fetal ball, squeezing her eyes shut, blocking out the image of the face. *You won't hurt me again. Not again. Not tonight.* A contorted, brown countenance and dark menacing eyes loomed before her like a specter. The large hands, like paws, reached for her.

She jumped, almost screamed when cool hands clasped her shoulders. Someone was in her room. She'd forgotten to block the door. Her body shook uncontrollably.

The hands were gentle this time, the voice soft. *Paul?*

Rayne dared to look up, open her eyes.

"Come on now, Ms. Holland," a woman dressed all in white coaxed. "Let's get you up off this cold floor and into bed."

The tag on her starched white uniform read, "Simpson." Rayne's mind began to clear. It was the nurse, the one who gave her the medicine that clouded her head, made her feet feel like lead boots, her heart crawl through her chest.

"Come on now." The nurse got her hands beneath Rayne's arms and pulled her to her feet, guiding her to the bed. "Sit right here. I'll get your gown."

The nurse pulled open the bottom drawer of the nightstand and took out a soft peach-tinted gown of cotton. She dressed Rayne as you would an infant, one incapable of doing for oneself.

I can do it, Rayne shouted, but Nurse Simpson couldn't hear her. *I can, I know I can.* As the soft gown slid over her head, a wave of helplessness swept through her, floated across her shoulders, caressed her breasts, and soothed her stomach.

"There. That's much better." Nurse Simpson tenderly pushed Rayne's hair away from her face, then lifted her legs and put them up on the bed, covering them with a thin white sheet. "You just lean back and relax. It's time for your medication. It will help you to sleep."

I don't want to sleep.

Nurse Simpson took two white pills out of the medicine cup on her tray and handed them to Rayne.

Rayne turned her head away, covering her face with her hair.

"You don't want me to have to get Willie in here, now do you, Ms. Holland?"

A sudden image of the burly orderly with his large hands, holding her down while Nurse Simpson pushed the pills past her sealed lips, exploded in front of her eyes. Her heart banged like someone trapped in a dark, black box begging to get out. Beneath the cotton gown, her body grew damp with perspiration.

Nurse Simpson pushed the pills forward.

I don't want to drift away, Rayne thought. *Please. I want to stay here — now. If I take those pills I won't be able to think, to hear the whispers, to write in my journal. I'm tired of being drugged.*

But then the vision of Willie, the feel of his big hands on her body, shot through her brain. Hands like those other hands. Rayne opened her mouth.

"Wonderful," Nurse Simpson praised, handing Rayne a cup of lukewarm water. "You rest, now. I'll be sure to check on you later."

The effects of the medication were swift and potent. Within minutes, the malaise set in, her thoughts churned through sludge. Her tongue grew thick, her eyelids heavy with a layer of cement fastened to her lashes. She wanted to fight it, but knew it was futile. She was tired. Sleep took over.

Pauline sat opposite Robert in a small, dimly lit café on Charles Street. The after-work crowd had thinned, gradually replaced by a dressier clientele. Pauline sipped a raspberry margarita. Robert pretended to drink his rum and Coke. He wasn't a drinker by nature. He'd seen what alcohol had done to his mother and had no intention of falling prey either by choice or by genetics.

Pauline was different when devoid of the sterile surroundings of the facility and out of her white garb, Robert quietly observed. Under the dim light that offered soft halos around her freckled, pretty face, she seemed more human. Feminine.

"How long have you had your own business, Robert?" Pauline asked over the rim of her glass.

"Almost ten years. Built the business from scratch with just me and one other guy. Now I have twenty employees. Funny, seems like I've been doing landscaping all my life." He took a short sip of his drink and looked off at a distant memory somewhere beyond her shoulder. "My grandmother got me interested in planting and tilling the soil when I'd visit her in Mississippi during summer breaks. I guess I just took to it. There's something soothing about working with the earth, seeing things grow, nurturing something from a seed." He blinked the images away. "And you?"

She smiled, her green eyes catching the light. "Twice as long as you, at least professionally. Years of schooling, study, and internships." She twirled the froth in her drink around with the hair-thin straw. "I grew up in New Orleans. My mother died when I was ten and being the oldest and the only girl I guess I learned how to run a house, take care of my father and my two brothers . . . and my uncle." *Men, they were everywhere in my life, in my days, in my nights. Nights were worst. He came at night, pretending to comfort me, make me feel better about my days, touching me in places that an uncle shouldn't touch. Putting things in places where they shouldn't have been, cutting off my air, pressing me into the mattress with his weight. The roughness of his facial stubble rubbing my young breasts nearly raw from the friction. The pain.* "Shush now. It's gonna feel real good in a minute," *he would whisper in my ear, covering my mouth with a big, heavy hand.*

Robert noticed a tic beneath her eye twitch several times then stop.

"I loved New Orleans but the opportunities I wanted for my career weren't there. I . . . had to get away," she said from a distance, then focused on Robert, forcing a smile. "I finally moved to Atlanta and worked in a community clinic for a while to get more experience. I heard about Cedar's at a medical conference and couldn't

82

wait to get here. Started about five years ago. I do private practice as well." She'd left out her experience at Johns Hopkins. There was no need for him to know, or question, what happened there. It was a bitter experience that left her scarred but resolved that she would not go down that road again, go against her medical judgment at the risk of her patient.

"Busy lady. How long have you been head of the psychology department?"

"Two years. I took over after Dr. Sorenson retired."

"That's a lot of responsibility, and power," he added, and saw her half smile. "There's nothing like the value of doing a good job, the sense of pride and self-respect it brings. You must enjoy what you do."

"Most of the time. Often it's very difficult. Especially when you still have to answer to higher authorities who don't always share your views." She thought about her boss and employer, Dr. Howell, and their constant clashing of wills, the underlying current of resentment between them that waited to overflow. "Sometimes I feel as though I'm not making any real progress with some of my patients."

"Is it like that with Rayne Holland?"

Her gaze held on to his for a moment,

searching behind the words. Her stomach momentarily tightened. "She'll take some time," she responded noncommittally.

"I'm sorry if I put you on the spot. I know I shouldn't be asking about your patients, but I was curious about her." He caught a fleeting image of Rayne standing in the doorway of his father's room. "I've seen one of her documentaries several times. Read articles on her and her family. It just seems so . . ."

"Tragic?"

"That's as good a word as any, I suppose."

"Bad things happen to good people every day, unfortunately."

He thought of his mother and sister.

Pauline took a long sip of her drink and tried to shake the dark feelings that brewed within her. "To be truthful, Rayne Holland was one of the reasons why I suggested we talk. You've asked about her before. Is there any particular reason why you're so interested in her?"

The tic picked up its beat again, Robert noted. He shifted in his seat, feeling suddenly uncomfortable, under scrutiny. He didn't like it. He didn't like her innuendos, that there was anything more than concern on his part. His gaze narrowed. "There's no *special* interest, if that's what you're getting at, Doctor. I was curious, that's all, especially knowing who she is and the work she's done."

Her mouth formed a smile of sorts. "As her doctor, I simply want to advise you that the last thing Rayne Holland needs right now is a distraction. I'm responsible for her care, her road toward health, and I would be lax in my responsibility if I didn't mention my concern."

"What are you saying, Doctor? Exactly."

"Rayne Holland is not well. You are. Don't confuse the two. For your own good and for hers."

"I don't think that's anything you have to worry about, Dr. Dennis."

She glanced at him for a moment and sipped the last of her drink. "That's good to hear." She checked her watch. "I really need to get home. I have a full schedule tomorrow."

Robert looked around for the waitress and signaled to her. "Me, too," he said, raising up a bit to get his wallet from his back pocket, and more than a little happy to get away.

"No. My treat. I *did* invite you."

"I like to pay my own way."

Pauline placed her credit card on the

85

tray the waitress presented along with the check. "I'm sure."

Standing side-by-side in front of their cars, caught in that awkward tableau of uncertainty, Pauline and Robert flipped through their rusty catalogue of exit lines.

"Thanks for the drink," he finally said.

"Sure. I hope you think about what I said regarding Rayne, Robert. I'm only thinking of her interests and well-being."

He slung his hands in his pockets. "I'll keep that in mind. See you on the grounds, Doctor. Good night."

"Drive safely."

"You, too." He opened his car door.

"Night."

They pulled off in opposite directions.

Through the shroud of drug-filled sleep, Rayne fought valiantly against the demons that plagued her. Her father, Edith, Paul, Gayle. Slaying each of them with fortitude, with the truth, laying open their ugly secrets. She could hear her own voice, not the soft placating lilt, but her real voice, one of force and determination compelling each of the demons to answer for what they had done.

One by one they fell, and the darkness, the heaviness that sat on her spirit began to lift, the misty veil of unreality began to dissipate and daylight crested the lush green horizon.

Rayne saw herself on the other side of the black, swirling gates, walking out into the world. When she turned to look back, all of them — her father, Edith, Paul, Gayle — ran to the gate, shaking it, screaming, begging her to let them out. Only she had the power to release them, to free herself. She walked away.

Rayne's eyes flew open, tried to adjust to the semidarkness. The only light was the sliver that slipped in beneath the door from the hallway, and the crisscross of beams that moved across the grounds, illuminating the single bed, the nightstand bolted to the floor, and the tiny shadow patterns of triangles and squares that spread across the floor.

Her heart thundered, her breathing ceased in her chest. She was still there. Trapped. And the shadow moved closer.

She screamed. From deep in her soul, she screamed. Agony, pain, unspeakable terror and sorrow tore through her, rose up and out in a keening wail. And no one heard her.

But maybe they did.

Five

The buttery smell of homemade biscuits filled the air of the Mercer kitchen. A gentle breeze blew in from the partially open window, mixing the aromas of bacon and eggs with the smell of green grass and red, rich earth. Edith moved gingerly around the country-style room, favoring her right side, her hip still sore from the blow it took against the counter.

Bill didn't mean it, she thought, laying the long strips of bacon on a warming tray as she spooned the scrambled eggs into a red-and-white porcelain bowl. *He's just hard that way sometimes. Hard like men are. He don't think much of his pushing and shoving. It ain't always easy for him to express himself, that's all. Sometimes he just lets his emotions run his mind and he don't think clear. He don't mean nothing by it,* she reaffirmed as a sharp pain shot through her hip with such force it clamped her eyes shut, stilled her fingers. Images of a terrified little girl, hunkered down beneath the bedcovers, shaking like a leaf, rolled behind her closed lids.

"Prayin' again, sugah," William joked, as he stepped right up behind her and kissed her cheek. "Or you just daydreamin' 'bout me?" He chuckled, pulled out a chair from beneath the rectangular butcher-block table and lowered his bulk into the spindle-back chair. "Got a job down in Smyrna." He poured a mug of coffee from the pot on the table, his huge hands almost able to wrap around the mug twice. "Nothing big, but the pay is good. Hank said the foreman down there is looking for a few extra hands. Gonna go down and check it out."

"That's real good, sweetheart. I'm sure you'll get something."

Narrowed eyes zeroed in on her back, and William could feel the old rage building in his gut like a smoldering forest fire. "What you say?"

The never-ending noose of tension tightened around Edith's throat, jamming the words there, shortening her breath. She turned toward him, forced a smile, her floral patterned housecoat hanging from her thin body like a wet sheet on a line. "I was just saying how I know you're going to get the job, Bill. You're good at what you do. Everyone knows that. Those folks in Smyrna would be damned lucky to have you. That's all I was saying." She twisted a threadbare dish towel between her hands.

William stared at her for a long, unbearable moment. But she dared not look away. Then he smiled as if the sun had suddenly burst through the dark clouds. He laughed. "That's what I figured you was tryin' to say." He shook his head, still chuckling, taking a long swallow of his coffee.

The coil inside her stomach began to loosen. Edith took a shallow breath and turned back to the stove. "How's this new job going to affect your visit to Rayne?"

"Who said I was gonna visit?"

"I just thought . . ."

"Didn't ask you what you thought, Edith, now did I. Food gonna get cold if you keep standing there. You know how I hate cold eggs." He watched her cross the room. "Why you walking like that?"

"Oh, my hip is hurting just a bit." She spooned some eggs onto his plate.

"Hmm." His eyes galloped up and down her body before he grabbed her around the waist. "Maybe I'll rub it for you later if these biscuits are as good as they smell." He ran his hand across her behind. "You'd like that, wouldn't you?" He pulled her closer.

"Of course."

"Bring me some of that bacon to go with these eggs."

"Sure."

Edith eased back over to the counter, fighting to camouflage her limp and the ache that shot through her with each step. She gritted her teeth, picked up the tray with the bacon, returning with it to the table.

"Rayne's just putting on another one of her acts," William said, biting into a crispy bacon strip, and waving the fork at Edith to make his point. "Always was one to make up something in her head and swear it was real. Ever since her mama died, girl ain't been right. You know it's true," he said, turning a glaring eye on his wife, daring her to contradict him. "You'd think Rayne would have turned out more like her mama. Looks just like her."

Edith lowered her gaze.

"But she ain't nothing like her mama." The muscles in his jaw clenched. "Nothing. Carol was one sweet woman. Loving. Kind. Not like that ungrateful daughter of hers. Carol would give her last to whoever needed it." He stared off to some distant spot on the flowered wallpaper. "When I first saw Carol at our high school dance, I said, 'There's the woman for me.' Prettiest thing I'd ever seen. Face like an angel. Wild black hair that ran down her shoulders, like puffs of cotton candy, and skin as brown as brown sugar and just as sweet." He ran his tongue across his lips.

Things had never been right since Carol died, he thought. When she closed her eyes and left him, he wanted to go with her. He wasn't sure how he would go on. Carol put a gentleness in his life that he'd never had before, made him see the softness in things.

He remembered the first picnic they'd gone on together, out near the lake. They were about nineteen, fresh out of high school and eager to take their place in the world.

"I packed us a picnic lunch," Carol announced that hot July morning, as she walked up his porch steps, a smile like sunshine dancing across her face.

"A picnic? Girl, I got chores to do 'round here."

She grabbed his hand, kissed his bulging knuckles, leaving an imprint of her ruby red lipstick behind. "There's plenty of time for chores, Bill. But we may not get another day like this one. Look at it," she said, turning her face to the heavens. "Sun shinin', hot breeze blowing off the lake, birds singin'. Come on, sugah," she cooed in that voice he couldn't resist. She pressed the fullness of her body against his.

"My papa's gonna skin me alive," he said, his resolve weakening with every stroke of her lips along his clenched fist.

"I'll fix it with your daddy. Come on, now, the day's getting away from us."

He blew out a breath. "All right, all right. Let me wash up and I'll be out directly."

She grinned in triumph. "That's better. I'll be in the car waiting."

That's just the way Carol was, spontaneous and full of adventure. She could wrap him around her pinky without even trying. He would have done anything for Carol, even all the kinky sex things she loved to do. Whatever it took to keep her happy. So when she turned up pregnant, he didn't even think twice about marrying her.

When Rayne was born and looked just like Carol, he was sure he was the luckiest man in the world. Now he had two of them. Until Rayne took Carol away from

93

him. When she was born, it was like he no longer existed. All Carol thought about, talked about, was Rayne, her beautiful baby girl. Where was all *his* attention, *his* lovin'? Gone. And it was all Rayne's fault. If it hadn't been for her, Carol would have still loved him, her heart wouldn't have gone bad. Doctors said she should have never gotten pregnant in the first place. It did too much damage to her already weakened heart. Her folks blamed him, too. They didn't want to have nothing to do with him or Rayne. But it wasn't his fault. He'd lost Carol, too.

It was Rayne's fault. Carol was gone and Rayne was still here. How fair was that? He glared at his wife and wondered what happened to the full-bodied woman he'd married, who now stood before him cowering and haggard-looking.

Edith saw the look that hovered in her husband's eyes, knew his thoughts. For all the years of her marriage Edith was well aware that she lived in Carol Mercer's shadow. Nothing she'd ever done or could hope to do would erase Carol Mercer's memory from her husband's mind. She knew she wasn't as pretty as Carol, or as graceful, or as smart. She'd always struggled with her weight and in her growing-up years she'd been tormented about her wide nose and short knotty hair. But she did the best she could. When William Mercer asked her to marry him, she finally felt worthwhile and deserving of being loved. She'd finally succeeded at something. She was somebody, not the ugly fat girl that the other girls teased and the boys ignored. When she married William Mercer she became somebody. She wanted to be all things to William, whatever it took. Yet, even sending Rayne away hadn't exorcised the ghost of Carol from the house. She was still in their bed, planted in William's heart, at least what was left of it.

Edith suspected what went on between father and daughter, how Rayne had taken on the role of the wife, waiting on William hand and foot, dressing up for him. That first year she watched in silence. And who knew how long this "thing" had gone on between them before she'd become part of the Mercer household? It wasn't right. So she did what was necessary to protect her marriage and the child. What choice did she have? Everyone thought she was jealous of Rayne. Maybe she was. But that wasn't the real reason. Never the real reason.

"Carol could cook, too. Damned good

cook. Make something outta nothin'." He laughed at the memory, derailing Edith's dark thoughts. "Yeah, those were good days. She knew how to make a man feel like a man," he continued, caught up in his own view of reality. He looked across the table at Edith. "You ain't eating." He forked a mouthful of eggs.

"Not real hungry this morning," she mumbled into her glass of orange juice.

"Hmm." William pushed his plate away. "Got to get going. Should be back late tonight." He stood, then leaned down and pecked her on the cheek. "I'll see what I can do about that hip of yours when I get back."

"Call if you're going to be really late."

He patted her on the shoulder and strode out, thinking how much different things could have been. It was all Rayne's fault. He stepped out into the blistering morning sun, stood for a moment on the porch, his gaze sweeping across the stretch of trees and rolling hills in the distance. *You reap what you sow*, he thought, stepping down. *You reap what you sow.*

Six

"Tracy wet the bed again last night," Gayle said, glancing at James's reflection in her dressing table mirror. She meticulously applied a stroke of coral-colored lipstick to her mouth — waiting.

James halted midway in buttoning his stark white shirt, set off by the richness of his honey-brown complexion. His dark eyes rose from the play of his long fingers to rest on her face in the mirror.

"How long are you going to let this continue? There's obviously something wrong."

"What would you have me do, James?" Gayle volleyed, priming herself for the accusations that were sure to come.

"Maybe try telling her the truth about what happened to Desiree, for starters."

"She's too young to understand."

"So you'd prefer to have her imagine God knows what instead? Desiree is dead, Gayle, dead. She needs to understand that. Having her think Desiree has just 'gone away' isn't doing her any good."

She spun around in the chair to face him. "Well, why don't *you* tell her that her best friend and her godfather died in a car accident and that her godmother has been committed to an institution?" Her voice, elevated, took on a crackling edge. "Is that what you want?"

"You obviously want to remain in the same fantasy world as Rayne and take our daughter right along with the two of you." He snatched his burgandy-striped tie from the bed. "Tracy hasn't been right for months but you refuse to see that."

"So it's my fault. Where do you fit in to all this?"

"That's what I've been trying to figure out, Gayle. You wanted to handle things your way, and I agreed. Now look at what's happened. I've been kept out of the equation."

"It's the way you wanted it. You've never involved yourself in what goes on around here."

"Maybe if what I thought and felt mattered, I would." He jerked the tie around his neck.

"This isn't about Tracy, is it?"

Their gazes remained fixed on each other for all the lost moments.

"It's about a lot of things, Gayle," James

finally said, relieved to say the words. "Tracy is only a symptom. You've been in this marriage by yourself for a long time now."

"What? Everything I do, I do it for us. How could you —"

"Everything is the way you want it. It has to be or else I get the cold shoulder." He glanced away, then back at his wife. "Why did you marry me, Gayle? Because Rayne got married?"

Gayle shook her head in denial. "Rayne has nothing to do with why we got married. I married you because I loved you. I still do."

"As much as you love Rayne?"

Gayle stumbled back as if she'd been slapped. "As . . . much as I love Rayne?" she stuttered. "What are you saying?"

Paul's tone was even, decisive. "Your whole life has always revolved around Rayne — what she has, her looks, her career. And now this."

"Now this!"

"This whole thing with Rayne has taken over our lives. You pretty much ignore both of us. You don't think Tracy feels it, that I feel it? All of your free time is devoted to running up to the hospital to see Rayne."

"Who else does she have, James? For God sake, why can't you see that?"

"What I see is *our* family, *our* marriage coming unraveled, and you don't seem to give a damn about it. And to be quite frank, you haven't for a long time. These past few months only make it more obvious."

The pulse in her temple pounded. "What are you saying?"

"You're no fool, Gayle." He took his steel-gray jacket off the hanger in the closet. "Maybe if Paul was still around you could talk to him about it, because you damned sure aren't talking to me." A victorious smile curved his mouth when Gayle's expression froze. "Yeah, I knew. I'm no fool either, Gayle."

Without a backward glance, he strode out.

The slamming of the bedroom door snatched Gayle out of her shock. She started to go after him, try to explain, get him to understand. Halfway to the door, she stopped. How could she explain something she didn't quite understand herself?

She laughed derisively. What did James think he knew? He could never know. No one would ever understand what she and Paul once meant to each other, what they provided for each other. Paul listened, really listened to her, and she to him. They'd been each other's support during the most turbulent times of their respective marriages. Between them was more than just friendship. Their bond was unshakeable. In some macabre way, they'd needed each other more than they needed their spouses just to get through their day.

Paul Holland. Her eyes clouded. She'd tried not to think about him. Too much pain. But all she had now were the memories. The taboo memories.

She'd met Paul Holland at the Marriott Marquee Hotel in New York during a business conference for black bank executives. At practically every seminar, they'd found themselves seated next to or near each other during those three days.

Gayle noticed him, she couldn't help it, but tried not to make it obvious. She was fascinated by the quickness of his mind, his ability to loosen up the tight-assed group leader, help a fellow colleague with a problem. Paul was a natural charmer — just the opposite from the reserved and practical James Davis — who found himself invited to any number of after-session gatherings. The combination of charming arrogance, intelligence, and good looks was an intoxicating brew. But it wasn't until the last day of the conference that they actually spoke.

"That was intense," Paul bemoaned as they exited a grueling three-hour session on corporate mergers.

"That wasn't intense, it was illegal. There must be a law against anyone talking that long and being boring as hell. My ears were buzzing."

Gayle massaged the bridge of her nose and slung the strap of her leather briefcase over her left shoulder, tenderly rubbing the right, and wondered why he'd singled her out — finally.

"Stiff neck?" Paul quizzed, slowing his long, almost cocky gait to match hers. "A hot shower is good for that. Let the water beat down on your neck. Even better is a follow-up massage. That will set you straight."

Gayle turned to look at him, wondering if he was coming on to her, or simply being helpful, noticing close up how handsome he was. He had a shadow of a beard, whether intentional or the sign of a long day, she couldn't tell. But she liked it. He was tall and slender, maybe six foot one. She could tell he was in good shape. With his jacket draped across his arm, his black leather belt cinching his waist, the outline of a muscular chest and flat, hard belly was clearly defined.

Her own stomach fluttered a moment when his eyes caught her staring. He grinned slightly, the right corner of his mouth lifting just a bit. His dark eyes set against sienna-toned skin sparkled even in the artificial light of the hotel corridor.

Gayle hadn't realized she'd neglected to answer his question about her neck until he asked again.

"A little," she finally replied. "Too much work, and too little sleep."

His brows drew together. "You're having trouble sleeping? I would think that these sessions would be enough to knock you out at night. It does for me."

Gayle nodded, rubbing her neck and her shoulder a bit more. "It's always hard for me to sleep in a strange bed."

His mouth curved in a half-smile. "Oh, I was hoping you weren't going to confess that you spent time in strange beds."

Gayle felt the heat rise to her face. She swallowed. "I suppose I should have added it's one reason why I don't like traveling and staying in hotels."

"Do you travel much for your job?" he said, smoothly changing topics.

"Usually no more than three times a year."

"I guess it must be hard on your family."

"I don't have a family. I mean, I have a family, but not a husband or anything."

Gayle thought about James and their almost engagement, their five-year courtship, their almost possible future. This man didn't need to know about that — her personal life.

"Where are you from?" Paul asked, pressing for the elevator.

"Savannah."

"So am I," he said, his expression lightening in surprise. "I thought I recognized the accent."

"Accent?" Gayle quipped, her pencil-thin brows arching in mock ignorance.

They laughed and stepped onto the elevator. The doors closed. They were alone. She inhaled the subtleness of his cologne.

"What floor?" Paul asked, leaning toward the buttons.

"Sixteen."

He pressed the dial and the conveyance rose in silence.

"Paul Holland." He extended his hand.

Gayle glanced up at him. "Gayle Johnson." She took his hand, and from that moment on they would be friends.

When they returned to their hometown, they stayed in contact, meeting often for lunch or dinner, chatting on the phone.

Eventually Gayle told him about her long-standing relationship with James and her frustration about the stagnant state in which they'd remained. But their relationship never faltered. Paul was always willing to lend a sympathetic ear, a shoulder, with nothing more passing between them than a chaste kiss on the cheek. Gayle thought she wanted more.

And then he met Rayne. Her best friend. Married her. Loved her. Loved her as always happened with men who met her.

Slowly Gayle returned the hairbrush to the tabletop, turned to face herself in the mirror.

She should have spoken up years ago. She hadn't. Rayne won Paul's heart without so much as lifting a finger. Rayne never realized how lucky she was to have Paul, how much he suffered during their marriage, the frustration he felt. He never came right out and said it, but she sensed that Rayne didn't satisfy him — not physically. Rayne never spoke of it either. But she could tell, tell by the words that were never said.

Still, she remained the friend, the confidant, oddly loving them both.

In the end, she married James. The one man who didn't have eyes for Rayne.

Seven

Pauline twisted the wand of the vertical white blinds to stem the flow of the afternoon sunshine. It was nearly three o'clock. Time for their session.

She turned away from the window and sat in the overstuffed side chair that was angled to the right of where Rayne sat. Pauline pulled her white coat closed, almost covering her navy blue suit beneath, and tucked a stray strand of her auburn hair behind her left ear. She placed her wire-rimmed reading glasses on the cherry-wood table.

The seating was placed in a conversational grouping, creating a sense of openness, friendship, accessibility. A five-foot-tall ficus tree drank in the sunshine from beneath the bay window.

The room was more rectangular than square, with a two-inch-thick midnight-blue carpet. Artwork by Jacob Lawrence, Elizabeth Catlett, Archibald Motley, and Romare Bearden hung throughout the room, showcasing the cool off-white walls. Her string of degrees from Wellesley, Columbia, and Johns Hopkins held places of honor on either side of the window, which overlooked the courtyard below.

I always liked this room, Rayne thought. *I want a room like this one day.*

"How are you this afternoon, Rayne?" Pauline placed her hands on either arm of the chair and leaned back against the thick cushion. "You fixed your hair. You look very nice."

Do I? Rayne's right hand rose halfway toward her head, then stopped. She put her hand in her lap.

"I always wished I had hair like yours," Pauline continued in her even modulation, thinking about her own baby-fine hair. "Wild and free. Do you ever feel wild and free, Rayne?"

Rayne's gaze slid toward the window and followed the flight of seagulls heading for the Mississippi River.

Sometimes, late at night, those nights when the shadows don't come, when I'm not afraid, I can make out the sounds and scents of the river. I feel its heavy mugginess rolling to a sluggish rhythm, embracing its deep secrets up and down the banks. I'm like the Mississippi. Full of dark history, debris, moving along be-

cause I must, carrying the burdens heaped upon my waves.

To look at the river, at me, they see beauty, strength, power. But beneath the waves is the unthinkable, the discarded, the remnants of times best forgotten, and not. I want to fly above it all like the gulls — wild and free. I do. I do. Tell her! the voice urged deep into her ear. *Tell her! I want to get out!*

Rayne slowly turned toward Pauline. The words rose in gentle undulations up her throat. "I am not free." Her voice sounded choked, like a phone momentarily losing its connection. She swallowed, struggled to control her racing heart.

A sudden joyous rush swept through Pauline. These were the first words Rayne had uttered to her since her arrival more than a month earlier. The small things, Pauline thought, an encouraging smile trimming her mouth. One small thing at a time.

"You're not free? Why do you think that is, Rayne?" Pauline held her breath, praying for an answer, any answer. Perhaps Rayne's response would answer her own haunting questions of being trapped, a feeling she knew all too well.

Rayne gazed at a place beyond Pauline's

shoulder. "Locked . . . inside myself. It's
. . . safe, here."

"It's safe to stay locked inside?"

"Yes."

"What outside frightens you?"

Rayne's voice turned childlike. "The shadow."

Pauline's heart thudded as a swift, sudden image of a dark figure looming above her flashed in her mind. "The shadow?" she repeated, to keep Rayne engaged. "Tell me about the shadow."

"It comes at night."

"Do you know what this shadow is?"

Rayne crossed her arms and legs, her eyes darting nervously around the room. She appeared to shrink inside herself.

You need to tell this woman what's going on, the voice inside her head whispered. *Tell her. Tell her.*

Suddenly, Rayne violently shook her head, her hair whipping around her face, as a strangled sob erupted from the center of her being. "It will hurt me if I tell," she finally gasped in a small voice.

Pauline felt the hair on the back of her neck tingle. Cautiously she leaned forward. "Rayne," she said softly. "Is the shadow here now, Rayne?" An overwhelming desire to protect Rayne from the shadows that haunted her filled Pauline. She wanted to protect her in a way that she had been unable to protect herself so many years before.

Rayne's throat worked up and down. Her voice was barely a whisper. "No."

"You're safe here, Rayne. I won't let anything happen to you. I promise. But you need to talk to me. Tell me what you see and why it frightens you, so that we can work to make it go away." She had to win Rayne's trust. It was crucial now.

Rayne began to tremble. Her eyes widened in terror. A heavy hand covered her mouth. The weight of the shadow pressed down on her, into her. She tried to scream, but she couldn't, she could hardly breathe. *You better not say a damn word to a soul, girl,* the raspy voice that haunted her dreams growled in her ear. That voice that came to her in the dead of night, then slid away before the sun rose to illuminate the dark secret of her shame.

"Rayne. Rayne, look at me," Pauline insisted.

Panic-filled eyes tried to focus on Pauline's face. If she could do that, focus, her vision would clear. It would be daylight and it would go away. "No one . . . will believe me," Rayne choked, the words coming from some hidden place.

"I'll believe you. Take your time, Rayne, just tell me what you see."

Rayne blinked, slowly coming back, the room easing into focus. She gazed around the office. It was daylight. Her breathing gradually slowed. Her heart stopped racing. "I . . . I don't remember. Just . . . fear," she whispered. Absently she touched her cheeks and looked in confusion at the tears that coated her fingertips, then looked across at Pauline, unspoken questions hovering in her eyes. Rayne pressed her lips together, trying desperately to recall what had happened. "Why was I crying?"

"That's what we're going to try to find out . . . together. We need to know what is frightening you."

Rayne's body involuntarily stiffened.

"It's all right, Rayne. Try to relax." Pauline walked to the small refrigerator and took out a bottle of spring water. Taking her time, to give Rayne a moment to compose herself, she poured the icy liquid into a plastic cup and returned to the couch, watching closely for any further signs of hysteria. "You've made enormous progress today. You're talking. That's important. It's the only way to get better. Do

111

you understand? You have to keep talking."

For a moment, she wrestled with an urge to tell Rayne her own story, the tortured tale of her trauma. It would cement their bond, the trust between them. Then Rayne would know she was not alone. But to do so would be risky, cruel, even manipulative. More important, it would be wrong morally and totally unprofessional. So she kept quiet with her burning truth.

She handed Rayne the cup. "Here, drink this."

Rayne looked up from her folded hands and shook her head. "Medicine. I don't want any medicine. Please."

"It's not medicine. It's only water. I promise."

Cautiously she took the cup and a tentative sip. She looked skeptically at Pauline. "The medication . . . can't think with them. Everything . . . is slow and hazy."

"Do you know where you are?"

Rayne nodded. "A . . . hospital . . . for crazy people. But I'm not crazy." Her eyes welled with tears.

"Do you know why you're here, Rayne?" Pauline asked gently.

She nodded. "I tried to kill myself," she answered in a flat voice.

"Yes. You slit your wrists. The medication is to help keep you calm so you won't harm yourself again." She waited a beat, debating on whether to pose her next question without pushing Rayne too far.

Rayne gazed down at her arms, turning her palms up, and saw the thin line of stitches on both wrists. Her body jerked as a tremor shot through her. She saw the glistening shards of the broken mirror on the bathroom floor calling out to her.

Pauline took a risk and decided to proceed. "Rayne. What happened that day to make you try to take your life? Can you tell me?"

Rayne's old bedroom, the one she'd grown up in, materialized in front of her. A light breeze blew in from the open window, gently ruffling the sheer off-white curtains. Lying in bed, she could look out at the stars that dotted the night sky. She thought of her daughter, her darling Desi. Desiree loved to count the stars on her little fingers and make wishes. It was a nightly ritual that mother and daughter shared. The scene in her mind suddenly shifted, flashed forward.

The bedroom door was closed. She always kept it closed when she slept. Had to. But she had nothing to fear, not now. Not after all this time. But the shadow of her past crept into her room that night while she slept, even as dreams of her daughter roamed through her head, polluting her precious memories with their weight and heavy hands. She had to make it stop.

"Paul and Desiree are dead," Rayne responded in a faraway voice.

"And you wanted to die, too?" Pauline pressed.

Rayne looked away. It was dark. The roads were slick from the rain that had pummeled the city in relentless fury for three days. They were coming home from an awards ceremony where Rayne had won for her latest documentary, *Back When We Were Free*. Paul was at the wheel, angry. She tried to remember why. She couldn't. Had she done something, said something? She couldn't remember. He was driving too fast. She asked him to slow down, but he wouldn't listen. He never listened to her, even when she pleaded. Desiree was asleep in the backseat. And then the lights were upon them and she screamed.

Rayne leaped up from the chair, wailing, "Nooo!" She ran to the corner of the room, turned in a frantic circle, her hands covering her face. "No!" She slid down the wall, curving her body into a tight impenetrable ball.

"Where are you, Rayne? Tell me," Pauline urged. Tentatively she crossed the room and lowered herself next to Rayne onto the floor, gently peeling the woman's trembling hands away from her face. "Look at me, Rayne."

Wild, frenzied eyes locked onto Pauline's face. Rayne grabbed the sleeves of Pauline's stiff white lab coat. "Don't let him hurt me. Please."

"Who, Rayne, who?"

"I promise I won't never tell," she said in a childish whimper, curling into a tighter knot.

Something deep inside Pauline gave way, rose up, and burned her throat. Her heart began to palpitate. Pain in her pelvis bent her over. Her head pounded. She struggled to control her rapid breathing. *What was happening?* A tingling fear crept up from the balls of her feet, settled in the center of her chest.

She'd heard that voice before. A frightened little girl voice. *Her* voice. Pleading. Again, the urge rose to disclose the secret that bound them, pour her heart out to the one person who would understand. But then Rayne would become the therapist and she the patient, their roles switched. Reason overrode emotion and she pressed on.

"Rayne. It's me, Dr. Dennis. Look at me, Rayne. There's no one here but you and me. Nothing to hurt you."

Slowly Rayne focused on Pauline's face. She looked around the room as if surprised to find herself there. "Nothing?"

"No. Nothing. Let me help you up." She took Rayne's hands, eased her to her feet, and put her arm around Rayne's shoulders. "This is enough for today. You did very well."

"Did I?"

"Yes. Now let's get you back to your room so you can rest for a while."

After settling Rayne in her room, Pauline returned to her office, entering the notes of their session in Rayne's case file:

First breakthrough in case. Patient became engaged in sporadic conversation though periodically fragmented by outbursts and apparent hallucinations of some past trauma. Fear of someone or something was prevalent. Unsure at this time if fear is directly connected to the deaths of her husband and daughter. However, I think not. Though sorrow is apparent. Deep terror of being hurt. Physical or emotional? Or both? At times, patient reverted to a childish voice. Believe that her underlying trauma is related to childhood. An abusive childhood. Patient requested to be taken off meds. However, that is not advisable at this time. Will consider a reduction in dosages and combinations if progress continues. An increase in therapy sessions is also warranted at this time.

Pauline signed and dated the entry, closed the file, and returned it to the file drawer before locking it. She returned to her desk, sat down, and covered her face with her hands. For those interminable moments, Pauline had felt the terror that Rayne had experienced. It was so powerful, so pervasive that she was still shaken from the effects of the encounter. She'd desperately wanted to reveal her own past, share her ugly secrets, and remove the weight that had held her captive on too many dark nights. This wasn't like her. She prided herself on remaining detached and objective in dealing with her patients. She inhaled a deep breath. And that's what she would continue to do. She must.

Pauline reached for the phone and dialed the home of William Mercer.

"Bill! Bill!" Edith called from the

kitchen window, hoping to catch him before he pulled off.

He stopped just before slamming the door shut on the battered blue Dodge station wagon.

"Yeah?" he shouted.

"That doctor from the hospital is on the phone. Says she need to talk to you right away."

William frowned, an uneasy heat turning in his belly. "What now?" he grumbled under his breath. With barely contained annoyance, he got out of the car and returned to the house.

Edith stood off to the side, pretending not to listen as she busied herself with mixing batter for corn bread. She pushed her thin graying hair away from the sides of her face with the back of her hand.

"How are ya, Doc?" he asked, full of congeniality.

"We had a breakthrough today, Mr. Mercer."

A nerve jumped in his cheek. "Whaddya mean, breakthrough?"

Edith listened carefully as she wiped down the already clean kitchen table.

"Rayne talked today. For the first time since she's been admitted."

"Is that right."

Pauline felt that sudden, disturbing chill roll through her in waves. Silence hung, momentarily, between them.

His voice held no emotion when he next spoke. "Guess that's a good thing there, Doc." He switched the phone from one hand to the other, stole a glance at Edith, and turned his back to her. He lowered his voice. "So what she have ta say?"

"A lot of it was disjointed . . . in pieces," Pauline qualified, her heart racing as if she'd been chased. She pressed on. "But what was most disturbing was a deep fear of someone or something. I'd really like you to come to Cedar's so that you and I can talk in person. I'm sure you'd be able to help me fill in some of the gaps in Rayne's life."

"Can't see how I can help you there, Doc. Rayne's been on her own for a long time."

"I understand. But I believe that something happened to Rayne during her childhood, during the time she was with you, and somehow an old trauma was triggered by the deaths of her husband and daughter." Pauline sensed that there was more to what William knew. He was hiding something. What, was the question?

A thin trail of sweat threaded its way

down William's hairline, finally anchoring itself precariously near his ear.

What had she said? William worried. What crazy story had she told this woman? He pondered the possibilities for a moment. Well, he obviously couldn't let Rayne just rattle on with God knows what, digging up shit that was best left buried, causin' trouble. Girl wasn't never nothin' but trouble nohow.

"You sound real serious, Doc, and I'm gonna take your word for it, you being the professional and all. I'd been thinkin' real hard about our last talk, and I was plannin' on payin' Rayne a visit. Sounds like now would be a good time. I figured Saturday. Yeah, Saturday. I'll come down there and we'll straighten all of this right out."

When Pauline hung up the phone, the sense that she'd opened a Pandora's box was as real as the tremors that shook her hands.

Eight

It was near midday. The August sun blistered the skies, engraving its mark on everything and everyone in its path. The grounds cried out in thirst, cracked in dry fissures from denial, then drank the cool water hungrily like weather-beaten sailors on shore leave.

Robert walked along the pathways, adjusting sprinklers and checking the shrubs and flora for any signs of damage from the unrelenting heat. He removed his dark shades, took a white handkerchief from the back pocket of his jeans, and scrubbed his damp face. He looked around, both hands now crammed into his pockets.

To look at Cedar Grove from the outside, one would never imagine some of the misery, the insanity, that lurked behind the ornate walls. Sometimes, as ashamed as he was to admit fear, the place, the people, frightened him. And he questioned himself.

How far away from illness, from madness, are we all? What is the final push to send us sailing over the precipice into a world of delusion? The idea intimidated yet intrigued him.

Yet even in his fear he had an empathy for these confined souls who were trapped, not by jackets, locked doors, and gates, but trapped in their own minds.

His instinctive nature had always been to nurture, to see things and people blossom. His work was merely an extension of his inner calling. It pained him to see anything or anyone hurt or ignored, begging for care and attention.

Where had he failed, then? he wondered. How could he have not done enough for his mother and sister? Day after day, year after year, he watched them wither. The soft petals of their womanliness dried up and blew away, until there was nothing left but hard stems and rotting roots.

He felt just as much a part of their deflowering as his father should have. The difference was Frank Parrish didn't. He never had. Perhaps his guilt is what finally ravaged his mind, reduced it to mere bits and pieces of the whole, never again to have the joy of a single coherent thought. But was even that enough? Yet he would do what he must. On his mother's deathbed, he promised he would.

Robert walked farther along the path in the direction of the man-made pond, passing the orderlies and nurses who watched the patients with a cautious eye. The atmosphere there, beneath the pondering willows, possessed the magic to ease the heaviness that sat on his spirit. That was the beauty of this place, even as it camouflaged its true intent behind the tall, concrete walls.

He slid his glasses back onto the bridge of his nose, then upward completely, shielding his eyes from the glare and from view.

Then he saw her. It was as if she'd mysteriously appeared — like an apparition — light, almost transparent. He watched her gaze follow the arch of the horizon as if trying to see what lay beyond. Then her face became shadowed by the storm cloud of hair, shielding her from view.

Robert watched her hair covering her face, and wondered why such a beautiful woman would want to hide herself from the world. Still, light appeared to radiate around her like an aura of energy, and the anguished expression of lost innocence in her eyes and that graced her face touched him deeply. Pain. Why is she so hurt? What horror had seduced her, making her its captive? He understood that his curiosity about her was not lust or desire, but sprung out of a humane paternalism. Oddly, he wanted to protect her as much as he struggled against it.

The shadow of his form spread slowly in front of her like water expanding across parched earth. Rayne put a hand to her forehead to shield her eyes as she looked up.

"How are you?" he asked, hoping that he wouldn't shatter her fragile calm, sending her scurrying away.

Rayne lowered her hand and turned her head back toward the beyond.

He spotted the floral-patterned journal, the size of a paperback novel, that lay unopened on her lap, and wondered what thoughts, what secrets, it contained.

"Pretty hot today," he continued, daring to take a closer step. "But you've got a great spot under this tree. I love it here, too. Relaxing."

She turned toward him, her head partially down, her hair slightly concealing the curiosity in her eyes. The corners of her mouth slightly trembled. *You've got to keep talking,* she heard the doctor say. *R-robert.*

Right? She thought she'd asked, but was confused when he didn't respond.

He smiled. "I've seen you," he said in a soothing voice, remembering the many times she'd timidly stood in the doorway of his father's hospital room.

She smiled shyly.

"I've seen some of your films, too. They're quite spectacular."

You've seen . . . my work? that voice in her head asked eagerly.

"They were brilliantly done. I envy that kind of skill, that kind of vision," he went on, allowing his body to relax, his mind to run free. Caught up in the mesmerizing memory of her work, the passion of it, he completely forgot the reason why she was at Cedar's, his only thought was expressing accolades to someone whom he'd admired.

Rayne listened to the energy in his voice, the sincerity, and the door to her closed consciousness creaked open. She felt safe for a fleeting instant. This man, this stranger, was the first person in weeks who didn't speak to her as if she were some backward child, or someone with "a problem." The beginnings of life bubbled inside her. She knew her sense of him was right. There was no danger here, nothing to fear.

I know you, too, Rayne thought, listening to Robert explain why he felt so strongly about the impact of her work on the film industry. Funny, but when she was working, creating, it was one of the few times that she felt whole, like a real person with a purpose. It was the one thing in her life that she could control.

"You've got to forgive me for rambling on like this." He chuckled. "I get like that sometimes when I feel strongly about something." He looked off toward the sky-line. "My work, I think, is who I am," he confessed. "There's something rewarding and soothing about seeing something grow from a tiny seed, or see a plant that was withering bloom with life."

Could you make me bloom? Rayne asked, or thought she did, but maybe not. *I feel like the plant that has withered, gone un-attended. Maybe you could . . . show me . . . what you do sometime?* The question, halting and uncertain, sprang forth so un-expectedly it surprised her. Had she spoken the words out loud?

"I'd like to show you what I do around here."

Her heart raced. Had he heard her silent question?

"Gardening, seeing things grow, is very

126

soothing. I think you would like it." He looked quickly around. "I mean if your doctor says it's okay."

In an instant, they were reminded where they were, who she was, and why she was there. She was a woman under care for a fractured mind, wounded in ways even she couldn't understand.

Rayne blinked, a stricken expression on her face as she looked at herself through his eyes. Then the sudden urge to flee rose within her with the swirling force of a gale wind. The fear of being close, exposed, letting someone in, overwhelmed her with an unexplainable dread. Her eyes began to dart around, seeking escape. Her hand fluttered to her throat where the pulse pounded against her fingertips. The present became a fog, the past taking its place.

Paul was gently reaching for me, whispering how deeply he loved me. "I want you, Rayne, body and soul." *He kissed me and I willed my body to respond. Willed myself not to be repulsed by the touch of my husband, the man I loved. I held my breath and closed my eyes. I could disappear and when I returned it would be over.* "What's wrong, baby?" *I forced my eyes open and there was such deep concern in his. His hand was on my breast, the other between my thighs. Tears squeezed from my eyes and I didn't know why. I didn't know.* "Rayne, baby, what is it?"

Robert watched her growing distress and his own alarms went off. She jumped at the touch of his hand on hers. He didn't need a scene, as much as he would like to keep talking to her. "Why don't I walk you inside?" he asked with a soft gentleness, pushing aside the images and voices in her head.

Rayne glanced at the hand extended to her. Slowly her vision began to clear and the past receded. *It's daylight. Nothing can hurt me now. It can't.*

She stood and he walked alongside her, carefully watching as they made their way toward the arched entryway of the facility.

"I don't think . . . I'm crazy," Rayne uttered as they grew closer to separating.

Robert almost stopped, so surprised was he by the sound of her voice. Instinct told him not to startle her, for he also heard the need for reassurance. But more important than that, he heard the ring of truth in her disjointed plea. Looking toward the entrance of the facility, he quietly said, "I don't think so, either. Don't let where you are define who you are. Only you can do that."

She stared at him for a moment, hugging the comforting words to her breasts. The tips of her fingers briefly fluttered across his hand. Then, suddenly, she turned and ran away.

Nine

Twilight, those precious moments in time when the end clings possessively to the beginning, when illusion is reality cloaked in a soft haze of waning light — uncertain but sure. This was the time Rayne feared most, those moments before night descended in a blanket of darkness, hiding secrets beneath its velvety caress. Night was not gentle.

She paced her close quarters, pushing the terrors away with sharp over-the-shoulder looks, a slap of her hand. They buzzed around her like hungry mosquitoes.

I'm so tired. Tired of being afraid. Afraid of being tired. Tired of being locked up inside myself — in here. But everywhere around me, wherever I turn, there is no getting away from myself.

Her father was coming tomorrow. The thought of "father" should comfort her, but she found none. Vague images of something gone terribly wrong shimmied through her when she thought of her father, saw his face in her mind, heard his voice. Her body seemed to stiffen in response.

Yet there was mixed in with this feeling a sense of abandonment, too, a sense of deep betrayal that left her unsteady. And at the core of those feelings was her father. Of that she was certain. But there were no solid images to accompany these feelings. Just that single, fleeting, terrifying glimpse of the man she called "father."

You can remember if you really want to, that voice whispered, the sound of it a low buzz in her ear.

Rayne put her hands to her ears, violently shaking her head, her hair fanning out like a storm cloud around her head. "No. I can't remember. I can't," she hissed between her teeth.

There was a light tap, tap on her door, startling her into immobility. Nurse Simpson stepped in before being asked, giving Rayne no time to harness her wild-eyed expression.

Judy Simpson left the door slightly ajar just in case there was any need to call for help. But for the most part, Rayne Holland was as quiet as they came. Except for those sporadic anxiety attacks where she'd find her naked, crying and balled up in a

131

corner, Rayne Holland was the perfect patient.

She was neat and clean, maybe obsessively so. And she never fought the staff like some of the other patients who went completely berserk and had to be restrained. Some of them would bite your arm or scratch your face if you got too close. Nurse Simpson had enough tetanus shots to prove it. But she knew how to handle the patients if the need arose. Every nurse considered the act of restraint an essential and necessary part of their training. This could be a very dangerous place. Not to mention the episodes with patients being taken for shock therapy. The thought of it made her cringe. Fortunately, that practice was reserved for the most severe cases, at least that's what she was told.

Rayne Holland was nothing like that. Electroshock wasn't something she'd have to endure. She reminded Nurse Simpson of a frightened child, forced to live in the home of relatives and trying to stay out of everyone's way.

Damn shame, Judy thought. Rayne Holland had been an up-and-coming filmmaker, one of a growing number of talented black women in the business. She remembered reading the news articles and seeing the television broadcasts of the accident that killed Rayne's husband and daughter, and thought at the time how horrific that experience must have been, especially following such a triumphant moment only hours earlier.

From what Judy could recall, Rayne and her family were returning from an awards ceremony honoring Rayne's new documentary.

Judy always wondered if the real reason for Rayne Holland's mental break was her guilt — that she'd been the one who survived. Perhaps.

But she couldn't concern herself with that. It was for the doctors to figure out. Still, she couldn't help but feel compassion for this young woman who had so much and lost it all in one fell swoop, including her mind.

"You have a visitor," Nurse Simpson said, keeping her voice even and pleasant. "Your friend Gayle is here to see you. Isn't that nice?" Nurse Simpson put on her best smile. "Come on now and see your friend. You don't want to keep her waiting."

Rayne silently followed the broad-shouldered nurse out of the room, down the cool blue corridor, taking surreptitious glances at the montage of patients who hovered — like planes waiting to land — in the doorways of their rooms, or who were being escorted to "treatment" areas. *Oh, yes, I've heard the screams,* Rayne thought, *but I never want to imagine what is being done to those people. Because if I do, it could be me.*

They proceeded past the nurses' station with its horseshoe shape and Peeping Tom monitors that provided twenty-four-hour entertainment, then turned left along the corridor to the visitors' room.

The room was actually quite pleasant, in a muted sea green with long soft couches in green and beige. Floor-to-ceiling windows, covered with mesh, gave a fractured view of the grounds below. For the entertainment of the patients and to distract the visitors from the real reason why they'd come to Cedar's, there were two twenty-seven-inch television sets mounted on either wall. Small group seating, with square tables bolted to the floor, allowed for card games or some therapeutic craft project.

Several patients were already in the room, some fully engaged with their guests, while others stared aimlessly or twirled their hands in what looked to be despair.

Gayle rose from her seat by the window when Rayne stepped through the doorway, and her first thought was that Rayne's hair was combed and that her eyes weren't quite so dull and lifeless as they had been the last time she'd visited. The realization instantly lifted her sagging spirits and she smiled as her friend drew near.

Gayle desperately wanted the old Rayne back — her friend. She needed someone to talk to, someone who would understand. With Paul gone and Rayne out of reach, her unhappiness was that much more difficult to endure.

Although Rayne had never been one who truly unveiled herself to anyone, not even to her, Gayle knew she could always count on Rayne to listen.

"Hi, hon," she said when Rayne stood in front of her, still beautiful, still unwell. Gayle leaned forward and kissed her cheek. She raised her hand to brush her hair farther away from Rayne's cheek, but halted in midair. The memory of the look that Rayne gave her on her last visit materialized before her and something inside went cold. But just as quickly as it had come, the sensation was replaced by delight when a shadow of a smile formed around the edges of Rayne's mouth. Gayle's throat tightened. She took Rayne's hand.

"Let's go outside," Gayle urged in a loud

whisper. "It's still beautiful."

The two friends walked hand-in-hand along the pathway that ran the circumference of the facility. If you listened closely, you could almost hear the sound of trees rustling in the light breeze.

To Gayle, this moment brought to mind the days of their youth, when everything seemed simple and they'd shared their plans for the future.

It was a couple of months before graduation, a gloriously happy and sad time. Graduation would be the first day of new beginnings, but the beginning of the end of the familiar.

Gayle hooked her arm in the curve of Rayne's. "Remember when you decided, two months before graduation, that you weren't going to college in Savannah? That you weren't going to be a teacher, but a filmmaker?" Gayle tossed her head back and laughed. "Girl, you could have knocked me over with a feather. I hadn't ever known you to change your mind about anything once it was made up. And it — you — scared the hell outta me. All I could think about was that my mother and father were going to flip when I told them I wasn't going to Georgia State, but going with Rayne to New York. Because you know I had to go with you.

"But you know what, sugah, to be truthful, the first feeling that came over me was anger. I was pissed. I was disappointed. I felt betrayed. I thought, *'How dare she do this to me? I'm supposed to be her friend and she didn't even tell me her plans.'* And you were just so matter-of-fact about the whole thing as if it were no more important than deciding to wear a different pair of panty hose. There was always a part of you I never understood, Rayne. A part that you kept guarded, even from me. But I'd come to accept it over the years as who you were, who we were."

Gayle tilted her head, pressing it momentarily on Rayne's shoulder. "We were walking along a path pretty much like this one when you made your announcement; remember, the path that ran around the high school? I think the only reason why my folks finally gave in and let me go was because you would be there. They always believed you were the sensible one, responsible. They trusted me with you." Gayle chuckled at the memory. "I guess I did need looking after. Remember my room?"

The image of Gayle's bedroom leaped into focus in Rayne's mind. It was a montage of color and chaos. Discarded clothing draped on doorknobs, backs of chairs, and frames of doors with an almost artistic zest. Used lipstick tubes and a rainbow of nail polish bottles dotted the top of the white lacquer dresser. Silk undies and sexy teddies mixed with sweat socks and flannel nightgowns ready to burst from the seams of the drawers, trying to become a part of the mad medley of Gayle's room, Rayne recalled, the ache of melancholy settling in the middle of her chest.

On more occasions than she dared to count, Rayne found refuge in Gayle's clutter, in her total disregard for order and discipline, which was so much the opposite of her world just across the street.

Gayle sighed. "I always envied you, Rayne. I wished that I was more like you, from your wild hair to the way you kept every class note in order. Yet there wasn't a stiffness about you. You know? Not really," she went on, needing to say the things that had been lingering in her mind. "I guess I figured that whatever it was you had, if I hung around long enough, some of it would rub off on me. Looks like it did, huh?" she asked with a false chuckle. "I'm a big-time corporate bank executive, my home looks like it belongs on the cover of a magazine. My husband is an engineer, my daughter a budding ballerina. I've kept my weight down to a size ten, even though I'll never see thirty again, and with regular touch-ups and a cut I can keep my hair looking decent."

They reached the bench that embraced the pond. Rayne sat down, looked out toward the water. Gayle sat next to her. The slight breeze fanned her bangs.

"I wish so many things were different, Rayne," she said, folding her hands in her lap. "I wish I could change things, do things differently. Make other choices." She turned her face away from her friend and thought about Paul — James — Paul — choices.

"You were always the quiet, take-charge one. You kept me in line, kept my world in some sort of order. I miss that." Her voice cracked. "I feel as if everything is coming apart, Rayne. There's no one to turn to. No one."

Gayle covered her face with her hands, ashamed and appalled at herself for dropping her problems in Rayne's lap as if she could help. However, the overwhelming urge to talk to Rayne was more powerful than reason, even though in her head she knew Rayne wasn't really listening. This whole thing was more symbolic, as if by its very act it could bring normalcy back into their lives.

"Why?" Rayne asked, her voice a hoarse whisper.

Gayle snapped up her head, her eyes wide and glistening, not daring to believe she'd heard Rayne. She stared into her eyes. "Rayne?"

"Why . . . are you so . . . lonely?" *I can almost see an image of you and Paul together. Is that why? Are you lonely because Paul is gone? What about your husband, James?*

But then that picture merged with the two of them working side-by-side at a SoHo diner in New York City so they could pay their rent. *Which picture is real? I'm not sure. I can't ever be sure.*

The images twisted together into a knot of perceptions.

But if Gayle was really my friend, there would be no pictures in my mind of her with Paul. There couldn't be. If she isn't my friend, then the picture of her and Paul is real and what I always thought we had doesn't exist.

Gayle's mouth opened, then closed. "Oh, God . . . Rayne." She pulled Rayne into her arms, holding her stiff body close. "I knew you'd be all right. I knew it," she said against Rayne's hair.

That's all I want, Rayne thought, *to be all*

right for the first time in my life. I want to be able to see life clearly, not through a prism. I want the shadows to be exorcised from my soul, the fear that constantly lingers in my heart to be punished for its years of torment, the emptiness that I feel to be finally filled. I want to be happy and whole, like I've dreamed of being since I was six. I need to know. I need to understand. But when I do, what will I see?

Gayle continued to ramble on excitedly about how wonderful it was that Rayne was getting better, that she would be out of there soon, that they could pick up where they left off. She would help. Anything Rayne needed she was willing to do.

Rayne listened in silence.

Ten

The morning sky was heavy with dark clouds that hung above the city of Savannah like rolls of fat on an oversized waist. The weather report predicted a downpour, bringing long overdue relief from the blistering heat. But it felt like something more. The air was charged with electricity, the sky illuminating in streaks of crackling light. Something ominous. The warning drumbeats of thunder could be heard in the distance.

Storms never boded well for the facility, Pauline thought, concern etching curves in her forehead. She tucked her hair behind her ears. The noise, darkness, and pounding rain were conductors for the patients, triggering any number of bizarre behaviors. The entire staff was always on full alert during thunderstorms, which unfortunately only added to the already unnerving tension.

She wished Rayne's father was not coming today.

Pauline poured hot water into a mug over a chamomile tea bag. She handed the cup to Rayne, who sat by the window gazing out at the gathering clouds. She took the cup, whispered her thanks, and brought the brew to her lips. Pauline poured herself a cup and sat opposite Rayne. They both gazed toward the outside.

"I don't really like days like this," Pauline confessed, taking a cautious step toward getting Rayne engaged, hoping to continue on their track of precarious progress. They'd met several times since the initial breakthrough and Pauline was finally beginning to feel that she was doing Rayne some real good. "I prefer the sunshine. Don't you?"

A blanket of silence wrapped around them.

Rayne's voice seemed to come from some distance. "We have to have days like this."

Encouraged, Pauline moved slightly forward, resting her arms on her thighs, her mug braced in both hands. "I suppose."

"Without the rain nothing would grow and every day would be more of the same nothingness."

"You're right. No matter how much we

like or dislike something, there's a place and reason for everything." She took a sip of her tea. "I spoke with Gayle this morning. She called me quite happy, actually. She said the two of you talked."

Rayne did not respond. *Talked?*

"I think it's wonderful that you're letting her reach out to you, Rayne. It's important to your recovery." She waited a beat. "How do you feel about your visit with Gayle?"

Rayne brought the mug to her lips. *At times, it felt like it once was between us,* Rayne thought. *I wasn't confined to a mental hospital. I was the friend to Gayle that I'd always been.*

"Something . . . is wrong between Gayle and me," she finally uttered.

Pauline set her cup down. "What do you think is wrong, Rayne?"

Rayne wanted to hide, to cover her face and hide. She gripped the cup in both hands, fighting the battle to block out Dr. Dennis and her questions behind the cascade of her hair. *Dr. Dennis said she would help you if you helped yourself. Stop runnin' away, girl,* the whispered voice warned. *Speak up!*

Rayne's hands shook as she brought the cup to her lips, just as a shard of lightning cut across the sky.

"Rayne, what do you think is wrong between you and Gayle?" Pauline gently repeated.

Rayne briefly shut her eyes and saw herself pulling the folded sheet of Strathmore paper from Paul's jacket pocket. She'd started to simply toss it on top of his bureau with his cuff links and change. Something stopped her. Instinct, maybe. Curiosity, perhaps. Confirmation . . . yes.

She wished she'd never read the words she'd dreaded to ever see or hear. Living in a safe fantasy, pretending ignorance, made life bearable.

"A letter," Rayne whispered, the word almost sticking in her throat. The tea sloshed over the top of her cup. A slow dark stain pooled in her lap. Rayne didn't seem to notice.

Pauline's first reaction was to grab a napkin and soak up the fluid. But instinct told her to wait, leave it alone, and allow Rayne to stay in that place just a bit longer.

"Let's talk about the letter. Tell me why it bothers you."

Rayne frowned, trying to make the words materialize. "Gayle wrote a letter to my husband, Paul," she blurted, then covered her mouth as if to keep any more words from tumbling out.

Pauline's right brow slightly rose. "Why does that disturb you, Rayne? What was in the letter to upset you?"

Rayne squeezed her eyes shut, then opened them wide, trying to make the words come into focus and stand out in the dark.

Her voice shuddered. "I don't . . . remember."

"Then let's talk about what you do remember, perhaps that will help. What do you feel when you think about this letter from your friend to your husband?"

Rayne flinched. She put down her cup on the round table and pressed her lips together for a moment before looking away. "Pain. Betrayal. Confusion. Anger. Something twisting inside."

"Are these feelings directed at your husband?"

Rayne hesitated. "No," she answered, her voice suddenly distant and detached.

Pauline made a mental note to explore that further. "These feelings you have about the letter are directed at your friend Gayle?"

Rayne's throat worked up and down. Her mouth trembled. "Yes! Yes!" She covered her face with her hands.

Pauline reached across the space and

stroked Rayne's back. "Good. This is good, Rayne. The only way to get beyond these feelings is to confront them, no matter how much you may want to run away from them. And I'll help you."

An explosion of thunder rattled the windows, followed by the whiplike crack of lightning.

The rain will come soon, Pauline thought. She could feel the tension brewing within the walls, simmering like stew, the vapors of discontent seeping beneath door frames and under noses. She glanced briefly at the cloud-torn sky, then back at her patient.

"If you can't remember what the letter said, Rayne, how can you be certain it was something bad?"

"I don't know how. I . . . just know. I can't remember the words, but I can't forget the feeling."

"Then let's focus on the feelings that you remember. Where were you when you found the letter?"

Rayne jerked at the sound of thunder and wrapped her arms around her body. "It was raining. A day like today — all day long. I was in my bedroom."

"How were you feeling that day?"

"Nervous."

"Why were you nervous?"

"It was the day of the awards ceremony given by the Black Filmmakers Institute. I was receiving an award for my documentary."

"Why did that make you nervous?"

"I don't like being on display — exposed." She turned her face away.

"So you were feeling nervous and a bit anxious about getting up in front of all those people."

"Yes. I really didn't want to do it. Paul insisted that I go. We'd argued about it all week." She balled her fist and pushed it to her mouth. Her voice dropped to a dull flatness. "He never listened."

Pauline watched Rayne's expression shift quickly from anxious and attentive to utter defeat, as if she'd been beaten without a weapon.

"Perhaps your husband didn't want you to miss out on such an honor because of unwarranted fears. Often the unknown is what frightens us. It's quite normal to be nervous and anxious in that type of situation. Most people are nervous when they have to face a room full of strangers. I know I am. I've been doing it for years and my stomach still gets in knots every time I think about making a presentation."

Rayne didn't respond.

"It's okay to be afraid as long as we don't let our fears paralyze us, Rayne. We have to find a way to use that energy in a positive way."

"You don't seem like you're afraid of anything."

Pauline rose and Rayne's gaze followed her to the counter where she refilled their cups of tea.

"Tell me what else you were feeling that day," she said, returning to the chair and handing Rayne her cup.

"That's all . . . really."

"So you had these feelings before you found the letter?"

Rayne nodded.

"Where in the room was the letter — on the floor, the dresser?"

"In Paul's jacket pocket," she answered blandly.

"Tell me about it. Take me through it step by step and tell me what you were feeling."

Rayne leaned back against the cushion of the chair, exhaled a long breath, and closed her eyes. "I was gathering clothes for the cleaners. I didn't really have time to do it, but I just wanted to — something to keep my mind off of the evening," she said, hesitating and seeming to weigh each word.

"Was anyone else at home?"

"No. I was alone. Desi . . ." She winced in anguish at the sound of her daughter's name. "She was next door playing with my neighbor's little girl."

"Go on."

"I was taking things out of the closet and I noticed a spot on Paul's suit jacket. I took it off the hanger and was going to put it in the pile, but then I remembered to check the pockets." She opened her eyes. "I found the letter." The words seemed to dance in front of her eyes, mocking her.

"When you were reading it, what were you thinking?"

Dear Paul. "That they were laughing at me for being so stupid — for not knowing." *I know I shouldn't be writing to you . . .*

"What did the letter say, Rayne? Can you remember now?"

Her mouth trembled and her breathing elevated, her nostrils flaring with each in and out. She reached for the teacup, then stopped. "Gayle wrote . . . how important Paul was to her, that she didn't know what she would do without him." *Although we're both married, what we have is even more precious . . .*

"What did you do then?"

"All the words became a blur. I guess I was crying. But I wasn't sad, really. I just felt betrayed. I never thought that Gayle . . ."

"That Gayle what, Rayne?"

"That she would have an affair with my husband . . . not after the things I shared with her."

"How can you be certain that your husband was having an affair with Gayle?"

"We . . . Paul and I . . ." She turned away, faced the window, the storm.

The rain had come, steady, pelting the window, insisting on getting in. The trees swayed, almost bending under the onslaught of wind and water, spotlighted by a showcase of white light.

"Talk to me, Rayne. I'm here to listen, not judge. What was it between you and Paul?"

"Why don't you act like a woman for once in your miserable life!"

"I . . . I couldn't, I wasn't a real wife . . . to him." She lowered her head, her body filling with shame.

"You talked with Gayle about this?"

Rayne nodded. "Not everything, just some things. She guessed the rest."

Pauline was reflective for a moment. "You never had the chance to confront either of them about the letter, did you?"

"No," she murmured. *Tell her, tell her. Tell her everything,* the voice urged.

I can't. I can't.

"You're dealing with a lot of unresolved issues, Rayne, in addition to guilt and feelings of betrayal. You're also dealing with speculation. The letter could mean a variety of things, and until you confront Gayle with what's on your mind, a lot of what's going on inside you will continue. Gayle needs to know, Rayne. And only you can do that — when you're ready." Pauline let out a breath. "We made a lot of progress today. I want it to continue. You may have noticed that you've been feeling a bit different lately, not quite so sluggish and unable to focus. I've made a notation on your chart to reduce the dosage of your medication. As long as progress continues, I don't see it as being a problem to continue with that line of treatment. Do you?"

Rayne stared at Pauline for several moments, hoping to be able to grasp the fleeting sensation of unease that had suddenly sifted through her. But the elusive impression was gone before she could wrap her mind around it and understand.

"Good." Pauline stood. "That's it for today. Nurse Simpson will see you back to your room." She put a hand on Rayne's shoulder as they walked toward the door. "I'm really proud of you and the steps you've decided to take. Just remember," she added, her free hand on the doorknob, "I'm here to listen and to help. As long as you continue to do the work." She opened the door. "I'll let you know when your father arrives. I want to speak with him first."

Rayne closed the door of her room behind her, crossing the floor to the window. The sky was dark, almost night, but it was in fact late morning. She could hear the sorrowful moans of the patients, the chilling cries that rose the hair on one's arms. She pressed her hands to her ears.

Coward. When you have the chance to speak up, you don't. Now what? That's what your problem is, always hiding . . . always . . .

"Shut up! Damn you. Shut up!"

She could feel a part of herself scurry to the corner, surprised at being scolded. But the taunting voice got in one last dig before settling down into the recesses of her subconscience. *Daddy's comin' . . . Daddy's comin'. You'll need me then. I betcha.*

Eleven

Gayle stood in the doorway, staring at her husband's form beneath the light blanket he'd thrown over his naked body. She stepped into the room.

"How many nights are you going to sleep in the guest room, James?" She wanted to sound strong and not as vulnerable as she felt.

James slowly lifted his arm that was draped over his eyes. "I hadn't really thought about it, Gayle."

"What are you trying to prove? You want to hurt me, is that it?"

James sat up, tossing a pillow to the floor in the process. "Do you hear yourself? This isn't just about *you*. There's a great big world out there, and hard as it may be for you to believe, it doesn't revolve around you. That's the problem. But you're so consumed with yourself, your job, your *friend*, there's no room for anything else."

He brought his knees up to his chest and rested his arms across them. "You haven't let me touch you in weeks . . . months. You're too tired, too busy, not in the mood. How do you think that makes me feel? I don't know what to do anymore. I'm tired of playing second, third fiddle in your life."

She folded her arms beneath her breasts, her nightgown inching up above her knees. "What . . . are you saying?"

"I'm saying . . . I want out. And I want Tracy." He looked her straight in the eye and she felt her knees give way.

"You can't mean that." Fear made her defiant. "I won't let you take Tracy."

James got up from the bed, took his robe, and slipped his arms through the sleeves. "Don't make this any more difficult than it has to be. We haven't had a marriage in far too long. Whatever needs to be worked out in Tracy's best interest is what we'll do."

Her body trembled. This was a man she didn't know. When had that happened? "And who decides that?"

James stood in front of her in the open doorway. "We see how the decisions you've made have affected our daughter. And it's my damned fault for not stepping in and stopping your foolishness in the beginning." He shook his head in disgust. "I may have put up with your single-mindedness, your lack of real love for me . . . because I loved you. Really loved you, Gayle. But now it's gone beyond me. It's affecting Tracy. And that I won't stand for. It's time for a change." He brushed past her and out the door.

Gayle stood rooted to the spot, held captive by forces that had spiraled out of her control. She covered her face with her hands. "What have I done?"

Moments later, the sound of the shower could be heard from down the hallway. Slowly, Gayle turned, hoping to see, what she wasn't sure, maybe yesterdays when things were different, better between her and James. Better, humph. Why didn't the word *good* come to mind? Had things ever been really good between them? How long had it been since she was actually happy, that they'd been happy together? She couldn't remember.

Maybe it was her fault, but it took two people to make a marriage work. They were both consumed with their own lives. They'd taken what they had for granted and grew apart as a result. The only thread that had held them together was Tracy. And when Tracy started coming apart, so did she and James.

Gayle slid down the wall and sat on the

floor, wrapping her arms around her knees. Her husband was leaving her. Her marriage was over. She shook her head, disbelieving the truth.

This isn't what she'd worked for. She'd spent too many years trying to convince James to get married, to marry her. To have someone who was only hers, to prove to everyone that she was wanted and loved. To have someone who didn't want Rayne first.

Tears of regret spilled over her closed lids. Everything always came back to Rayne. Always. For as long as she could remember.

She'd been terrified when Rayne came back to Savannah, more beautiful and mysterious than ever. She was certain that once Rick met her he'd fall head over heels for her just like every other man. But he didn't. She didn't give him a chance, didn't wait around to get hurt. She'd dumped him first. She'd seen the looks he'd thrown Rayne's way when he thought she wasn't paying attention. She politely answered his questions about Rayne's background and read beneath the surface. When she told him it was over, he truly looked stunned, hurt, and Gayle almost took back what she'd said. But some irrational place in her heart told her it was only a matter of time before his full attention was turned toward Rayne. Gayle went through a series of short-lived romances that last year of school, all of which she politely exited before what she perceived was the inevitable. At one point she'd become so obsessed with losing to Rayne that she would initiate the conversations about Rayne to her at-the-moment beau. None of them passed the test, except James Davis.

"You don't have anything to worry about, Gayle," James said one night when they'd parked down by Lake Charles. "I'm not interested in Rayne Mercer. She's pretty and all, but she's . . . I don't know . . . strange."

"How can you say that? Rayne is not strange," Gayle threw back, half in defense of her friend, the other half elated that he didn't want Rayne.

"Did you ever really look at her? I mean really look? It's like she's staring right through you sometimes. It's spooky."

Gayle cuddled closer and let his fingers dance along the inside of her half-opened blouse. "She's just thoughtful, that's all. Most men find her intriguing."

"I don't. All I want to concentrate on

now is finishing school, going to college for my engineering degree, and finding a good-paying job."

Her heart thumped. "What . . . about us?"

James kissed the top of her head. "We have plenty of time, sugah. I want things to be right before we think about anything long term."

"Long term. You mean marriage?"

"Yeah."

Gayle sat up in the seat, pulling her blouse into a bunch in her fist. "So I'm supposed to wait another five or six years until you think things are right?"

"Sugah, if it's meant, we'll be together."

"What do you mean *if* it's meant?"

"Time changes people, Gayle. Right now, you think you want me, and I feel the same way. But we both need to go to college, get out in the world. Make sure what we feel for each other isn't some puppy love but the real thing that can stand the test of time."

He pulled her into his arms and took her chin into his hand, turning her to face him. "I don't want to go into marriage with any regrets, any 'if only' and 'I wish.' It has to be for good. And I have to be sure. I want our marriage to be forever."

At that moment, Gayle was certain she couldn't love anyone more than she loved James, and she showed him, right in the backseat of his father's station wagon.

Right after graduation, James left Savannah to attend school at Howard University in Washington, and she and Rayne headed to New York. They called each other constantly and visited at every opportunity. They made it through those four years by sheer determination. She came out of school with her degree in banking and finance and he with one in engineering. Gayle was sure the time was right. She'd paid her dues; she'd waited.

"The time's not right, Gayle," James announced one night over the phone, when she'd broached the subject of marriage again. "Not yet. I need to get settled in a stable job, save some money. You can't eat love, sugah, that takes bucks."

So she waited, found a job at First National Bank, and dug her heels in. Within the first year, she'd been promoted twice. James was working for a growing company that designed and maintained Web sites for international corporations. They were inching up the corporate ladder. Finally, James asked her to marry him.

And then she met Paul. He was everything that James wasn't. He was exciting, so easy to talk to, and there was something almost dangerous about him, something daring. For all his outright sexiness, he never made a move toward her. Always treated her like a lady. However, her loyalty to James kept her from speaking what was in her heart, so they remained friends, more than friends.

When Paul married Rayne she realized that any hope she may have had for them was over. Rayne had the brass ring once again, without even trying.

"You'll always be my best girl," Paul said to her as they stood outside the chapel following the wedding, more handsome than ever in his black tux and snow-white shirt. "You're important to me. That's never going to change."

"I'll always be your friend. I'll be there for you, no matter what."

"I know that, babe. That's why I love you." He kissed her lightly on the lips, before turning to join the reception on the lawn.

She didn't realize until months later what the test of their friendship would mean.

They'd met after work one evening for drinks at their favorite café, Clary's, in the historic district.

"I don't know what to do, Gayle. It's just so frustrating. I feel like I'm going to hurt her. But I love her. What's wrong with me?"

Gayle stretched her hand across the table and took his. She leaned forward. "What's going on?"

Paul looked away, his expression pained and saddened. This wasn't the same happy-go-lucky man of a few months earlier.

"I don't even know how to say this."

"Just say it."

"Something's wrong with Rayne."

Her pulse began to pound. "Is she sick? What's wrong?"

He shook his head. "No. No, nothing like that. It's just . . . well . . . let's just say that things haven't been working too well inside the bedroom."

Gayle frowned. "What do you mean?"

Paul took a sip of his Scotch-and-water, staring into the contents of the glass. "She won't . . . she can't seem to give herself to me unless . . ." His voice trailed off. "I can't talk about this. I shouldn't be talking about this. Forget it, babe. Forget I said anything, okay?" He gave her a crooked smile, downed his drink, and ordered another.

Gayle stroked the top of his hand. "She's

probably just overwhelmed with the idea of being a wife and starting her film career. That's all. You know how intense and focused Rayne can be. Just give it some time."

"Yeah," he muttered, sounding cynical. "Does she ever talk to you about *it*?"

Gayle thought about the few conversations she and Rayne had about Rayne's marriage. For the most part, Rayne claimed to be happy, though it never showed on her face, in her voice, or in her eyes. The subject of intimacy never came up. If Gayle would tease her about "getting it regularly," Rayne would totally shut down and change the subject. At times, Gayle felt as if Rayne was hiding something. But she was always like that. There was a side of Rayne that she never opened and shared. Gayle had grown used to it over the years. Paul would have to find a way to deal with it as well. And she was more than happy to give him whatever support he needed.

"Rayne doesn't really talk to me about the . . . personal aspects of your relationship. I suppose she feels it's between the two of you."

The tight line between his eyes began to ease. "How are things with you and James?"

She shrugged. "About the same. James seems to think he has to squirrel away a fortune before we can get married. And quite frankly, I'm tired of waiting."

Paul chuckled. "You've got to give the brother credit. He wants to make sure he can give you the kind of life to which you will easily grow accustomed," he teased, his smile flashing.

"Very funny."

"Aw, come on. James is a decent brother. I'm sure it'll be worth the wait."

"I sure hope so, Paul, I really do."

"You want me to talk to him?"

"No. He, uh, doesn't need to know that you and I talk so much." She brought her drink to her mouth. "I don't want him to get the wrong idea."

He looked at her for a moment and a silent pact was made between them that would forever color the course of their lives.

"You're right," Paul agreed. "No point in planting any seeds."

"No, not at all."

"To friendship," Paul said, raising his glass.

Gayle touched her glass to his. "To friendship."

When she and James married nearly a

year after Rayne and Paul, they still met at Clary's once or twice a week, saw each other at conferences, and talked by phone during the business day. Yet the longer it went on the easier it became for both of them to turn to each other instead of to their spouses — because that was the way it had always been between them.

Gayle slowly raised her head from the cradle of her arms. And this was what it had cost her — her home, her husband, and possibly her daughter — and maybe even Rayne, the only person she'd been able to both love and envy. All for the want of a man she knew she could never have. How would she ever be able to make this up to everyone she'd hurt in her selfishness — in her lifelong quest to be like Rayne Mercer-Holland, even going so far as to vicariously live her life through Paul?

There was silence from the bath down the hall. Moments later, James emerged, the lower half of his body wrapped in a mint-green towel, his slightly protruding belly giving evidence to the years that had passed between them.

James turned to look at her, curled up against the wall. For a moment there was a flash of compassion, maybe even love, in his eyes, and then it was gone. He crossed the hall and went into the bedroom they'd once shared, closing the door behind him.

With great effort, she pushed herself up from the floor. Maybe she would spend the day with her daughter. It had been far too long.

By the time Gayle had showered, dressed, and walked down the hall to wake Tracy, she was gone, and so was James.

Twelve

"I don't think you need to be driving all the way out there in this weather, Bill," Edith said, wiping her hands on a towel. "It's supposed to get worse before it gets better."

He cut her a look from the corner of his eye. "That ain't for you to say, Edith. The doc says she needs to see me 'bout my daughter. Seems to me you'd want to make sure I took care of that."

"I only meant that I was worried . . . concerned about you driving alone in this bad weather, that's all. You know how reckless other drivers can be. That's all."

"Hmm." He patted her on the behind. "That's real thoughtful of you, Edith. But I don't think you have anything to worry 'bout." He put on his raincoat and took his hat from the rack by the door. "I'm gonna take care of everything."

William stepped out onto the porch and looked up at the sky. He smiled. *Perfect day for a drive,* he thought.

The drive was about a solid hour and a

half on a good day. William figured that by keeping within the speed limit he should still make it in under two hours. He enjoyed driving in the rain — him against nature.

As he drove along the water-laden roads, he hummed an offbeat blues tune. Music always put him in a steady frame of mind, helped him to think. He'd need to have his wits about him today. No telling what that uppity doctor would try to trick him into saying, or what lies that damned daughter of his had told. Yes, he had to be clearheaded. They wouldn't fool him into saying anything.

His gaze narrowed. It was a day just like this one when Edith found Rayne on the bathroom floor, blood and broken glass everywhere. There was no reason for her to have done that to herself. He'd only been trying to comfort her, make her feel loved and wanted, especially after losing Paul and Desiree.

But she'd fought him like he was some kind of stranger. *Ungrateful.* He'd opened his home to her, given her a place to stay after the accident. Edith cooked for her and washed her clothes. And what does she do: tries to kill herself. *Fool.*

Rayne never did have the toughness of

her mama. No, sir. All she had of her mother was her looks.

Something deep inside twisted, cutting off his air. He slammed his fist against the steering wheel, needing to hit something, someone. How could she do this to him — to them? How?

No one could understand what they'd shared all those years. No one. Most times he didn't understand it himself.

Rain pelted the windshield, bouncing in an uneven rhythm. William stepped on the gas, jerking the station wagon forward, raising a tide of water on either side, splashing the windows. That's how he felt now, like plowing through something.

William ran a hand across his face. He was never sure where the anger came from, the rage, then the need to punish, then seek comfort. When had it all started? When he was ten, sixteen, twenty?

He frowned, the music now turned off in his head. Funny that those numbers, those ages, would come to mind. Was it at age ten when his father tied him down to the bed, his rib broken by his father's swift kick at sixteen, his first brush with the law at twenty? William could never tell when the beatings would come or for what reason; if it was something he'd said or done or if it was something as simple as his father having a bad day and no one else to vent his hostility out on but him. He, in turn, held his hurt, rage, and confusion sealed tight in his chest, only letting it explode like lava spewing from a volcano when he couldn't take it anymore and had to release the fury he felt. He'd pick fights with strangers on the street, in the classroom, in the neighborhood, which would cause more beatings and kicks by his father, which only sent William back out into the world looking for someone to absorb his pain. A night in jail after a brawl in a local nightspot only hardened him even more.

He couldn't recall all the details, the reasons why. All he knew was the flame that had become lit in his belly that he had to keep putting out. Carol had been the only one to temper that flame. But she'd left him, and that pain was greater than any other.

Visibility was becoming more difficult. The combination of heat and rain created a haze that hung over the city like smoke from an extinguished fire.

Even his thinking grew foggy. Images shifting in and out. First Carol, then Rayne, and back again between the folds of mists. Alternately he would see the plain face of Edith emerge with her secret accusing looks. Whatever happened, he decided, blinking to clear his vision, he couldn't let Rayne continue with her lies, her version of the truth. He stepped on the gas, creating another tidal wave. When he looked up ahead the ghostly outline of the facility was coming into view. Yeah, he'd straighten this all out in no time.

At the gate he was stopped by a security guard, then directed around the back to the visitor's parking lot. When he walked through the front door, he was stopped again and asked to sign in and show identification.

"You lookin' at that driver's license like you don't think it's me," William said with an ash-dry chuckle.

The guard looked him over one last time and compared the carved face in front of him to the one in the tiny photo. His expression neither rose nor fell as he handed back the license. "It's my job . . ." He glanced at the signature. "Mr. Mercer. Can't be too careful."

"You ain't expectin' crazies to be comin' *in*. I'd think you'd be more worried about them gettin' out." He cackled at his own joke.

The guard's face remained stoic. "Right

down the hall to the left is the elevator. Show your pass to security, they'll take you straight up to the sixth floor."

William took the plastic-encased pass with the metal clip and fastened it onto his shirt. "You ain't the friendly sort. Somebody should see about that."

William turned and proceeded down the corridor, determined to speak to someone about the rude way he was handled. *Some damned nerve.*

When he reached the elevator he was subjected to the same process before being cleared to go up. Upon reaching the sixth floor, the security guard from the elevator slid a plastic card through a side panel on the door and it whooshed open, allowing him entrance.

The sounds, noises he couldn't quite place — shuffling sounds, whispers, muffled wailing, garbled conversations amid the ping of electronic instruments, most he couldn't name — blended into some unidentifiable vibration and flowed through him in a nauseating wave.

A cold sweat began at his hairline and trickled under his armpits, down his back, blotted his chest. He suddenly felt as if he'd been running from the devil under the moonlight.

"Can I help you?"

The businesslike voice slowed down the rapid racing of his heart. Now it just knocked, hard, wanting to leap out of his chest.

William looked down into filmy pale green eyes shielded behind too-thick lenses, magnifying them to cartoon size. The ridiculousness of it made the tendrils of fear recede on a gust of laughter.

The pale eyes squinted, suddenly leery of the burly clean-shaven man. "Sir, is there something funny?" The woman shifted the clipboard chart from her left hand to her right.

"I'm sorry," William muttered, swallowing down his laughter. "I was looking for Dr. Dennis."

The duty nurse looked him over. "Is she expecting you?"

He glanced around, then back at her. "You don't think I'd come up here for any other reason 'cept if she was expectin' me, now, would you?"

She jutted her short chin and the taste of lemon seemed to fill her mouth. "What is your name, sir?"

"William Mercer. My daughter's here. Rayne Holland."

Her cartoon eyes widened. "Rayne

Holland is your daughter?"

"That's right."

Nurse Simpson joined them. "Need some help, Cynthia?" Simpson looked from one to the other.

"This gentleman is Rayne Holland's father. He has an appointment with Dr. Dennis."

Judy Simpson gave him a quick once-over, trying to see any similarities between father and daughter. There were none. And for someone who was obviously damp all over from the overwhelming heat, he gave off a chill as if someone had opened a deep freezer.

"I'll walk with you to Dr. Dennis's office," Judy offered. "It's right this way." The quicker she got him into Dr. Dennis's hands, the better she would feel.

The two didn't exchange a word on the short walk down the corridor, which was odd to Judy. Never once did he ask about Rayne. Maybe he was part of her problem to begin with, she thought, tapping on Dr. Dennis's door.

"Come in," Pauline called from inside.

Judy opened the door, stepping slightly to the side to let William pass, and she felt that chill again. She didn't like it. Not one bit.

"Dr. Dennis — Mr. Mercer, Rayne's father, is here to see you."

Pauline looked up from the pages on her desk and slid off her glasses. She closed the folder and stood, extending her hand to him.

"Mr. Mercer, glad you could make it, especially on a day like today."

"Is that right," he said, stepping into the room and taking her hand in his large one when he reached her desk.

"It is pretty rough out there."

The right side of his mouth curved up. "It ain't so bad. Not so bad," he added, correcting himself. "I kind of like this weather."

Pauline released his hand and came from behind the desk. *Interesting.* "Please." She extended her arm toward the couch. "Sit. Can I get you something to drink: tea, coffee, or something cold?"

"Coffee would be fine."

She crossed the room to the counter and poured a cup of coffee. "Cream, sugar?"

"A little of both."

Her flesh began to tingle. She turned. William was right behind her. A gasp clung in her throat. The damp scent of him engulfed her.

"Didn't mean to scare you there, Doc,

175

just thought I'd help." He took one of the cups from her hands, just before they began to shake.

"I . . . didn't hear you come up behind me." Heat flushed her face.

He laughed. "Lotsa folks say that. Guess I just have a light step, huh?"

The edges of her mouth flickered. "Let's sit." She moved toward the easy chair, sitting opposite him.

"As I said on the phone," she began, setting her cup on the table, knowing that the wobbling cup in her hand would be a clear indication of the uneasiness she felt. "Rayne has finally come around. The progress during the past week has been slow but steady."

William crossed his left ankle over his right knee. "Is that right." His dark eyes probed her.

Pauline cleared her throat. "I'd like you to tell me all you can about Rayne's childhood and adolescence, Mr. Mercer. I'm not at all sure that Rayne's attempted suicide was directly related to the deaths of her husband and daughter. But something much deeper. Perhaps the accident was the catalyst for her attempt, but not the central reason."

She leaned back, secure now in her domain, reached for her cup of tea, and brought it with a steady hand to her mouth. "I believe your recollections would be extremely helpful."

The cup rattled slightly in his hand. He put it on the table. "Like I said before, there's not much to tell. Rayne was just a regular kid. She went to live with my sister, Mae, when she was 'bout sixteen years old."

"Why was that?"

"I was married again."

Pauline waited for something more. It didn't come. "You sent her to live with your sister because you remarried. Is that correct?"

William leaned a bit forward and his response came from somewhere dark and menacing, a place Pauline dared not go. "Yeah. That's right."

In response, a quick torrent of rain rapped on the window, demanding to be let in. Pauline felt a chill that began at her feet and ran up her back. She drew her white coat closer around her body. "How did Rayne feel about being sent away?"

"She felt fine 'cause that's the way it was."

"What do you mean?"

"Simple. You tell a child to do somethin',

177

then they do it, and like it."

"I see. So you never talked to Rayne about her feelings or explained to her why she was being sent away?"

"No reason to."

"Rayne was six when her mother died, correct, Mr. Mercer?" She watched the muscles in his face begin to flutter.

He reached for his cup of coffee, then changed his mind. Pauline took a sip of tea, watching him over the rim.

"Just turnin' six," he mumbled, before looking away.

"Were Rayne and her mother —"

"Carol," he corrected her, with an edge in his voice.

"Carol — were they close?"

His jaw flexed in and out. Pauline could almost hear his teeth grinding against one another.

"Some folks might say that," he said.

"What would *you* say?"

His eyes flashed at her, then narrowed, drawing his brows close. "That's all she ever thought about," he uttered in a grumble. "Night and day. Carol never went anywhere without dragging Rayne along. She even put her in the bed with us some nights," he spat.

Pauline witnessed the frames of softness,

rage, doubt, love, and hate pan across the screen of his face, one quickly taking the place of the next. She only wished she could slow down the machine of his mind to get a better view.

"Did your wife work, Mr. Mercer?"

His head jerked in her direction, snatched back to the present. "Carol didn't have no reason to work. I took care of everything she needed. If she wanted something all she had to do was ask. Understand?"

She understood. Perfectly. "Of course." Observing him clench and unclench those big, meaty hands, she shuddered at the idea of anger ever being behind what they were capable of doing. "Was Rayne a good student?"

"So her mama said." He reached for his cup, this time taking a swallow of the luke-warm coffee. "Carol took care of that kind of thing."

"What about after she, your wife, died — did you take more of a role in Rayne's activities?"

The blood rushing to his head darkened his face. "You sayin' I didn't have no time or no interest in my daughter?"

Pauline gently gripped the arms of her chair. "I'm sure that's not what I said, or implied. It's apparent that your wife,

Carol, was the primary caregiver and you the provider. I'm curious to learn whether you took on more of the role of caregiver to your daughter. To do both is a difficult job for anyone. I admire those parents who can do both."

She watched his body begin to decompress, the swelling anger released with the pinprick of her carefully chosen words.

"I'm glad you can see that, Doc. Most folks can't appreciate how hard it is for a man to raise a girl child alone." A drop of perspiration dripped onto his pant leg. "She clung to me, you know — after Carol." He wiped a hand across his face. "I loved Rayne and all, but I had to work. Man's got to work. Well, she didn't seem to like that much, always whinin' and cryin' and clingin'. Carol spoiled her, is all. Rayne needed some growing up. But I did the best I could."

William looked across at Pauline for the first time since the start of his monologue. "You can understand that, Doc."

"Of course. Marrying Edith must have taken a lot of pressure off you."

"I didn't say nothin' 'bout there being any pressure."

"You're right. What I meant to say was that since you were married you could

180

concentrate on being the provider."

"That's right." He bobbed his head in agreement, and rubbed his palms along the thighs of his pants, wondering why the doctor kept her office so damned hot. He'd have to tell her about it before he left.

"How did Edith get along with your daughter?"

His mouth wrinkled into some indiscernible expression. "Fine."

"Then why was Rayne sent to live with your sister? It seems that a semblance of a normal life had returned when you remarried."

William's features became entangled with one another. The series of expressions knotting and unknotting. He leaned forward, just a bit, but enough to envelop Pauline in his maelstrom. "I do what I know to be best for my family, Doc."

Pauline scrambled to escape the sudden sense of suffocation. She pushed herself up from her seat. The need to remove herself rose within her with such stunning force that her legs felt unsteady beneath her. For an instant she was a little girl again, scurrying to the corner of her bed, out of her uncle's reach.

"Can I refresh your coffee?" Pauline asked, taking in a lungful of air.

William's gaze rode languorously up from her legs, meandered a moment at her center, and took a rest stop at her breasts before coming to a complete halt on her face.

"No. Thanks."

Pauline turned away, crossing to the counter. Her entire body was vibrating like aftershocks from an electric charge. There was a menace about William Mercer. Not in anything he did or said directly, she reasoned, refilling her cup, but his presence, the soullessness in his eyes, the barely-there malice in his tone. He was a dark cloud ready to burst, showering everything and everyone in his path. She'd felt it from the first moment she'd spoken with him. But being in the same room with him only confirmed her worst fears. He was the terror that haunted Rayne day and night. There had been no one to protect Pauline from her uncle Thomas, but she would protect Rayne from her father.

"I really ain't got a lotta time, Doc," he said when she'd returned to her seat. "You been so busy askin' me questions, I ain't had the chance to ask you anything."

"What would you like to ask me?" She leaned back, pulling her white coat tighter to ward off the pervasive chill.

182

William wiped his damp hands on his pants legs again. "What kind of things Rayne been sayin'? She tell you why she tried to kill herself like that?"

"As I mentioned on the phone, I believe much of Rayne's fears stem from her childhood and the recent trauma has served to bring those fears to the surface. That's why I wanted to talk with you. And in answer to your other question, no, she hasn't told me why." Pauline watched for any change of expression. "Do you have any ideas?"

A path beneath his right eye ticked. "No. I figured it was what you doctors said, past . . . trauma stress." He folded his arms.

"Yes. Post-traumatic stress disorder is still a possibility." She paused a moment, put her index finger to her lip while she framed her question. "Do you think Rayne has some guilty feelings about her mother's death?"

His mouth flinched. "Carol died of a bad heart. Doctors said the strain of the pregnancy only made it worse. She had to take medicine every day after that girl was born."

"Did you or anyone ever tell Rayne this?"

"Tell her what?" he hedged.

"That her mother's already bad heart

183

was made worse by the pregnancy and ultimately led to her death?"

William shifted his weight in the seat. "I . . . might of . . . said somethin' once or twice."

"Did you or any of your acquaintances ever talk about the deaths of her husband and daughter with her? Or in her presence?"

"I tried to talk to her. Sometimes at night when I'd get home from work, she'd be up in her old room curled up in bed, you know. Just like when she was a little girl. Only she wasn't little no more, she was grown." His mouth jerked, his hands opened and closed. "She looked just like her mother laying up there, especially in the dark," he rambled on, trapped in his own vision. "So sometimes I'd be feelin' real bad for her and I'd sit on the side of the bed and talk to her, rub her back."

Pauline followed the thin line of sweat that traced his hairline and slid along the side of his face, down to his ear.

"I tried to talk to her about the accident, see if she could tell me what happened. But she wouldn't or couldn't."

William's voice began to dim and Pauline suddenly saw herself at fourteen. *It was night. Summertime. She was alone in her bedroom, afraid of the footsteps that were sure to come. A dark presence loomed over her in the night while she slept, covered her mouth and warned her to be silent.* "This is our secret. Mine and yours, little girl. Now, let's see what you have for me tonight . . ."

"Is there anything else, Doc? It's getting late. I'd like to see my daughter."

Pauline blinked, her eyes focused completely on William Mercer's face. For a split second, she saw him as the dark presence above her, touching her, violating her. She wanted to run, needed to get away. But reason took hold, chasing her fears to the corner of her mind.

She cleared her throat, took a long, deep breath to slow the rapid racing of her heart. "Certainly." She got up and crossed to her desk, pressing the intercom for the nurse's station. "Yes. This is Dr. Dennis. Would you bring Rayne Holland to my office? Her father is here. Yes. Thank you."

Pauline looked up. "Rayne will be here shortly. A nurse will bring her."

"You're gonna be here?"

"Is that a problem?"

"I thought I'd get a chance to see her — alone. It's been a while. I wanted some private time with her, see how she's really doing."

"You'll have a chance to speak with her alone before you leave. But before that happens I'd like to be present to monitor her response to you."

William's gaze narrowed to slits. "Is that right."

Pauline wrapped her arms about her waist to stave off the chill. He was too close. She could barely breathe.

He pursed his lips, his cheeks concaving, giving him a predatory look. "Why is monitoring needed? Don't sound right to me. That's my daughter. You think I'm gonna upset her or somethin'?"

"I would hope not, Mr. Mercer." She raised her chin. "But my first responsibility is to my patient. Once I'm assured that she can handle the visit, you can have some time with her."

He slowly rose from his seat like something from the depths of the sea, his presence taking up space, air. He ran a finger across his right eyebrow as he spoke. "I'm not happy with the sound of that, Doc. Not happy. I come all this way. I should have some rights. No reason for you to be settin' watchin'. Sounds to me like you don't trust me with my own daughter." He angled his head to the side. "Is that it, Doc?"

186

Pauline watched his hands open and close, felt her chest being squeezed with his every move. She felt he enjoyed his power to unsettle her, to make her uneasy. He smiled evilly, as if reading her thoughts.

A bolt of lightning ripped across the near black sky, illuminating the room in bright white light.

Pauline jumped at the short bang on her door, then exhaled a silent sigh of relief. William turned toward the door.

Rayne walked in first, looking from Pauline to her father. Her step stuttered for a moment.

"Go in, Rayne," Judy Simpson coaxed gently, patting Rayne on the shoulder.

Rayne counted each step it took for her to cross the floor, concentrating on patterns in the wood. If she could count off the panels, one . . . two . . . she wouldn't have to think about the man in front of her. She could pretend she wasn't afraid. Three . . . four . . .

William severed the distance between them. "Hey, sugah."

Rayne blinked rapidly. She'd lost count. *I'm right here, girl. I won't let nothing happen to you on my watch,* the voice inside her head whispered. *Let me handle this.*

The racing of her heart began to downshift. William stood in front of her and everything around them began to recede into the background. She stood in the room but on the outside. Removed and safe.

William wrapped his arms around her statue-stiff body and pulled her close.

"You promised," he whispered in her ear before kissing her cheek and stepping back. "You look good, sugah," he said, perusing her from head to foot. "The doctor said you're making progress — and talking. That's good. Real good."

Pauline observed the exchange, the vacuous expression on Rayne's face, the almost unnoticeable tremor of her body, held so rigidly that to move her might cause her to crackle like dried autumn leaves.

The air in the room could no longer contain them, like shoes that were too tight, pinching, squeezing no matter how you tried to adjust to the fit. The contents wanted to break free.

Pauline came from behind the desk to stand beside Rayne. "Your father and I have been talking, Rayne," she began in her soothing tone, snatching a glance at William, whose marble expression was smooth, etched, and cold as ice. Not the face of a man who loved his child — or anyone, for that matter. "Why don't we all sit down?"

Rayne took the chair closest to the window.

"You can go now, Nurse Simpson. Thank you," Pauline said.

"I'll be on the floor — if you need me," Judy responded, giving Pauline a yellow-light look of warning.

"I'm sure we'll be fine," Pauline replied, forcing a tight-lipped smile.

Judy looked from one to the other, knowing that she must follow instructions. But her instinct was to stay. She gave William one last stare, then turned and left, praying with each footfall. There was something about that man that affected her like bad food. Her stomach churned.

After everyone was seated, Pauline began.

"I asked your father to come today, Rayne, in the hope that he could fill in some of the gaps. And we need your help, too."

Rayne focused on her folded hands, linking and unlinking her fingers. *You promised.* A hiss in her ear.

Pauline saw Rayne's expression contract as if she'd been stuck with a needle. "Is that all right with you, Rayne?"

Rayne turned to look at her father, the kind of expression a child gives when seeking approval to speak. *Interesting,* Pauline thought.

"It's . . . fine," Rayne murmured, keeping her gaze lowered.

"Good." Pauline sat back against the cushion of the chair and crossed her legs. "How much do you remember about the day you cut your wrists?"

William jumped up. "I thought you said we were gonna talk about her childhood."

"I believe what happened to Rayne is all part of the same problem, Mr. Mercer." She turned to Rayne. "Can you remember?"

Slowly William returned to his seat.

Tell her, tell her. This is your chance, the voice urged. Rayne stole a glance at her father, whose face was as furious as the storm that raged just beyond the window, and she felt herself move farther into the background, closer to safety. And then the words began to flow from that hidden place . . .

"I was very unhappy," she began, speaking in a halting voice. "I'd been thinking about Paul and Desiree and . . . wondering why I'd been spared." She

190

paused for several moments as the buried feelings rose then settled within her. She gazed toward the window. "It was a day like this . . . I'd been . . . crying most of the night. I felt so lost, helpless. Everything was coming apart." She looked up at Pauline, her eyes filling, almost pleading for a reprieve.

"Go on, Rayne."

She took a breath. "I was in my room . . . at my father's house." William shifted in his seat. "In bed." She closed her eyes, seeing herself curled in bed, burrowed beneath the quilt. Even though it was warm for that time of year, she felt chilled to the bone . . .

The house was silent. The only sounds were of nature trying to find a way in through any opening, banging and whistling against the doors, rattling the windows.

But there were no human sounds of activity: footfalls in the hallways or on the stairs; the muffled sound of voices in conversation; the aroma of baked bread or frying chicken to tempt your palate. Nothing. The only presence was the shell of herself, and in realizing that, she understood in truth just how empty the house was. Because in that moment she felt as if she no longer existed — her reason for being had lost its validity.

Lying in bed, eyes swollen from hours of tears, Rayne began to question her worth, her purpose. All her life she'd battled with feelings of inadequacy and abandonment, feelings of having to measure up to the idealized image of her mother, a woman whom she could never replace.

She'd been the cause of her mother's death. Her father said so, more times than anyone should have to hear.

"If it wasn't for you, your mama would still be here," William yelled the night following her mother's funeral, the words tumbling over one another in one long syllable of accusation. "You took her from me. You!"

He stood in the open doorway, illuminated only by the light from the hall. To her six-year-old eyes, he appeared like a giant black shadow towering and dangerous, with unimaginable power . . .

She crouched in the corner of her bedroom, her knees pulled up to her chin, her thick hair shielding her face, hoping to hide from the poisonous verbal assault hurled at her. The smell of the alcohol he'd been drinking all day filled the room, rocked her stomach. But she knew she couldn't throw up. So she tried to hold her breath as the smell enveloped her and she grew woozy.

Pulling her arms tighter around her knees, she hoped to stop the shivers that relayed up and down her body.

The smell grew stronger and when she dared to look up, her father was standing above her. His eyes were red like a poorly shot color photograph. Her stomach rushed to her throat. She felt the burn of bile fill her mouth.

He stepped closer. "Carol," he slurred. "Come on, sugah, get up off the floor." He stretched out his hand.

"I'm not . . . Mama, Daddy. I'm Rayne," she whimpered.

William squeezed his eyes shut, then opened them. His face twisted in anguish and he threw his head back and let loose an agonizing wail that sent rivers of terror surging through her.

Suddenly he grabbed a handful of her hair and wrenched her up from the floor.

"Aagh!" She screamed in agony, sure that he'd torn her hair from her scalp.

Like a rag doll, he tossed her across the room. She landed sprawled on the bed, her peach-and-white dress hitched up around her waist.

William's red eyes were glazed with pain and fury, but then something else, something more menacing, hovered there. And even in the innocence of her youth, Rayne somehow understood that her father no longer saw her at all. *She* had disappeared.

He stumbled toward her. She tried to get away, but there was nowhere to go. She scrambled to the corner of the bed. "Daddy, please. Please, Daddy. I'll be good. I promise."

Tears streamed down her face. Her head throbbed. Her body shook as if controlled by an unseen force. She knew he could hear the pounding of her heart because it was the only sound in the room, thudding, banging in an unnatural rhythm.

He unhooked the buckle of his belt and pulled it with a snap through the loops that held it in place.

"Da-ddy!" She covered her face with her hands and screamed until her throat was raw, her voice barely audible. Her body quivered helplessly as he spread over her.

Pain. Pain. Pain like she'd never experienced before ripped through her, ringing her ears, tearing her flesh until everything was black and empty and her body throbbed and burned as if tossed in hot oil.

When she opened her eyes, she was alone in the dark, afraid to move. The strange stickiness sealing her thighs. She curled into a ball, covered her face with her hair and cried for her mother. She cried for something taken from her, for which she had no name.

That's what she thought about on the afternoon that she cut her wrists. That and all the other times that followed.

And when she thought she was alone in her grief and her shame, the terror rose again when she realized she wasn't.

"Why you all crouched up in the bed?" William asked from the doorway of her bedroom.

Rayne stiffened, then slowly sat up, pulling her robe tightly around her body.

"You need to get yourself up outta the bed. Laying up in here ain't gon' change a thing that done happened. You got to get on with your life."

With the back of her hand she swiped away the remnants of tears from her face. "What life do I have, Daddy?"

"Don't be silly. You still here, ain't cha? That got to count for somethin'."

She turned her face away.

"Look at me when I'm talkin' to you, girl."

Her heart banged in her chest. Slowly she turned to face him. He came closer. "Why you all covered up in this heat?" His gaze ran up and down her body. "Humph, humph, humph. Look more like your mama every day."

He came closer, close enough for her to smell his sweat.

She could feel herself shrink.

He stroked her hair, running his hands across the crinkly waves. "Always did like your hair. Pretty. Feels like cotton. Just like Carol's."

She grew smaller.

"Sometimes she'd let me press my face in it." He sat down on the side of the bed.

She was a little girl again, weak, small, intimidated by the man who should protect her. "Daddy. Don't." It was a six-year-old Rayne whose voice she heard.

William heard nothing. He pulled her to him, burying his face in her hair. He rubbed his hands up and down her back.

"I'm gon' make everything all right, sugah. You trust me. I will. Don't you cry 'bout nothin'. Haven't I always taken care of you? That's a man's job, baby." His stroking grew more aggressive.

I'm not going to let this happen again, the voice had snapped. The voice that always came, stepped in, and shut her down so she wouldn't feel, wouldn't hurt, wouldn't remember.

William's large hand encircled her waist, then moved upward. "I'ma take care of you," he whispered into her hair. "Anytime I want."

Something inside her gave way and everything she'd ever endured, all the hurt, loneliness, and silent agony rose up in one ball of strength that propelled him onto the floor.

"Don't you ever touch me again!" She stood above him for the first time in her life and in that split second of changed places, she felt free. She wanted to hit him.

William's face contorted into a mask of animal rage. "You ungrateful bitch!" He scrambled to get up and tried to grab her as she ran from the room and down the hallway.

He was mere steps behind her. She could feel his breath on her neck. She ran for the bathroom, slamming the door an instant before he reached it.

His fist banged against the door, shaking it in its hinges. "Come outta there. Now!"

"Go away!"

"You think you can run from me? Huh?" He began to laugh. "You can't stay in there forever. You're gonna come out sometime and when you do I'm gonna teach you a lesson you'll wish you never had to learn. Ungrateful." His fist slammed the door again. "Come out here, dammit. You know you like it. Just like your mama. The two of you are just alike. Always want it. Always."

Then the anger became choked in sobs. "I'm sorry, sugah . . . I . . . didn't mean to hurt you." His fingernails scratched at the door. "You know that. I love you. Please let me make it up to you. Please."

Silence.

Rayne held her breath.

"I said I was sorry. I guess that's not good enough. But you just remember this one thing: you're mine. And I'll do with you want I want, when I want. And you'll like it."

Rayne was no longer sure if it was her heart she was hearing, or the sound of his footsteps on the stairs.

Shaking, she turned away from the door. Her legs limp and trembling, she stumbled toward the sink, catching the rim in time to keep from falling.

Her gaze rose and she saw her image reflected in the mirror.

I'm gonna teach you a lesson . . . Bitch . . . You know you want it . . . Just like your mama . . . You got to come out . . .

"N-o-o!"

From the sink Rayne grabbed the hairbrush and crashed it against the mirror, hoping to obliterate the shame and ugliness that was her. But when she looked down, what she saw were pieces of her image multiplied hundreds of times in the shards of broken glass, taunting her like a house of mirrors at her feet. Everywhere she looked, there she was, pitiful, weak, broken.

She crumbled to the floor surrounded by countless fragments of herself, no longer able to put the pieces back together again.

She wasn't certain how long she sat there, replaying the reels of her life, the loss of her mother, her innocence, her home, her husband and daughter, her career, herself. All she knew was that she could not relive those scenes ever again.

Pauline watched, her skin tingling, transfixed as Rayne had thrashed about, sometimes screaming, talking incoherently, often sounding like a pleading child begging for mercy.

Now Rayne sat on the floor in the

middle of the office, reaching for something unseen, then looking from one arm to the other before slicing at her wrists and screaming until she passed out.

"Rayne. Rayne," Pauline called gently.

I don't want to open my eyes. For once sleep is peaceful. I can see the pond just beyond my window, the willows that hang their heads, the riot of color bursting all around me, and Robert who said he would teach me one day. But if you stay asleep, the voice whispered, *you'll never see the garden again. Never have the chance to experience its beauty or life beyond the swirling black gates. Never be able to tell to them what happened to us and punish . . . him. Wake up! Don't be a coward. Wake up!*

Slowly Rayne opened her eyes. Everything in the room seemed hazy and out of focus as if she were viewing the world from behind a cloudy camera lens.

She blinked several times and realized that she was still in Dr. Dennis's office, lying on her couch.

"Are you feeling better?" Pauline asked.

Rayne tried to speak, but her throat felt oddly raw, as if she'd been screaming. "Yes. I think so," she said, sounding like sandpaper on wood.

Pauline brought a cup of water to her

lips and helped to raise her head. "Here, drink this."

Rayne took several sips, then turned her face away. "Thanks." She stiffly pushed herself up into a sitting position. Her body ached as if she'd been beaten. "What happened?"

Pauline watched Rayne's face carefully. "That's what I was hoping you would tell me."

Rayne's eyes darted around the room. "Where's my father?"

"I sent him to wait outside."

"Make him go away."

"Why, Rayne?"

"Just make him go away."

Pauline pushed out a breath and stood. "I'll be right back."

"What's going on?" William demanded as soon as Pauline approached. "Did you see what went on in there?"

"Yes, and if you'll just calm down I'll explain everything to you."

"Explain. How could you let somethin' like that happen? You said she was gettin' better. She ain't better, she's worse. And it's your fault. I'm not gonna have it. I'll speak to your boss about this. I'll have her taken outta here."

He was beginning to cause a scene. Several nurses stopped what they were doing to listen.

"Mr. Mercer, please, calm down."

"There's nothin' for me to be calm about. You ruinin' my child. I won't have it. I'm next a kin and what I say goes."

He stalked off, pushing an orderly against a medicine cart on his way.

Pauline briefly shut her eyes, turned, and went back into her office. She put on her best smile.

"Your father just left. I explained to him that you needed some rest."

"I'd like to go to my room now," Rayne said in a detached voice.

"Of course. We'll talk again tomorrow."

Once inside her room, Rayne walked to the window. Below she saw the dark image of her father walking with his head bent against the wind and rain, across the grounds of the facility to the other side of freedom.

She shivered.

"I'm going to send Nurse Simpson in with something to help you relax, Rayne," Pauline said, from the door.

Rayne turned quickly from the window. "No. Not tonight. Please."

"You've had a rough afternoon. It will help."

"I can sleep on my own."

"Rayne, I —"

"Please, Doctor. Just this once."

Pauline knew she was going against her better judgment, going against standard procedure, especially following a session such as the one Rayne had been through. But something stronger than her medical knowledge compelled her to forego what she knew was the right thing to do. She understood, perhaps better than anyone else, the trauma that Rayne endured. Maybe by bending the rules a little, it would help her patient get what she needed to recover.

"All right. This time. We'll see what happens." And for the first time since she'd had Rayne Holland as a patient, she saw her almost smile. "Try to get some rest." She turned to leave.

"Dr. Dennis."

Pauline stopped, looked over her shoulder, her hand inches away from the door. "Yes?" She turned and her heart slammed in her chest.

"Got a cigarette?"

An unnatural coolness crept into the room, slipped up Pauline's spine.

Pauline held Rayne's steady gaze for a long moment before closing the door behind her. Cautiously she stepped forward. "Rayne?"

Rayne tossed her hair behind her shoulders in a sultry gesture, brushing the rest away from her face. Her expression was serene, challenging. The corner of her mouth curved, almost alluring. Every gesture was intentionally seductive.

"Whew, isn't it hot, Doc?" she asked in a tone Pauline didn't recognize. The voice was hard with a worldly edge, not the often timid voice of Rayne. *Her* Rayne.

Rayne began to unbutton the top of her dress.

"Button your clothes, Rayne."

"You got a cigarette? I'm having a nicotine fit and it's hot as hell in here," she said, ignoring Pauline's command.

"When — did you start smoking?" Pauline asked, watching in fascination the almost imperceptible changes, the subtle assurance in Rayne's body language, the look of mischief in her eyes.

"Oh, I guess I was about sixteen. The year they sent us away."

"Us?"

"Yeah. Me and Rayne." She turned toward the window, peered between the mesh patterns.

"*You* and Rayne," Pauline repeated.

"And what's your name?"

This *other* Rayne faced Pauline. Her gaze was pinched as if she were looking directly into the sun. She put her right hand on her hip. Her mouth slowly spread into a smile.

"Don't be silly, Doc. You know who I am."

Then, as suddenly as she appeared, like an apparition, she was gone. The change was stunning, definitive.

Rayne blinked, the hard stance of her body softening like ice cream left out too long. "I think I'll lay down for a while. I guess I'm more tired than I thought."

Slowly Pauline nodded. "Do you still want that cigarette?"

Rayne frowned. "Cigarette?" She chuckled lightly. "You know I don't smoke."

"Yes. You're right. I don't know what I was thinking."

"Are you okay, Dr. Dennis? You look — strained."

"I'm fine. Just a lot on my mind. You get some rest. We'll talk later." She glanced at Rayne, turned, and left the room.

Pauline sat behind her desk, shaken by the events of the session and its aftermath. What she'd witnessed with Rayne Holland, practitioners spend years hoping to see.

For the most part, multiple personality was something many psychiatrists read about, but rarely had an opportunity to treat. Splits in personality were triggered by something devastating that the central self cannot handle. And now she understood why William Mercer never answered her question about why he sent Rayne away after he remarried. And what she'd just witnessed in Rayne's hospital room was only the tip of the iceberg, for both of them.

Thirteen

Gayle thought she would go mad with worry. One minute she was certain that James had taken Tracy and was gone for good. The next minute she convinced herself that he'd just taken her for a drive. But to where in this storm?

She paced the kitchen, absently arranging and rearranging the dishes stacked in the drain. *Nine-thirty in the morning.*

It was after eleven when she'd begun emptying the kitchen cabinets; nearly three by the time she finished sorting through the clothes in all the closets of the house. Huge black plastic bags of long-forgotten outfits sat like overstuffed bean bags in the foyer.

She'd lost count of the number of times she'd gone to the window believing that every other noise was James's car pulling into the driveway.

Maybe she should go out and look for them. What if something had happened on the road?

Images of twisted metal and wailing sirens whirled through her head, setting her off on another frenzy of reorganizing.

She checked her watch. It was almost five. She peered between the slats in the teal-green miniblinds. The rain had slowed but still refused to give up and go away without a last-ditch effort.

How did things get like this? she wondered, putting a load of laundry into the washing machine. Maybe her marriage wasn't perfect, but it wasn't so horrible that it was no longer salvageable.

Gayle closed the door to the washer and turned the dial, the sound always reminding her of a creaky safe. The machine hummed to life.

Crossing her arms, she walked through the laundry room, which was situated between the kitchen and the den, and out into the living room. Five-thirty, according to the antique grandfather clock that Rayne had given her and James on their second-year anniversary.

I hope time will continue to bless your marriage with happiness, the inscription read.

Gayle was so touched by the warm sentiment, so unlike Rayne, that she'd cried. For so many years, she'd always questioned the depth of Rayne's feelings for her, and

208

often wondered if Rayne viewed her as a friend or just someone in her life. She'd always been so hard to read, especially when her emotions were involved.

That was why she couldn't have been more stunned when Rayne told her that Paul had asked to marry her and she'd accepted.

They'd been at Cousins, a trendy after-work bar and grill in the heart of Savannah that sometimes offered a great jazz band. Gayle had finished a grueling day at the bank. Having been only two months earlier promoted to senior-level status, they piled the most complex corporate mergers on her in the hope that she would screw up, believing that she didn't belong in that neck of a man's world. She wouldn't give them the satisfaction of falling on her face. She worked harder and longer than anyone at the bank. She would prove to all of them that she deserved her job. It was her daily mantra: "I will succeed."

Her head was pounding when she called it a day at six. She needed a drink. She'd wanted to call Paul, but since he'd begun seriously seeing Rayne their time together had diminished considerably. She'd reluctantly begun to back off. So she did the next best thing: she called Rayne, hoping that if Rayne was with her, she wouldn't be with Paul.

"I'll be in the studio until at least eight," Rayne said, speaking into a headset as she supervised the staging of her next shot. "It's really crazy around here today. I need to get this finished. We're reaching the ceiling of our budget and the crew is ready to revolt. I — No, put that desk to the left of the set," she instructed in midsentence. "Sorry. How about eight-thirty at Cousins?"

"Sure. I'll go to the gym for an hour. I could stand to burn off a few pounds of attitude and frustration."

"Don't hurt yourself — Yes, perfect, right there. — Anyway, I have something I want to tell you," she said, returning her attention to Gayle.

"Yeah. What?"

"We'll talk. Listen, I've got to run. The natives are restless. See you later."

Before Gayle had a chance to press any further, she could hear Rayne's voice receding, calling out instructions, their conversation and her already put aside and compartmentalized. Gayle slowly replaced the receiver.

Gayle arrived at Cousins a bit before eight and had to wait for Rayne before being seated.

It was rare that Cousins would be this crowded on a Tuesday, Gayle thought, cooling her heels at the bar with a raspberry daiquiri.

"What's the occasion tonight?" Gayle quizzed the bartender, while taking a sip of her frosted drink.

The bartender wiped down the counter, filled a bowl with peanuts, made change, and mixed a martini, all at the same time Gayle would have sworn under oath, amazed at his versatility.

"Word started buzzing late this afternoon that Ray Brown was going to sit in on bass with the house band." He washed glasses as he spoke. "Place has been hopping."

Gayle smiled crookedly as she peered over her shoulder. He was absolutely right. Virtually every table was taken and the short line she'd recently stood in was now out the door. If Rayne didn't show up soon, they'd lose their quasi-reservation.

Gayle checked her watch. Eight-twenty. Rayne had ten minutes. She took a long sip of her drink just as Rayne tapped her on the shoulder.

"Sorry if I'm late," she said in her usual breathy voice. "I didn't think we'd ever get finished. It's going to be an incredible piece of work, Gayle. I can feel it," she said, her dark eyes wide and shining with excitement.

Rayne's work was the only thing Gayle had ever seen her express any real emotion or enthusiasm about. When she was working on a script or talking about what she visualized on the screen, or directing, Rayne came alive. There was a vibrancy about her that was contagious, undeniable. Her world of film seemed to be the only place where Rayne felt truly at home, a part of something. Everything and everyone else in her life merely existed along the fringes of her life, never really gaining access.

"How much longer do you think it will be?"

"Probably another six to eight weeks. There's so much information and so much I want to say in the film."

"Did you decide on a final title yet?"

Rayne smiled proudly. "*The History of Black Women's Rights in America.*"

"Hmm. I'm impressed."

"You'd better be," she teased, then looked around. "What's going on tonight? It's like rush hour." She pressed her duffel bag to her chest and slid between two bar stools to let a couple pass.

"Ray Brown is playing with the house band tonight," Gayle said, mentioning the jazz bassist proudly.

"Now I'm impressed."

"I got a table. Since you're here we can be seated."

As they made their way to the other side of the room, Gayle was confident in her designer business suit, workout body, and Italian leather accessories. She couldn't help notice the open stares and admiring glances Rayne received from the men around them. Even dressed in her standard baggy jeans, an oversized denim shirt, and not a stroke of makeup, she still drew men to her like an oasis in the desert. And yet Rayne didn't seem to notice or care. She never had.

Gayle raised her chin a notch higher and took a seat at their table.

"Are we ordering dinner?" Rayne asked. "My treat, since we're celebrating."

Gayle leaned forward, wide-eyed and eager, her momentary brush with envy forgotten. "Come on and spill it. You know I hate suspense."

Rayne paused a beat. "Paul asked me to marry him and I said yes."

For a split second, Gayle felt as if the world had come to a standstill. The music stopped playing, the voices grew silent, and all movement ceased. She wanted to scream.

"What? Congratulations!"

She was dying inside and prayed that it didn't show. *God, please don't let it show.*

Gayle took Rayne's hands. "Be happy, Rayne. I'm happy for you."

Rayne's smile seemed forced, or maybe Gayle only imagined it, wanted it to be something else, something it wasn't.

"Thanks. I hope so."

Just like that, she made her announcement and as quickly changed the subject back to her work, which was fine with Gayle. She wasn't sure if she could handle any details of the whys and hows.

It was always so easy for Rayne, Gayle thought. How many times had she wished she could so easily rid herself of anything distracting, bothersome, or not equally as important as whatever was happening — now — right this minute.

Gayle drew in a long breath. What would Rayne do now? Gayle pondered as she sat curled on the sofa, the television on mute, the rain tapping against the window. What would Rayne have done if Paul had threatened to leave her and take Desiree?

But Paul would have never left, no

matter how unhappy he had claimed to be, how unfulfilled. Beneath it all, she knew that there was a part of Paul that was totally captivated by Rayne. And for him that almost inexplicable attraction teetered on the brink of love and hate. He'd loved the inaccessibility of Rayne, her beauty, her budding status in the film industry and the prestige it brought him. And because of that he'd hated himself for being so vulnerable to a woman.

Did Rayne ever know his true feelings? Sometimes she wondered if it even mattered to Rayne.

But what was equally sad was that Gayle never told Rayne what she did know — the things Paul shared — not really, not in depth. It was almost as if by keeping those confessions she could keep a part of Paul that Rayne could never have.

God, what kind of woman am I? What kind of friend?

She got up from the couch and crossed to the window, pulling back the curtains, then the blinds. "Please come home," she prayed.

It can't be like this. I can't be like this. James and Rayne have always treated me with love and kindness. Look what I've done to both of them.

Tears of shame and remorse filled her eyes, overflowing onto her cheeks. In harmony against the window, tiny pellets of water splattered, sliding down the pane to pool on the sill. Beyond, a static display of headlights twinkled against the fall of night. And a darkness settled over her, submerging her into a bottomlessness that swirled outside her window, that sucked her in, imprisoned her in the muddy waters of her conscience. She had to find a way to make it to the surface, save herself, her marriage, and maybe rebuild a real friendship before she drowned in regret.

When Gayle next opened her eyes, evening had sneaked into her home, making itself comfortable among her furnishings, moving quietly through the rooms, casting soft shadows.

The rain had ceased, magnifying the quiet.

She rubbed her eyes and slowly massaged her shoulders, which had tightened while she slept curled up on the couch.

Then all at once the burn of something wrong engulfed her. She sat upright, looked around the shadowed space.

Quiet, too quiet.

James and Tracy had not returned.

Her heart banged against her chest and the fear that was laid to rest during sleep awoke with the ferocity of a hungry bear.

Gayle jumped up from the couch and hurried to the window, praying to see James's car pull into the driveway. And the phone rang.

Retracing her steps, she snatched the phone from the cradle that rested on the antique cherry-wood table.

"Hello?" Her greeting rushed out in a breath of hope.

"It's me."

"James. Oh, thank God. I've been so worried. Are you both all right? Where are you?"

"We're fine. I'm at Mitchell's house."

Gayle's fear was quickly replaced with annoyance.

"Your brother's house! Have you been there all this time? You could have called me, James. Don't I deserve that much respect?"

"You know what, Gayle? I've had a lot of time today to do some serious thinking. I was calling to apologize for what happened this morning. I wanted us to talk, really talk. But I can see it's pointless with you. The only person you want to hear is yourself."

"That's not true and you know it."

"I don't know anything anymore, Gayle. Especially about you and what's happening to our marriage."

"James —"

"We'll be staying at my brother's house tonight. Tracy's having a ball with her cousins and Gina is doting all over her. Tracy needs a woman's touch."

Turning the other cheek did not diminish the sting of his words. He said it to hurt her and he'd succeeded.

"James, please. Don't do this. Don't use Tracy."

"I'll do whatever I think is best, for myself and for Tracy."

"And what about me?"

"You should have thought of that a long time ago, Gayle. Good night."

Before she had an opportunity to protest, the dial tone hummed in her ear.

She threw the receiver across the room, shattering the glass of the china cabinet. The same cabinet she'd spent hundreds of dollars restoring above James's protests.

"We have other expenses that are more important than fixing up some tacky cabinet to satisfy your whim," James had said as they'd stepped outside of an antique shop in the historic center of Savannah.

218

"We have plenty to take care of our bills," Gayle responded, brushing aside her husband's concerns.

"Be reasonable. We just took out an equity loan to redo the house because you wanted it. You just traded in your car for a brand-new one, and the dentist said Tracy will need braces."

"We both make plenty of money, James," she said, opening the passenger side of her new Lincoln Town Car. She'd let James drive, she'd thought. He liked that — being in control.

"That's not the point." He slammed the car door and gunned the engine.

Gayle cringed as the powerful engine roared to life.

"We won't have any money if we keep spending it every time you see something that strikes your eye."

Gayle turned her head to stare out of her window, the lush greenery, cobbled streets, array of shops and fountains playing tag in front of her eyes, one picking up where the other left off.

James was so pessimistic at times, a money watcher. So what if she was extravagant? She wanted to live well and live comfortably. Rayne did.

Paul bought Rayne anything she wanted,

anything he thought would please her. Their home was exquisite. And she never heard Paul complain about the money Rayne spent, which she knew was substantial. But Rayne, of course, never seemed to notice, or care. She seemed to take what she had as a given, something she deserved, and was being compensated for. And the more she seemed oblivious to the treasures around her, the more Paul showered her with them.

At times, Gayle believed that Paul was trying to buy Rayne's love, to lease her affections.

"How many diamond bracelets can one woman wear?" Gayle questioned him one day over lunch at Clary's, trying to keep the rancorous jealousy out of her voice.

Paul smiled shyly. "To be honest, it's a makeup gift." He looked away briefly. "We, uh, had some problems." He shrugged and ran a finger around the collar of his starched white shirt, avoiding Gayle's eyes.

"You do a lot of that," she replied, not understanding his sudden nervousness.

His eyes finally met hers. "What does that mean?"

"It means, every time I look around you're either buying Rayne something because you two have had a fight, or she's depressed, or you're trying to make up for some infraction or the other. Your walls can't hold another piece of art. You've re-done the house twice. She has more diamonds and jewelry than she'll ever wear — and never does anyway."

A deep crease sliced down between his brows. "Funny, I thought we were friends. I thought you were Rayne's friend. But it sounds to me as if you're jealous." He stared at her for a long moment.

Gayle forced a laugh. "Don't be ridiculous." She leaned forward and put her hand atop his. "All I'm saying is that I don't want to see you get hurt," she offered, lowering her voice to an intimate whisper, forcing him to draw closer. "Let Rayne love you because she loves you, not because she feels obligated to you for all the things you've bought her."

"Do you think that's the way she feels? Obligated?"

Gayle paused, hearing the note of hurt in his voice. "Paul, I couldn't tell you how Rayne feels about too much of anything. That's just the way she is. Closed. But you know that." She pressed her point a bit further. "You knew that when you married her."

Paul released a long breath. "I guess that

was the attraction," he confessed. "Still is. Sometimes her elusiveness is the greatest turn-on in the world," he said, his voice layered with emotion, making it heavy and thick. "Other times she makes me so crazy — I lose myself, don't know who I am." He gripped his glass.

"What do you mean?" Gayle watched the veins pulse in his hand.

Paul blinked, bringing Gayle back into focus. He shook his head, chuckled lightly. "Nothing. Just running off at the mouth." He tossed down the last of his drink. "Forget it."

But Gayle didn't.

Many nights she lay awake next to her own husband wondering what went on behind the closed doors of Rayne and Paul's bedroom.

Something inside of her knew — thought she knew, but was unwilling to accept or even to contemplate it. It was easier if she didn't think about it — the possibilities. To acknowledge the existence of her darkest thoughts would give them power and life. Once that happened, the tide of events would be unstoppable. And then she would be forced to decide whose side she was on.

Instead, she found a way to run from the

possibility of the truth, not be seduced by knowledge. She surrounded herself in a cloak of envy and longing, constantly altering it to keep the temptation of truth at bay. She, too, hid behind things, just like Paul, just like Rayne.

The Lincoln had screeched to a halt at a red light. She'd glanced at James from the corner of her eye. She'd get the china cabinet herself, she'd decided, no matter what he said, which is exactly what she'd done.

Gayle looked at the broken glass now — sparkling like cut diamonds on the floor, the pieces of her life — thinking about that day then, and where she was now: among her things — alone.

Fourteen

Brilliant rays of sunshine streaked through the patterns on the window. They nudged Rayne in the ribs, slipped beneath the sheets, and tickled her belly, tried to get behind her lids, then settled for warming her in a bath of light.

Morning, she thought, through the haze of filmy dreams that were quietly tiptoeing away. She tried to snatch them back, but they were too quick, leaving behind only a whisper of their existence.

With reluctance, she opened her eyes, blinking against the crisscross patterns that skipped around the room. For an instant she actually felt good, her spirit light as if a long-carried weight had been mysteriously carted away during her repose.

Stretching, her body awakened by degrees: from the bottom of her feet that flexed and pointed; her slender legs that rose toward the ceiling then glided back to the mattress; her loose pelvis that did a languid rotation; the back that arched,

224

pushing her breasts against the thin cotton gown; up to her neck that stretched the muscles against soft flesh. It was a slow, erotic dance, a ritual that paid homage to a new day.

As she looked around the room, for the first time in months her head didn't feel as if it were submerged underwater, her thoughts disjointed and floating aimlessly. A night without being weighed down by medication had given her the first sense of clarity since she'd been confined.

She sat up, a sense of the possible taking its place beside her on the single bed. She stood and walked with it toward the window, pressing her hand against the glass.

There he was. Robert. She'd thought about what he'd said to her, kept the words with her, close to her heart. She was more than this place, the circumstances that captured her. No man had ever said that to her — that she had value.

A feeling of ease gently flowed through her, settling her in a way. Her gaze followed him as he checked the manicured shrubs and potted plants for water damage.

He seemed so gentle to be a big man. Big at least by her standards. But his large hands and broad shoulders didn't intimidate. Rather, they gave her a sense of protection and comfort — that his body would shield, his hands heal.

She'd never felt that way about any man, she thought. Not even about her husband, Paul. He'd been almost gentle once, but her fears, her ghosts, her secrets awakened his beast. In a way, what they had was familiar. An ugly truth. She fed the beast.

Rayne turned away from the window. What would *something different* be like? How does it feel to love and be loved without hurt and pain?

That's the way she felt about Desi. The fleeting image of her little girl floated before her. Her baby — the only thing that anchored her, let her know that there was goodness in her. She knew what love was when she held her baby, when Desi ran to her at the end of the day, held her hand, and told her a secret. With Desi's death her capacity to feel vanished. Yes, she knew a kind of love because of her child. But never a woman-and-man love. Never that.

Perhaps all she could evoke in a man is the beast, the rage. But she believed that there was something deep inside of her that knew she could be so much more. She could care. She could love. She was worthy.

But she was afraid. Afraid to reach out and try, only to discover that what seemed new was only more of the same. To discover that would be more than she could bear.

Perhaps Robert would show her some things today — how to make things grow, to find a way to care again. She wanted to — today. She wanted her soul back. She wanted to be like the roses he tended, the buds ready to bloom, the damaged edges clipped off, the thorns trimmed, no longer able to hurt. She wanted to try. She wanted to try while her head was clear, before the shadows returned and the little white pills slid over her tongue and sent her back into that hazy world where nothing was as it appeared.

Quickly she bathed and dressed, forced down a bowl of cornflakes and asked Judy to escort her onto the grounds.

"You're up and out mighty early," Judy Simpson said, walking beside Rayne down the corridor to the elevator.

Judy slid her identification card through the slot on the door.

"I . . . just have . . . an urge to be outdoors," Rayne responded between breaths of exhilaration.

Judy turned toward Rayne as the door

slid open, stunned and pleasantly pleased at hearing Rayne's voice. She sent up a silent thank you. "Did you rest well, dear?"

Rayne released a faint smile and nodded.

Judy patted her shoulders. She could only imagine what had transpired the previous day between Rayne, her father, and Dr. Dennis. She couldn't imagine it being pleasant, having witnessed his outburst in the corridor. She glanced at Rayne from the corner of her eye. There was something different about her today. Rayne had been on her service for a bit more than three months now. At first she thought Rayne Holland would be another lost cause, forever in and out of institutions, on a lifetime of medication.

But there was a resiliency about this young woman, an underlying toughness that belied her exotic, almost serene, beauty. She was a fighter, a survivor. Even in her months of silence, Judy believed it was more rebellion than illness — her way of coping and to hell with everyone else. She had a strong feeling that Rayne Holland would walk out of Cedar Grove one day and be just fine.

"I'd . . . like to sit on the bench for a while," Rayne said timidly, almost as if she were afraid of being reprimanded, as they stepped out into the humid Georgia morning.

"Of course. I'll be around if you need anything."

"I'll . . . be fine."

Judy patted Rayne's shoulder again, and returned inside, secure in the knowledge that there was plenty of staff on the grounds to keep an eye on things.

Rayne took her favorite seat on the bench beneath the willow tree. For a moment she gazed up at the forlorn arms seeming to seek someone or something to embrace. Then she opened her journal.

That's how I feel today, she wrote in a steady hand. *I feel the need to embrace. My daughter awakened those feelings — those instincts in me. After Mother died, I'd lost the urge to touch or to be touched. The want of closeness had been stripped from me, peeled away layer by layer until I lay raw and bare.*

When I'd met Paul at the Christmas party that Gayle dragged me to, it was the first time in years that I'd felt any emotion toward a man.

Paul was gentle with me, his touch

soothing, his voice a caress. Not like the men I'd known before who'd wanted to possess me, to get beneath the protective veneer.

He was different when we'd danced together that first time. The lights in the ballroom were low, twinkling like the constellation. Music didn't play, it floated. Glasses tinkled. Champagne flowed. Laughter blended into a symphony of song.

"I'm glad to finally meet you," Paul had said as he led me onto the dance floor. "Gayle talks about you all the time."

He eased me into his arms, not too tight, but comfortable, easy, and I felt an immediate aura of safety.

As I moved against and with him in time to the music, for the first time a man's touch didn't repel me, make me feel ugly and sick inside.

Yet there was an underlying fear, a quiet dread that at any moment the ugliness would rear up and grab me by the throat, squeezing the promise of happiness out of me.

"Gayle tells me you're a filmmaker."

"Yes. Just starting out, actually."

"What type of films do you make?"

"Documentaries."

"Hmm. I'd think you'd be more commercial."

My skeptical gaze rose and was stopped by the sincerity in his eyes. "Why would you think that?"

"Money. Prestige."

"I'm more interested in bringing a message to the screen. Something with purpose." I fought down the truth of his comment, but not hard enough. Maybe I needed to hear what he was really saying. "Financing is difficult for feature films. Especially for an unknown."

"What about backing?"

"It's difficult when you have no one who can vouch for your work. That's one reason why I'm going the documentary route until I can make a name and get the financing I need for a major project."

"Have you done anything yet?" he asked.

"About my film?"

"Financing. Do you have any?"

"No. Not enough to get it done."

The music eased down and drifted away. Paul stepped back but didn't release me.

"I want to get to know you better. See some of your work — and you."

I looked across the dance floor, beyond Paul's shoulder. Gayle was sipping a drink, talking to James, but she was looking at me — staring at Paul. At the time I didn't understand. I do now.

I turned back to Paul then. "I think I'd like that."

He gave me the most disarming smile and I felt a warmth inside. "Do you like jazz?" he asked me.

"Pretty much."

"I go to this really great spot on Thursday nights. They're throwing a New Year's bash. I'd love to take you if you don't have plans. But you're probably busy."

"I've never gone out on New Year's."

"Neither have I," he said, his confessional secret easing mine.

The music from the band hung between us, crying out that last note you didn't want to end, hoping instead for the chorus.

"Maybe we can break tradition. Together." He stepped up to me, sweeping me into a slow drag.

I inhaled the male scent of him,

mixed with smoke, perfumes, and colognes, the aroma of food and wine tossed together into that slow drag dance.

I heard the chorus line, not the end of my song. A night to remember.

And I didn't want to forget, would never forget that first night. It was what held me together when the times between us grew insane. Like his arms did that night. I tried to conjure up that first dance during our marriage as if it would somehow make the dread of night go away.

So that is where it began with Paul Holland and me — out on the dance floor on a Christmas night nearly nine years ago. I wanted him to be my salvation, my knight, and at first he was — in the beginning. When did things begin to change? I wasn't sure. I'm still not. It remains a haze, as if a part of my life with Paul is shrouded in a veil.

Many times I asked myself what it was I felt for him and he for me. I needed safety. In me, he saw something I could never give. Myself. I didn't know how. I didn't know who I was, not really. Maybe never.

The only thing in my life that made sense, where I had control, was in my work. Behind the camera, viewing the world I'd created, one in which I was not at its mercy. There I could give birth to the scenes, the message, shape them in my image — shedding the veils — for all the world to see.

Until Desiree. My beautiful baby girl — conceived in violence, born to love. Yes. That was when I first understood the power of love, what it meant to want to give willingly of yourself for the good of someone else.

I was almost whole, and then she was gone.

I'm rambling. When I'll look back at these pages, they won't make sense. But I know I need to put my thoughts and feelings down as I see them. As they come.

I was wrong to think Paul could save me. And he grew to resent me for it, maybe even hate me — just a little. The only one who could save me was myself.

I tried and failed.

So here I am.

Sometimes, sitting here on the grounds — with grass as green as

Far Eastern jade, the jutting sentinels of trees pointing accusingly toward the open azure sky, dotted with cotton ball puffs, the distant flap of birds' wings soft as a fetal heartbeat — I forget where I am, why I'm here. And I almost smile.

Today is one of those days. I forget because I need to, want to more than anything, because during those lapses, those intermissions from reality, I can have those precious moments when the emptiness doesn't consume me, and then it doesn't hurt quite so much.

A shadow pans across the pages of my journal, growing, skewing the view of my world.

"Good morning."

I knew he would come.

Rayne glanced up at him, covering the wounds of her conscience with her hand. "Hello."

"Beautiful day after the one we had yesterday," he said, taking a white handkerchief from his back pocket and wiping the sweat from his face.

A dark patch, the size of a child's fist, crested beneath each arm. Twins almost.

It was hot. Waves of heat fluttered up from the ground, seemingly attempting to escape.

She closed her journal.

"How are you today?"

"How . . . is your father?" she asked in answer.

Robert felt his body coil. He didn't want to think about the man on the sixth floor. Not today. He knew he'd visit later. Sit by the bedside, listen to the meanderings, the truths. But not now. Not in this space.

"Mind if I sit down?" Robert asked.

Rayne moved over a bit, made room on the short bench.

"It's beautiful in this spot. I can see almost everything from here," Rayne thought, wishing she could push the words out of her mind and into the summer air.

"Is that what you're writing about?"

She looked at him curiously. Had she spoken the words out loud, or did he truly have some secret power to read her thoughts? "No," she murmured — at least she believed she did. She put the journal beside her thigh, away from him. "How old do you think this tree is?" The words burst past her lips, surprising her with their sudden arrival. She looked up at the willow that canopied them. Her heart pounded.

Robert shrugged. "You can only tell for sure if you cut it down. Count the rings."

"To . . . destroy something to find out how long it's lived. People are like that, too."

How could she know what was in his thoughts? he wondered.

Suddenly she wanted to unbutton her blouse. Her hands gravitated toward the top button. Her fingers played with its smoothness. She curled her fingers around it, breathed a bit faster.

"Are you all right?" Robert asked, breaking the spell.

Ashamed. Dirty. Her eyes began to burn. *Don't cry, girl,* the voice warned. *Just answer the man.* "Fine. Just . . . hot."

"Let me get you some water." He got up, walked briskly across the lawn to his van parked on the other side of the facility.

Robert returned with a plastic cup of water. A lone ice cube melted by degrees.

"Drink this. You're probably overheated."

Rayne raised her eyes to meet his and brought the cup to her lips. The cube of ice teased the outer folds of skin. She wanted to wrap them around it. Suck it until it was only a cool memory. She slipped the diminishing cube of ice into her mouth, drawing on the last of what it had to offer. And then it was gone.

"Thank you." She handed him the cup.

Their fingers brushed.

"You seem different," Robert said.

"How?"

"You've . . . opened up."

"Like a bud?" she asked in an almost childish voice.

He smiled. "Yes."

The heat hung between them now, like that last note on Christmas night. On the dance floor. That first night, when she wanted to hear the chorus. Who would sing it?

"You said you'd show me one day how to tend the garden . . . make things grow." The music was fading. She wanted to hold on.

He stepped closer.

Rayne's eyes followed him, captured how his long, hard body moved, folded itself, stretched muscular legs as he sat beside her, absorbing her, the air and space around them.

She was the cube of ice, melting under his heat — drawn in and consumed by him. Her heart rose and fell. She wanted to run, get away from this thing that she knew would only hurt. But the macabre fascination with its power held her transfixed.

"I haven't had a chance to talk to your . . . doctor about me teaching you."

Rayne looked down at her hands rather than the pity that would be in his eyes. She was confined. That was the simple truth — and they both knew it.

The last note reached its apex. In a breath it would be gone if she didn't sing the chorus.

"Maybe I . . . could watch," she said, the note of hope reaching out like a prayer.

He looked at her a moment, remembering sitting in his bedroom window every night for months, praying that his father would return so that his mother would stop crying, his sister would stop whoring, and the hollowness in his stomach would be filled.

Day after day he waited to see that familiar figure turn the corner and put his key in the lock. Then everything could be as it was. Yes, Robert knew how Rayne felt.

"Everything is a process," he said. "All the ingredients have to be right if they're going to work. Growing things is no different than your life or mine." He looked at her. "You have to tend it, care for and about it. When anything or anyone is cared about, it blooms, flourishes. And you need patience. Sometimes the first try fails. So you try again until you get it right."

"Don't you ever get tired of trying?" she asked.

"Sure. But I don't let it stop me. I can't. And neither should you. I'm sure you don't want to shoot a scene over and over. But you do because you know the next time will be better. Then when you get it just the way you want it, there's no greater joy than to see your vision, your work, a reality."

She listened to the simplicity of the words, the truth of them. These rare times spent with Robert provided her with something she'd never had — nurturing. He listened to her, not only her words but in the things she didn't say. He understood what rested in her heart. What would her reality ultimately be? she wondered. Where could she begin?

"We can start now, if you like," he said, as if reading her thoughts. "At least you can watch until I get a chance to talk to your doctor."

Her eyes brightened, or maybe it was the sun. He couldn't be sure.

"Yes. I would."

"Come on, then. I'll show you the rose bushes first. They're beautiful when handled right."

For an instant their gazes held that last note.

Hope started with a rose.

Fifteen

The telephone buzzed.

Pauline jotted her last note in Rayne's case file, then pressed the flashing red light. "Yes." She picked off her glasses, set them down on the desk.

"Dr. Dennis, Dr. Howell would like to see you in his office," the duty nurse said.

Pauline inhaled quickly. "Thank you."

Reginald Howell was the psychiatric chief, rarely seen, his presence always felt. *He* was Cedar Grove.

Dr. Howell had studied with some of the greatest minds in the world. A devout follower of Freud, he didn't take kindly to the latest innovations of modern psychotherapy, and looked upon many of the new practitioners as charlatans — practitioners such as herself who followed the modalities of Jung, known to many as the father of modern psychotherapy. Although Freud and Jung had been fast friends and colleagues, their relationship became fractured when their basic beliefs and practices for treatment began to diverge. The same was true of her and Dr. Howell. They'd become intellectual adversaries.

But time and necessity compelled Howell to accept the unacceptable and staff his hospital with a balanced cross section of therapists.

Although Pauline was head of her department with a staff of more than twenty, having risen up the ranks over the years, her tenure meant nothing. She still had to answer to Reginald Howell. And from experience, meetings with Dr. Howell never boded well for the invitee.

Steeling herself for the confrontation she was certain to come, she left her office. Deciding to get some air instead of taking the connecting tunnel that linked the two wings of the hospital, Pauline took the route across the grounds.

Halfway, she stopped short, spotting Rayne and Robert near the rose bushes.

She could almost see their expressions from the distance — happy. What she didn't see, she imagined. *Intimacy. Hope. Beginnings.*

She had every right and responsibility to find out exactly what was happening between *her* patient and a hospital employee. Stop it before it grew. It was as if Rayne and Robert's momentary idyll was a microcosm of her own desires to steal a moment of guileless happiness. The realization disturbed her with the strength of its simplicity.

Her pager went off. She checked the number on the LED screen. It was Dr. Howell. She looked once more toward Rayne and Robert, pushed her concerns aside, and hurried on her way.

"Come in," the voice behind the door commanded.

Pauline stepped into the room and knew the full meaning of power.

Reginald Howell was a bear of a man. Towering more than six feet five and tipping the scales at three-hundred-plus pounds, his stature alone demanded attention.

Opulence surrounded him. Imported rugs, cut crystal, and hand-carved furnishings adorned the spacious office. A complete library containing rare books and signed first editions were the envy of many. It had been rumored that his collections were worth millions, but he'd never been interested in selling. He relished being sought after — for his mind as well as his possessions. Like her uncle — and his things. Her muscles tensed at the thought of any conflict with Reginald Howell.

Reginald Howell didn't bother to look up when Pauline entered. He'd heard the mating of metal as the door closed, knew she would come. They all did. That's the way he liked it.

But there was something about Pauline Dennis that consistently disturbed him, put him on edge and on the defensive. He didn't like it and he didn't like her. Even if he had to admit that she was brilliant. Brilliance always intrigued him.

Arrogant bastard, Pauline inwardly fumed, teetering on the precipice of his acknowledgment. Waiting.

She loathed men like Reginald Howell. Men who believed they were above all others. That those whom they deemed beneath them were never worthy of their precious time or attention — minor annoyances to be dealt with.

Who dealt with him? she wondered. All therapists were encouraged and required to seek therapy themselves, to rid their minds and spirits of the pain and illness of their patients.

What was it like to hear and see the mighty Dr. Howell humbled into revealing his darkest thoughts, exposing his fears and weaknesses? Whoever held that key truly understood the full measure of power.

Pauline cleared her throat.

Reginald peered at her over the rim of his half-framed glasses, indicating with a gesture of his pen that she was permitted to sit in the chair stationed at the side of his desk.

Pauline sat, crossed her legs, and waited.

Reginald removed his glasses and lay them next to a stack of files and reference books. He turned his leonine head in her direction.

"I received a very disturbing phone call today, Dr. Dennis."

Pauline raised her chin. "And what might that be, Doctor?" She already knew. It was like an ache in your joints just before a storm set in. You felt it coming.

His mouth twitched seconds before his eyes narrowed. "About you, Doctor. And what the complainant feels are unethical practices, performed by you."

"What is it that I've allegedly done?"

His face flushed a bright crimson. "At the very least, Dr. Dennis, you've offended a family member of a very important patient," he seethed through bared teeth, his voice on simmer, which only magnified the cadence of his drawl.

Pauline folded her hands in her lap, refusing to be intimidated, and leaned forward. "Why don't we simply cut to the chase, Dr. Howell? Rayne Holland's father contacted you. He said he would. And do you know why he called, really called? Because all of a sudden what was happening in that room was no longer about Rayne Holland. It was about him. And it scared the hell out of him."

Reginald pursed his lips, his blue eyes flashing with barely contained curiosity. "Explain yourself, Dr. Dennis."

Pauline released a long breath. "From everything I witnessed yesterday, I believe that Rayne Holland had been sexually assaulted by her father." She paused to let the information digest, holding back what she'd witnessed in Rayne's room. Rayne's fractured personality had been created to protect her from something — her father, she was sure. But Pauline would protect her now.

Reginald relaxed against the cushion of his high-back leather-and-wood chair. He ran his hand across his mouth. Held it there, then lowered it to his lap. "How did you come to this conclusion?"

"By everything I saw in that room. Rayne Holland transformed into a terrified little girl, a girl frightened to death of her father."

"Why couldn't she have been reliving a spanking? Why sexual assault?"

It was always this way between them, Pauline fumed, struggling to maintain a level of calm, coming together in a battle of the mind over treatment methods, pharmacology, Freud vs. Jung, new vs. old. He seemed to derive some sort of bizarre pleasure from belittling the staff, questioning their judgment, their treatment — making them question themselves. Not this time. His vision was not superior.

"Dr. Howell, I have three degrees in psychology. I've practiced for more than fifteen years. I've had papers published in medical journals around the world. I've studied with some of the best minds in psychology." She stood, looking down on his shock of steel-gray hair. "I know abuse when I see it. And I assure you I'm not at the stage of my professional career where my observations and actions need to be questioned. Even by you, Dr. Howell."

He glared at her for a long moment, caught between outrage and admiration. There weren't many, if any at all, who dared to challenge him.

"I'm quite aware of *your* qualifications,

Dr. Dennis, or else you wouldn't be employed in *my* hospital." He folded his hands. "However, this *is* my hospital. You *are* my employee. And as such, *my* decision is the only one that counts. Dr. Dennis, right now my main concern is Mr. Mercer and his accusations, which could turn into a nasty lawsuit. Lawsuits, Doctor, do not please me. Not at all. Nor do the doctors who cause them." He leaned back. "I will give you the opportunity, because of your *qualifications*, to rectify this problem."

"Rectify the problem?" She heard her voice rise an octave before she could snatch it back and bring it down. "Rayne Holland is not a *problem*. She is my patient, a human being who has been traumatized and abused. A woman who is trying to find her way back to health. I intend to help her accomplish that. And the hell with that bastard of a father of hers and his accusations!"

She turned and stormed out of the office, leaving the door swinging on its hinges.

Reginald watched her retreating form through the open doorway, full of fire and ethical morality.

He smiled. Pauline Dennis was one of the most brilliant doctors he'd worked with over the years, but he'd be damned if he'd ever tell her that.

Pauline sat behind her desk, her fingers clenched around her black ballpoint pen. Her entire body trembled with fury, pent up like a tornado trapped in a ramshackle barn, ready to splinter.

Domination, tyranny, and absolute control were enemies she'd fought against all her life — with her brothers who treated her like a servant, her father who never believed she would amount to anything . . . her uncle who used her body at will.

As the only female in a household of men, she'd learned long ago that if she allowed it, she would be and remain at the mercy of men, as she once had been.

To battle that, to overcome the guilt of her submissions, her subservience, she'd entered into a field where she could help those who had suffered emotionally, physically, mentally. She'd cast aside her dark shadows, kept them locked safely away where they could no longer hurt or touch her.

But it was days like today, and men like Reginald Howell and William Mercer, who resurrected all the old demons, unlocked the door, and set the past on a rampage into her present.

She'd never told anyone about what had happened to her as a young girl, not even her therapist. She never even whispered about her uncle's carnal abuse of her young body or his threats to hurt her if she ever told. He'd said he was teaching her how to give pleasure to a man. But it was to be their secret. Over time she grew to expect the door to her room to open on Friday night, the smell of alcohol to fill the air, for the heavy body of her uncle to slide between her sheets, slip his hand between her thighs until she became wet and ready for him to take what he'd come to get. It was shame that prevented the words from leaving her lips. She knew that. It was fear of discovery, of being seen as broken, used, damaged goods, in her profession and in her life that kept her from revealing her dirty secret — the rage that she knew would erupt if she released the words.

Her fingers clamped tighter around the pen. Its tip bore into the soft, white-lined paper, carving black jagged fractures into the smooth finish. The pressure duplicated the scarring on the pages beneath.

She would not relinquish control. Would not. Not ever again. Not to any man. *She* would save Rayne Holland. Her way.

The black plastic pen snapped in half.

Sixteen

"Thank you . . . for today," Rayne softly murmured, hoping that he could hear her thoughts. She rose from her crouched position near the trimmed hedges.

"I enjoyed it." Robert wiped his hands on the fabric of his jeans, his dark brown face glistening with perspiration.

The air grew cooler. The time between them had passed. For now.

"I should . . . go back." Rayne tucked her journal under her arm. *They'll come for you if you don't,* the voice whispered. Her eyes darted quickly around the grounds, imagining the guards bearing down on her, dragging her back to her room, humiliating her. She didn't want that, didn't want the reality of her existence to crowd out her fantasy.

Robert glanced at his watch. "Visiting hours."

Say something, girl. Don't just run away. Speak up! "Your father . . . will you see him?" she asked, the words coming from some faraway place.

"I should. Sometimes he knows I'm there." He looked away.

The cape of his sadness hung on her shoulders. She wanted to say something, do anything to lift the weight. But how could she when she still could not rid herself of her own burdens?

Helpless. Again.

Rayne reached out to touch his cheek, wipe away the lines of worry from beneath his eyes, but stopped halfway when he looked back at her.

The brackets around his mouth softened as he smiled. "Maybe tomorrow. If the weather holds up, how about if we meet by the bench after lunch?"

She didn't want to feel hope, that warm glow of maybe, but she did.

Robert smiled outright. "It should be good and hot by then. I'll be sure to bring plenty of water."

Rayne studied him for one slender moment, memorizing their day together, then turned and hurried toward the entrance.

Robert watched her until she was gone. There was so much about her that he wanted to know. He wanted to find out her favorite color, places she'd been, her fondest memory. He wanted to know who she was before she came to Cedar's, who she could be when she left. And as much as he tried to deny it, he wanted to be there for her when she did. She challenged him in ways she was totally unaware of. In her, he could perhaps redeem himself. Do for her what he was unable to do for his mother and sister. Maybe.

He bent down and picked up his shears, rose, and looked out across the grounds. His men were packing up, heading home. The hospital staff escorted some of the patients back inside. Others found their own way.

Everyone had a destination. He looked up at the building. Lights began to twinkle in the windows.

Where did he have to go and to whom? Nowhere, and to no one.

How long had it been this way? he questioned, moving toward his van.

For the most part, his work kept him satisfied, fulfilled in a way. He tried not to think about the other things. His mother. His father. His sister.

He opened the door, got in behind the wheel, turned on the engine.

His mother. Lena Parrish was the kind of mother any child would want. All his friends said so, for as long as he could remember . . .

★ ★ ★

"Your mom is cool, man," Mike, Robert's best friend, was saying as they walked home from school.

Robert shrugged, pretending the comment meant nothing much, but inside it made him feel special. "She's awright. Gets on my nerves, though."

"Yeah, but she's home when you get in from school. Lets your friends hang out at the house. Takes us all out and stuff. My moms never does nothin' like that. She's always 'too tired,'" Michael singsonged. "You're lucky, that's all," he added.

Robert glanced at him from the corner of his eyes. It wasn't cool to check someone out if they were going to break down. Not a guy. But that's how Mike sounded, like he was going to cry or something.

"You awright, man?" Robert asked.

"Yeah." Mike sniffed briefly, then picked up his bebop step. "I just wish my moms didn't have to work all the time, you know."

"Yeah."

Maybe they *were* lucky, Robert thought. Most of his friends didn't have their real dads around. A lot of them were on public assistance, or got food stamps. He knew because he'd seen his buddies in the store trying to look cool passing that Monopoly-looking money to the cashier.

That could never happen to his family.

Robert and his sister, Nicole, never really thought much about their way of life. It's just the way things were. Dad worked and took care of the expenses and their mother stayed home and took care of them.

Robert's father, Frank, had a good job as a truck driver. He was gone a lot of the time. But when he came home, it was always like Christmas. He brought presents home for everyone. They'd all go out together and have fancy dinners at restaurants, go to the movies, even to plays.

Lena and Nicole would just fall all over themselves when Dad came home. They really missed him a lot when he was gone, but not more than Robert did.

But he would just wait his turn. He knew his dad would take him to the side for a man-to-man talk, or come up to his room just before bed, like he did that last night.

"How's things been around here, son?" Frank asked, sitting on the edge of Robert's single bed.

"Pretty good." Robert turned on his side so he could see his dad better.

Frank was a medium-built man, no more

than five nine, five ten. His penny-brown complexion was clear and always clean shaven. There was not too much of anything in particular about Frank Parrish. But what Robert liked best about his father's face was his eyes. They were large and dark, so dark they appeared black. They could be warm when he was telling tales of his road trips, and laughing. Or spark like hot coals when he got angry. That wasn't often. For the most part, his father was an easygoing man who worked hard and loved his family.

He looked up at his father. "I'm trying out for the track team at school," he said, the pride in his voice making it deeper.

Frank patted him on the thigh. "That's my boy. Always was faster than a greased pig." He laughed, then gave his son a serious look. "How you been doing in your studies, boy? I don't want to have to go up there again behind you."

Robert shifted beneath the sheet. "I'm tryin', Dad, I swear."

"Don't swear, just do it. I'm expectin' great things outta you, Bobby." He looked at his son for a long moment, a look Robert would never forget. "You're growing up real nice, son. I'm proud of you. Really proud. And I want you to promise me you'll keep doing the right thing."

Robert's heart began to race. He sat up. "What's wrong?"

"Just promise me."

He was getting scared, but wasn't sure why. He had that uncertain feeling you get in your chest when you know something is about to happen, something that would change your life, but you can't stop it because you don't know what it is.

"I promise, Dad. But —"

"And I want you to make sure you take care of your mother and your sister. You're the man of the house when I'm gone." He patted Robert's thigh again.

But instead of letting his ego inflate with his father's breath of confidence filling him, he wanted to grab his father, hug him, and tell him to make the twirling sensation in his belly go away. All he could do was nod his head.

"That's my boy. Now get some sleep and don't forget what I said."

He stood. To Robert, he appeared a giant, tall, strong, and invincible.

"I'll be heading out very early in the morning. I probably won't see you." He hesitated. "Remember that I love you, son. Always will."

"Love you, too, Dad."

"Get some sleep," he said, his voice suddenly battling exhaustion and failing. He switched off the light and pulled the door almost closed, letting the light from the hall peek in through the sliver of an opening.

Robert leaned back against his pillow. The smell of his father's Old Spice cologne still hung in the air.

That was the last night he saw his father until more than twenty years later, when he'd located him in a nursing home for the indigent.

Robert opened his eyes and slammed his fist against the steering wheel. The burn in his throat kept him from howling out his anguish, lament over the lost years, the unexplainable. He looked toward the facility and the lights that beckoned him.

He missed his father. He'd missed him most of his life. There'd been no one to teach him to be a man, what it meant. He'd had to put the pieces together himself and never felt as if he'd succeeded. How could all that lost time ever be regained?

It couldn't. He knew that. That's what made it hurt so bad. Aw hell, he was just being a sentimental fool. What was he thinking? He'd gotten weak for a moment, a little boy again who needed his dad.

Too many nights he'd replayed that last conversation, smelled his father's scent, and wondered what he'd done to make his dad leave — to abandon them all.

Would he ever know?

Will you see him tonight — your father? Rayne's voice was right in his ear.

He looked toward the facility again. Maybe tonight would be the night. The one that would answer the questions, fill in the blanks.

His hand was on the car door handle. He pulled it toward him. The door popped open. He paused for a moment then shut the door. Robert walked across the grounds and into the facility.

"Good evening, Mr. Parrish," the duty nurse greeted.

"Hi, Cynthia. How are you?"

"Can't complain."

Robert angled his chin toward the corridor. "How is he today?"

Cynthia's brows rose to half-moons above her light-green eyes, framed her glasses. "Actually, it was a good day for him. He knew where he was, even listened to some music." Her expression softened. "He asked for you."

"Really?"

"Yes." She smiled. "Go on in. He'll be happy to see you."

Robert hesitated. There'd been so many almosts, maybes, he didn't want to get his hopes up only to have them collapse like dominoes around him.

"Thanks, Cynthia."

When he reached the door to his father's room, Frank looked up and Robert could see the light of recognition glimmer in his father's eyes. The edges of his mouth wobbled in uncertainty as Robert drew closer.

"Hi, Dad." He took his seat by the bed. "How are you?"

His words meandered out of his mouth, took their time reaching their destination. "Not too bad, son. I was out in the hall earlier. This is a big place. Get lost in a minute."

Robert grinned. "Yeah, you sure can."

"You're looking pretty good. I was hoping you'd stop by. I wanted to talk to you."

"About what?"

Frank blinked, hesitated, trying to gather up his thoughts. But they were so quick, flying away like dry leaves blown by an autumn wind.

"How's your mama and Nicole? They haven't come to see me."

Robert's stomach knotted for a moment. Whatever hope he had that tonight would be the night for answers crumbled at his feet.

"Mama's dead." He blew out a breath of regret. "Nicole's been gone for a long time."

Frank looked at his son, trying to make sense of what he was hearing. Waves of confusion ripped across his brow. Frank's mouth opened, then closed. His thin hand gripped the metal rail of the bed. "Not my Lena." His large dark eyes begged to be filled with a reason why. "I was waiting for her to come. Thought she was upset with me about getting sick — not telling her. You know how your mama always fussed with me about taking care of myself." Water seeped out from the corner of his eyes. "She was fine when I left."

Robert felt as if he'd been slammed in the gut. Reality and illusion clashed. What was it that his father did know and understand? Had he not known all these years that his mother was dead? If he did, would he have come home? Or was it that he really believed that he'd just seen her, as if it were only yesterday and not twenty years ago?

Robert wanted to be angry, to shake

some sense into the old man, make him remember. But the part of him that still longed for the times gone by, remembered the man his father had once been, softened the knot of hate that had grown inside him like a cancer, eating away at his feelings for this stranger who had sired him.

And then revelation took his hand and held it, leading him along a path he'd fought to avoid. As he witnessed his father's anguish, he realized Frank Parrish was just as trapped by the past as Robert had allowed himself to be. Frank was held captive by his mind, Robert by his heart.

How different were they — really?

He took his father's hand and held it, the first time he'd done so since he was a little boy. When he felt his father's thin fingers wrap around his hand, he felt his soul open up and shift. This was his father. His father.

Slowly, Frank opened his eyes and appeared to have aged five years in a matter of minutes. "You always were my big boy," Frank said, his voice as weak as the faded colors of an ancient portrait.

Robert pushed down the knot in his throat. He'd spent most of his life hating this man who had given him life. He's spent his days wishing him ill, because he never understood how you could love someone and simply leave them.

The seed of his pain and loss had been planted deep, tended over the years, fed by the waters of his resentment.

Frank's mist-filled eyes held on to his son's, searching for the key that would unlock the memories — release them, make them clear.

"Why, Dad? Why did you leave me — us?"

Frank blinked, tried to focus. He almost smiled, his mind fighting its battle between reality and fantasy. "You know I have to work, son. That job takes me on the road." He shook his head. "You know how much I love you all. Hate to leave. But a man has to take care of his family. It's not easy, you know. Especially for a black man. Might be better up North." He nodded his head as if accepting the reality. "You'll see when you grow up and have a family of your own. Nothin' harder on a real man than not to be able to take care of his family. Just don't feel like a man. It's important to feel like a man."

Frank's gaze drifted off to some distant place that Robert could not see.

The moment had passed.

Robert patted his father's shoulders,

shoulders that he'd once believed could carry any burden. "Get some rest, Dad. I'll see you tomorrow."

"Yeah, yeah. I got a big job tomorrow. Gonna bring you and your sister something nice and a new dress for your mama."

His eyes drifted closed, his voice faint. "Don't forget to do your homework."

An unwanted tear fell from Robert's eyes, staining the white sheet. "I — will."

"Tell your sister it's time to be gettin' inside now. Dark out there . . ." A shadow seemed to settle over the older man's craggy features as he shifted his failing body away from the small boy standing near him. He hoped he didn't have to remind him again about that damned homework.

Seventeen

Pauline moaned in her sleep.

She was standing next to Rayne. Both of them faced a huge mirror. Their images were at once clear, then hazy as if they'd been smudged. But as they stepped closer, hand-in-hand, their images began to shimmy, becoming vaporlike, mixing with each other. For a brief, terrifying moment they merged and only one figure was reflected.

Rayne.

Pauline's eyes flew open. Her body was damp with sweat. The thin, yellow nylon gown clung to her breasts, dipped into the damp hollow of her stomach.

She was exhausted. Every muscle ached as if she'd been running for miles without rest. Rayne Holland's case had infiltrated her life, entered her dreams, something that never happened before. The dream unnerved her. It was reminiscent of the classic Bergman film *Persona*: two women, one silent, one gregarious, one ill and one well; over time their personalities merged, two persons battling for one soul until one became the other.

Pauline tossed the sheet aside and sat up, momentarily covering her face with her hands.

What was happening?

In the years that she'd practiced, there'd been cases that had gotten to her, tested her, kept her awake at night. But Rayne's case had tapped into a part of her that she'd worked for years to keep submerged.

She saw herself in Rayne, what frightened her, identified with the past that had stained her soul, disfigured her spirit. And the more she probed Rayne's mind, assembled the pieces of her journey toward healing, she felt her own life begin to change shape.

Was she superimposing her own traumas onto Rayne, believing what she wanted to believe, hoping to fix her and in turn fix herself? Was she allowing the nature of Rayne's illness to cloud her medical judgment?

"No." She stood. She was a better doctor than that. Of course she empathized with her patients. It was only human. But she was professional enough to keep herself separate, see things for what they were.

But her life was becoming like the dream. The closer she came to uncovering Rayne's mysteries, the nearer she drew to confronting her own. And she was afraid.

She finally made it into the bathroom and turned on the shower full blast. Standing under the pelting spray, she hoped to wash away the doubts, to cleanse her fears.

She knew she needed help. But to do so, to reach the core of who she was in order to move forward, would put her under the microscope, dissected and inspected, open to criticism and pity. She couldn't do that to herself. She'd have to find a way to be strong, for herself and for Rayne.

That's what they both needed now.

Pauline tightened the belt around the plain white cotton robe, trying to recall where she'd picked it up or if it was an after-thought gift from one of her estranged family members.

It certainly had no sex appeal, she thought, padding into the sunny lemon-yellow kitchen. Not that it would matter. She couldn't recall the last time she'd been in a relationship with a man that would re-quire he see her in a robe, threadbare and plain or otherwise.

What did that say about her? she wondered, sitting at the bar stool counter with a glass of orange juice. It said, *You don't have a life outside of your work.*

She sipped her juice as the coffee brewed, drip by drip, in the background. Her patients were her relationships. They consumed most of her time and energy. No man outside of her profession, and often in it, could understand how important they were to her. How she felt it was her duty to heal them. It was a compulsion that devoured her, even at the expense of her own lovers.

Lovers. That was always difficult. Opening herself, giving of herself to someone else. She'd never known how that truly felt.

She took another sip of her juice. There had been someone once. Scott Lancing. They'd met during her residency at Johns Hopkins in Baltimore, Maryland. He was handsome, brilliant, and ambitious, and he went after Pauline with the same dogged determination that he pursued his work.

Funny she should think about Scott after all this time. It was a part of her life that she'd guiltily enjoyed but lived to regret.

She should have seen the trouble coming, but she was too blinded by his attention and accolades of her skills. Scott picked her out of the crop of new residents with the same care one would when selecting the perfect rose from a dozen that looked just like it.

"You have great potential, Pauline," he'd said to her one afternoon at the end of her shift.

Pauline returned a case file to the duty nurse. "Thank you, Doctor."

"Please." He placed his hand at the small of her back, extended his other in the direction of his office. "Why don't we talk inside?"

That was the day her life irrevocably changed.

Pauline shook her head, scattering the visions. It was a time best forgotten — what she'd done, been a part of. But there were days and times like today when she became wary, distrusted her instincts.

Shaky fingers buttoned her cream-colored blouse, put on her navy slacks and matching jacket. As she examined her reflection, a sudden sensation of dread wrapped around her, squeezing the air from her lungs. She saw Rayne's face in the mirror, terrified and accusing. Pauline turned away, grabbed her car keys, briefcase, and hurried out.

Her day began with a steady flow of activity. But the lack of sleep, compounded with the disturbing dreams, were playing havoc with her nerves and her mind. She found herself snapping at the hospital staff and only half listening to the string of patients. Her fourth cup of coffee for the day wasn't helping and she still had a group session to conduct.

Walking down the long pale-blue corridor, the people and images around her took on a surreal feeling. She felt as if she were standing outside of herself, a surveyor of the landscape of life. The voices and sounds around her were muted, as if she were listening to them through a filter. She felt the wild racing of her heart and a dampness that covered her body.

Maybe she needed to take a break before conducting the group session, just sit down and relax for a minute, try to pull herself together. She continued down the corridor with the intention of retreating to the staff lounge and closing her eyes for a bit, meditate. But before she reached the lounge, she was accosted by Nurse Simpson.

"Dr. Dennis, thank God I found you."

Pauline stopped short. "What's wrong?"

Judy looked around, then lowered her voice. "Can we go somewhere and talk privately?"

Pauline studied the tense expression on Judy's otherwise controlled face and was immediately alarmed. "Of course."

The instant the door to Pauline's office was closed, Judy launched into the horror of her story.

"I was reviewing the charts this morning, like I do every day when I come on duty," she began. "And I picked up Rayne Holland's chart. And that's when I saw the notation from Dr. Howell."

"Dr. Howell? Why would he make notations in Rayne's chart?"

"Exactly. That's what I thought. But that's not the worst of it. He's ordered electroshock therapy for her."

"What!"

Pauline knew and had seen the effects of ETC. Electroconvulsive therapy, as it's called in clinical terms, virtually fries the brain, killing off entire sections with high-voltage electricity. ECT was generally used as a last resort when all other forms of intervention and medication have failed. All options had not been used with Rayne. The entire process was traumatic at best, with the patient being given an IV of Brevital, an anesthetic to silence them, then succinylcholine, a muscle relaxant, is administered through the IV to prevent

271

broken bones or a cracked vertebrae. A rubber block is put in the patient's mouth to keep him from biting his tongue and a mask is placed over his nose and mouth so that the brain isn't deprived of oxygen, while the electrodes are placed on the temple. Although the electric currents charge through the body only for an instant, it's sufficient to cause a grand-mal seizure lasting up to twenty seconds. Whole areas of a patient's life are erased as if they'd never existed — "curing" him. As radical as the treatment was, it was used much more than necessary at Cedar Grove. And Dr. Howell always initiated the order, more for a show of power than a means to a cure. But this was the first time one of her patients at Cedar's had been subjected to Dr. Howell's God complex.

She wouldn't allow that to happen to Rayne.

"When is it scheduled?"

"This afternoon," Judy responded, her own anxiety rising along with Pauline's.

"Have you seen Dr. Howell on the grounds?"

"No. He's not in today. But he left specific instructions with the shock team that the procedure was to be taken care of

272

today without interference . . . specifically from you."

Pauline straightened. The gauntlet had been thrown, the treatment protocol of her patient overridden. Had this been what she'd been feeling all day — what the dreams had been alluding to?

To go against Dr. Howell would end her career. Any hope of working at Cedar Grove would be crushed out like a bug beneath the toe of a shoe. And her chances of working anywhere in Georgia would be eliminated. He would see to that. She'd be forced to start over, rebuild her practice, her reputation, somewhere else.

Everything she'd done, all the work, the energy, the time, and sacrifice was to reach this point in her life, the top of her profession. And with one pen stroke, one word, it could all be destroyed by one egotistical man hell-bent on besting her.

She'd faced this uncertainty once before in her life with Scott. Damn him and what she'd allowed to happen. She'd lived with her weakness, her indecisiveness for nearly a decade, and the shame of it hadn't lessened with time.

Linda Cole had been her patient, diagnosed as bipolar and she was a brilliant artist with incredible promise. Pauline had been treating Linda with medication and psychotherapy for nearly six months, and felt that she was making slow but steady progress. But her colleagues believed otherwise, with Scott Lansing the driving force. No one dared to question his decisions or his judgment for fear of the repercussions.

Pauline knew in her heart, knew in her gut, that what was proposed for Linda Cole was wrong. It went against every instinct she had as a physician. But she'd allowed her feelings for Scott, her drive for success, and her desire not to question the status quo to keep her from doing what was right — stopping them, by any means necessary.

The ECT administered to Linda Cole had unquestionably cured her symptoms, but any hope of her resuming a career as a painter was removed, along with a host of memories that made her who she was.

Pauline remembered all too vividly the day Linda was released on an outpatient basis — a ghost. And she'd lived with her guilt every day since.

"Where is Rayne?" Pauline asked Judy.

"I believe she's in her room."

Pauline's thoughts raced. She must decide, and quickly. Was she willing to risk it all?

"I need you to do something for me. Take Rayne out onto the grounds. Keep her out of the building until I beep you."

"What are you going to do?"

"That's what I'm trying to figure out. Just do as I ask. Please. And don't say anything to anyone."

Judy nodded and hurried out the door.

For several moments, Pauline remained where Judy had left her, vacillating between personal ethics and professional suicide.

Then she picked up the phone.

Eighteen

Gayle was sitting in the kitchen staring into space when James and Tracy came through the door.

"Mommy!" Tracy squealed, running across the linoleum floor into her mother's arms.

"Hey, baby." Gayle held her close while looking over her head and into James's stony expression. "Hi," she murmured to him.

"She wanted to see you." He hung his jacket on the back of the kitchen door and it took all Gayle had not to point out that it didn't belong there.

"Have a good time at Auntie and Uncle's house?" Gayle asked, holding Tracy at arm's length, subtly giving her a good once-over, looking for signs that she hadn't been cared for — something she could hold against James. She could find nothing.

"Auntie washed my hair and sat me between her knees to braid it." Tracy giggled.

"Like you used to do," she added innocently.

Gayle's eyes flashed toward her husband to catch the hint of satisfaction on his face.

"I was a big girl," Tracy whispered. "I didn't wet the bed."

"That's wonderful, baby." Gayle brushed her hair. "I knew you could do it."

"Why don't you go on upstairs, sweetheart," James said, "and get out of those clothes. I'll be up in a minute."

"Can Mommy come, too?" Tracy looked from one parent to the other.

"Sure," James said.

Tracy skipped out of the kitchen and up the stairs.

James turned away from Gayle and toward the cabinets, opened one, and took out the jar of coffee. "It didn't feel good being away from you, Gayle," he said, keeping his back to his wife. "I never thought things would get like this between us."

"Neither did I."

James turned to face her. His voice was heavy with the weight of the years and dreams they'd shared together, no longer made light by hope but laden with sorrow. "What happened? How did we let it all get away from us?"

Gayle slowly stood, watching the lines of hurt and confusion etch a path across James's handsome face. She crossed the short distance between them, reached up, and touched his cheek. Briefly his eyes shut, then looked down at her. "I'm not sure, James. All I know is that we can't live like this. This isn't what we dreamed about." She lowered her hand to her side.

James walked past her and sat down. "I know I wasn't your first choice," James said, finally speaking the words that taunted him.

Gayle felt her heart knock in her chest. She held her breath.

"If you could've had your way, you would have married Paul Holland. I know that." He turned to look at her over his shoulder, a shaky smile wavering around his full lips. "But I fell in love with you, Gayle. Been in love with you since high school." He looked down at his folded hands. "I just believed that once I got my education and my career on the right track, we could make a life together — I could make you happy. That's all I've ever wanted." He shook his head. "But enough just never seemed to be enough. No matter what I did."

"James —"

"No, please let me finish." He blew out a breath. "It seemed that all you really wanted was Rayne's life. Whatever it was that she had, you wanted it, too. The house and everything that went with it, the stellar career, *the husband.* You didn't even want kids until Rayne had Desiree."

As much as she wanted to refute what James said, she knew she couldn't. It was all true.

"Why, Gayle? What is it about Rayne that makes her life so perfect and yours incomplete? Look what it's gotten her. I've never believed for a moment that Rayne was actually happy — about anything. For all that she seemed to have, she was always empty inside. But that never seemed to matter to you."

How could she explain something she barely understood herself? How could she tell this man, her husband, how much she'd envied Rayne, how in her presence she always felt so inadequate? Yet even with these feelings, Gayle was drawn to her, drawn to that something inside of Rayne that was needy, and it was the only thing Gayle ever felt she was good at — filling a need.

"I don't even know where to begin, James," Gayle began slowly. "I don't think

I've ever said out loud some of the things that have gone on inside me, my real feelings."

"Try. I want to know. If there's any chance of us salvaging what we have, we need to be honest, Gayle, even if it hurts like hell. Nothing can be worse than the way things have been between us." His gaze held hers for a moment. "Give me a reason to stay."

Gayle stood rooted to the spot, silent and unsure, ashamed of the words forming in her mind. She was afraid to speak them, understanding what they would say about the person she was.

She released a heavy sigh, looking out through the backyard window. "For as long as I can remember, I never felt good enough about anything. My parents were so caught up in the beauty and brilliance of my brother, Nathan, that they hardly noticed me unless they needed me to do something."

"Your brother?" James's expression wrinkled in confusion. "You never told me you had a brother."

"It was, and still is, too painful. A part of my life that I've kept to myself. Nathan was five years older than me. It could have been light years and we couldn't have been further apart. My father treated him as if he were the heir apparent, and my mother virtually waited on him hand and foot." She held her glass tighter. "He died when I was thirteen. Nathan and a bunch of his friends had been to a frat party. Everyone was drinking. The driver of the car was the only one who survived."

Gayle said this all in a flat sameness, as if reciting a string of chemistry formulas. Just data, no emotion. James was chilled by her indifference, yet mystified by this aspect of his wife's life he knew nothing of, and the reasons why she chose to keep it from him.

"Why haven't you ever said anything to me?"

Gayle refused to look at him. "I couldn't."

"Why, Gayle?"

She swallowed down the knot in her throat, blinked away the burn in her eyes. "Then . . . you might see that part of me that I hate . . . and hate me, too, like they did. I — there was a part of me that was glad he was gone, and that maybe my parents would finally love me."

"Gayle, baby." James got up from his seat, came around the table, and took her in his arms. "I could never hate you, Gayle," he whispered against her hair.

"Never. I love you. I'll always love you. Please, just talk to me. Whatever it is. We're supposed to be a team, me and you. I can deal with anything if you just talk to me."

Gayle cried against her husband's shoulder, cried out her years of loneliness, her feelings of inadequacy. She cried out her confusion about who she was and, most of all, shed bitter tears for what she'd done to her marriage and to this man who loved her without question.

"When I met you," James uttered, "all I could see was this confident girl-woman waiting to bloom. She was strong and decisive. She wanted a career, a husband, and family, and wasn't taking no for an answer. And she wanted to be the very best at everything she did. But she was also giving, willing to listen to anyone's tale of woe. Ready to help out everyone who asked, even at the risk of sacrificing herself in the process."

He took her hand and they sat down. "Remember when I first started college and got laid off from my part-time gig?"

Gayle nodded, a shaky smile curving her full mouth.

"You took all the money you'd been saving for your first car and gave it to me so I could pay my tuition and stay in the dorm." He looked deeply into her eyes, his gaze scanning her face. "I never forgot that, Gayle. All I could think was how wonderful you were, how selfless. And I knew I intended to do whatever was necessary to make you happy. I still feel that way. If you'll let me, Gayle. If you'll open yourself up to the full possibility of who you are and let me love you — completely."

Gently, James pulled away, raised Gayle's chin with his finger. "Listen to me. We need some time to talk, really talk and work this stuff out between us. I'm going to pack a bag for Tracy and take her back to my brother's house. I'm sure they won't mind taking her to school in the morning."

Gayle pressed her lips together and simply nodded.

James left her there in the kitchen while he went about the task of trying to put their marriage back together.

Alone in the kitchen, in the house, Gayle reflected on the years and events that had led to this moment of comeuppance.

She'd never voiced her innermost feelings and uncertainties. She'd been too ashamed to admit the ugly things she felt about herself. But she wanted them out, to cleanse herself of the virus that had infected her over the years. She wanted happiness, wanted to feel joy. She wanted to save her marriage, she knew that now. She could only pray that she had what it took to do that, and that James would be there to catch her when she fell.

Her calico cat brushed against her leg, meowing. Absently she reached out to brush its coat as the phone began to ring. She decided to simply let it ring, allowing the answering machine to pick it up, not having the will or the energy to deal with even a banal conversation.

When the voice of Dr. Dennis came through the machine, Gayle stiffened to attention.

"Mrs. Davis, this is Dr. Dennis from Cedar Grove. I'm calling about Rayne. Please call me as soon as possible. It's quite urgent. I —"

Gayle snatched up the phone. "I'm here. This is Mrs. Davis. Has something happened to Rayne?"

Pauline released a silent sigh of relief. "Mrs. Davis, I'll get straight to the point. I need to get Rayne out of here, immediately, and I need your help."

"Me? I don't understand. What do you mean get her out?"

"It's quite involved. But if I don't move her today to someplace safe, we could lose her."

"You're scaring me. Tell me what's happened."

"Do you know anything about shock treatment?"

"Not really, only what I've seen in the movies."

"Magnify that by one hundred. That's what's been planned for Rayne. It will essentially erase parts of her brain — her memory." And perhaps the Rayne that had been born to save her, Pauline thought.

"What are you talking about?" Gayle's fear escalated her voice, gave it that caustic, grating edge. She knew it but was helpless to make it stop.

"Dr. Howell, the head of the hospital, has ordered a series of shock treatments to begin today."

"Aren't you her doctor? You can't let something like this happen. Don't you have any power?"

"Dr. Howell has made sure that I don't. Please, Mrs. Davis, I don't have much time."

"What do you want me to do?" Gayle asked. "Call someone, talk to this Dr. Howell?"

"I want to bring Rayne to stay with you — just for a little while. She needs to be with someone and in an environment where she feels safe and comfortable. You're her best friend. I can't think of anyone else."

Gayle's mouth opened, then closed. Her first instinct was to say yes, of course she would help. But then she thought of James, of her marriage, and everything that was on the line — her own salvation. How could she bring Rayne into the midst of that — her being the seed of what was already wrong? Planted here, in her home, it would grow like a weed, strangling everything in its path. That, combined with the reality that Rayne was not well. What if she had some sort of "episode"? What then? What in heaven's name would James say?

"I know this is asking a lot, Mrs. Davis," Pauline said, cutting off the lengthy silence. "I want to help her. And as her friend so should you."

Pauline knew she was fighting for her patient's life. She also knew the strength of her own will. She gave in and gave up once. She wouldn't let Rayne down, too.

"How can you ask me something like this?" Gayle suddenly shouted, wanting to slam something, do anything to make the doctor go away.

"Gayle," Pauline said, using the intimacy of her first name to reach her. "You are Rayne's friend. Her only friend. She has no one else. I can't send her to her father. She needs a safe place to heal. To get better. Don't you want that for her?"

"Of course. But —"

"You were the one who told me how long you two had been friends. You told me to make her better, that I didn't know the Rayne you knew, that the world was beginning to know."

"Why are you doing this to me?"

"What am I doing, Gayle, asking you to take a stand? Asking you to back up what you profess?"

Gayle squeezed her eyes shut. "I can't." There — she'd said it. "I can't do it, Dr. Dennis."

"You can't do what, Gayle?" Pauline pressed on, undaunted. "Face what's really going on inside of you? Face Rayne with who you are, the kind of friend you are?"

"You don't know anything about me."

"You're right. Only you know. And maybe Rayne."

Gayle gripped the phone tighter. "What has she told you?"

"None of that matters. It's between you and Rayne. You say you love her. Show her, Gayle, really show her, maybe for the first time in your lives." She paused, then tried once more. "I'm risking my entire career, everything I've ever worked and slaved for to help Rayne because I believe in what I'm doing. What are you willing to risk, Gayle?"

The question, like a powerful gust of wind, stirred the embers of her conscience, rekindling the flame. Before her stood the essence of who she was, who she would choose to be. Seeing that, facing herself in the light, frightened her as nothing else ever had.

She had a choice: stamp out the fire and turn away, or walk through the flames and endure the agony of being stripped to the bone.

James's parting words rang in her head. *Confident, strong, decisive. Your reasons were pure and from the heart.*

Which woman would she finally be? For once this was not about helping someone else to fill her own need. It was about helping herself.

What *was* she willing to risk? At that moment she knew. *Everything.*

"When will you bring her?" Gayle finally asked.

Nineteen

Pauline shoved the last of her case files into her briefcase, and hurried from her office, completely focused on what must be done. She would not allow her thoughts to be clouded with the repercussions of her actions. To do so would paralyze her, and leave Rayne open to the barbarism that awaited her.

She understood that she was not only saving Rayne Holland, she was saving herself. She was restoring that part of her eaten away by guilt.

Yes. It was guilt that propelled her. It propelled her to heal all those who came under her care, to somehow make up for what she did not do for Linda Cole. But this final act was one of true absolution. And she needed to be cleansed in order to be free.

Pauline glanced over her shoulder as she approached Rayne's room, certain that at any moment her plan would be revealed and she'd be hauled away.

She tapped lightly on the door and stepped in, wondering which Rayne she would find.

Motionless, Rayne sat in front of the window in the one chair in the room, staring out onto the grounds below. Pauline realized with aching clarity what a poignant portrait she made. The backdrop of bursting color and life beyond the framed window, juxtaposed against this single, solitary figure.

She's come for me, Rayne thought, watching the activity beyond her reach. *I know she's come to help me. I heard the nurses' whispers, saw the looks of shock and pity on their faces. I should be grateful, I suppose. But perhaps erasing the memories will finally chase the shadows away, block out the fear.* Maybe.

"Rayne," Pauline called softly.

Slowly, Rayne turned her head. "I've been waiting for you."

Pauline walked into the room, satisfied with who she saw. "I need to explain some things to you."

"I know," she said, her voice devoid of emotion.

Rayne's eyes trailed Pauline as she crossed the final distance and sat on the side of the bed.

"How much did Judy tell you?"

Rayne tried to clear her thoughts, remember the words Nurse Simpson spoke, halting and somewhat panicked.

"She said that you were going to take me away from here. That you didn't want the treatment that Dr. Howell prescribed. Electric shock."

"Yes. Shock treatment can work in some cases and for certain patients. Patients who are out of control. Patients who have lost the ability to handle their actions and emotions."

"You don't think I'm one of those patients?"

Her question hung suspended in the air, like the final note of a Billie Holiday ballad — crying out in pain.

"No. I don't." Pauline leaned forward. "You can get well, Rayne. I know you can. You've made wonderful progress. With time I know you'll be fine."

Everything takes time, she heard Robert whisper. *You need patience.* Rayne searched Pauline's face, looking for clues, for answers beyond what was said. It was what she did with a script, looked beyond the words, the scenes, to see what was truly being conveyed. Deciding if what was offered held some unspoken message. Her message. What was Dr. Dennis's real message?

"What's going to happen to you?" Rayne asked.

The question, for a moment, left Pauline without words as the harsh reality of what she was about to do loomed before her. She looked away, then directly into Rayne's challenging gaze.

"Let me worry about that."

In that simple declaration, Rayne fully understood the meaning behind the words. Pauline Dennis was willing to risk everything to save her. And she was not certain she was worthy of that sacrifice. Why was she really doing this?

Rayne turned away, focused on the crisscross patterns of the mesh screen in the window, momentarily enraptured by the intricate wire design. "I — can't let you do this. Not for me."

Pauline stood, walked toward Rayne, and bent down in front of her. She gently clasped Rayne's chin and turned her head. Her tone was firm, unbreakable. "Listen to me. You're worth the risk. I know you believe you're not. But I do. I'd rather deal with any consequence than live my life with my conscience if I allowed them to inflict this on you. You have your whole life ahead of you and it can be a good one." Her voice softened. "Trust me. Please, Rayne."

Rayne wanted to cover her face with her hair, run and hide from the possibilities, the future that Pauline offered. *Get out while you can,* the other Rayne whispered. She swatted away the buzz in her ear. "How will I live with *my* conscience?" Rayne asked.

"The same way I'll live with mine. Day by day."

For a heartbeat, the two women looked upon each other, held in place by the crossroads. Knowing that whichever path they chose would irrevocably change the course of their lives.

"Where . . . will I go?"

Pauline released a long-held breath. "I talked with Gayle. She wants you to stay with her."

There was movement outside the closed door. Pauline froze. Her eyes darted toward the door. Then the noise passed, moving down the pale-blue corridor.

"We need to leave, Rayne." Her voice was low and insistent.

Rayne felt her heart tumble in her chest. She was safe here. Outside she couldn't be protected. The shadows would come again. Her body trembled.

Pauline clasped Rayne's hand. "I'm going to get your bag."

"I — I can't."

Pauline squeezed her hand, willing her strength into Rayne. "You can." With her free hand, she removed the syringe. "This is just a mild sedative."

Rayne shook her head wildly, but no sound came from her mouth. Her hair spilled around her face. *Please don't,* she screamed in silence.

Pauline deftly squirted the plunger. The geyser of fluid leapt into the air. She grabbed Rayne's arm and quickly inserted the needle.

Rayne's entire body contracted in a short spasm, then slowly unwound. Within moments, a light haze covered her eyes. Her body grew limp, no longer her own. *Help me.*

Pauline rose, went directly to the closet, and took out Rayne's small duffel bag. "Come. We have to hurry," she instructed, taking Rayne by the arm and leading her toward the door.

The thump of Pauline's heart beat in her temple. She held her head erect, her shoulders proud, looked straight ahead. This was just an ordinary stroll on the grounds with her patient, she said with her eyes to anyone who questioned her with theirs.

They reached the door to the end of the corridor. Rayne's step grew more sluggish, measured.

"It's quite beautiful out today, Rayne," Pauline said, sliding her metallic card through the slot in the door. "We'll sit on the bench by the pond," she continued, for the benefit of the orderly who'd come up behind them. "The air will do you good."

The door slid open. The trio continued down the corridor toward the elevator.

"How's your patient today, Dr. Dennis?" the orderly asked as the elevator doors sealed them in.

Pauline turned and forced a half-smile, barely meeting his questioning blue eyes.

"Coming along quite well." She tightened her grip on Rayne's arm, feeling the slight tremor beneath her fingertips.

He nodded and looked ahead.

The elevator stopped on the third floor and two nurses and a wheelchair-bound patient boarded. The two nurses chatted softly.

Pauline felt a trickle of sweat slide down the line of her spine. Rayne moaned weakly.

Just a few more minutes, Pauline silently chanted. We'll walk down the path and to the parking lot. She heard the jangle of her keys in her smock pocket when Rayne's body swayed lightly against her. Just a few more minutes, she repeated. She grew damp beneath her arms.

The doors slid open. Her stomach muscles knotted. They stepped out.

All around them was movement, sounds of equipment, the click of locks, the beep of machines, noises. Danger lurked everywhere. At any moment they could be stopped.

Pauline wanted to run. She wanted to drag Rayne by the arm and run. But she couldn't. Instead they walked slowly, casually, as if this were simply another day.

But it wasn't.

Daylight burst around them. Nature's music played its symphony. Water trickled, the grass glistened.

The parking lot was a hundred yards away. It could have been in another world.

"It's not too much farther," Pauline said in a hushed whisper, the sound of her shoes rhythmic and precise against the concrete — Rayne's steps uneven and halting.

"Not — Gayle," she mumbled.

"Just relax. We're almost there."

Her pager went off. She walked a bit

faster. "We really should hurry." She glanced over her shoulder, expecting security guards to be running behind her. Any minute a hand would clamp her shoulder. Stop her.

The lot was directly ahead. Her mouth grew dry.

Rayne's legs suddenly wobbled. Pauline braced her around the waist. "Just hold on," she urged, wishing she'd taken a wheelchair.

Her car was ten feet away. Almost there.

She reached into her pocket and pulled out the keys, looked around one last time. No one was in the lot. She opened the back door and helped Rayne inside. "Just lay down and rest," she said, her voice coming to Rayne like a soothing bedtime story.

I'm so tired, Rayne mused, her thoughts tumbling atop one another like dominoes stacked too high.

Every scene appeared clear, one following the other, like frames in a movie. *Only my film is unedited,* Rayne thought. *The pieces didn't make sense. I want to cut and paste them together, but I'm so tired. The weight of my own thoughts is holding me down.*

Pauline took a blanket from the trunk

and placed it over Rayne's limp body. She walked briskly around to the front and opened the door, tossing her briefcase onto the passenger seat. She turned on the ignition.

Her pager went off again. They were looking for her.

She stepped on the gas and eased out of the lot.

"Just rest," she whispered to Rayne as they approached the exit gate. "Relax and rest."

Pauline eased up to the gate and showed her parking pass. The guard tipped his plastic brimmed hat, barely noticing her. She pulled off and out.

The gates swung shut behind her.

They were free.

Almost.

Twenty

Gayle paced. She went upstairs and checked all the rooms. She came back down. In the living room, she walked to the window, peeked out between the slats in the blinds. She paced.

Why didn't she call James and tell him what she'd decided to do? She ran a hand through her hair. Her bangs were growing too long, she mused abstractly. She'd have to make an appointment with her stylist soon.

In the kitchen, she turned on the water and filled the teapot, setting it on the stove, turning the flame up high.

Yes, she'd have some tea. Some herbal tea to soothe her nerves.

Why was she so nervous? She was doing the right thing. The only thing. James would understand. She'd explain everything when he came home. If only she could explain it all to herself. Now it seemed her real reasons for agreeing were unclear even to her. But the doctor's words had goaded her, dared her almost.

Perhaps this would be a way to bridge the gap that had been forged between Rayne and herself. Maybe she could, by doing this, find a way to rid herself of her guilt. The guilt of wanting what was never hers.

They were both women now, women with a history behind them, secrets that bound them. A strange kind of love that held them together yet kept them apart.

For years she'd tried to understand the silent power that Rayne held over her. Tried to understand her own need to give in to that power, submit to it, and let it consume her.

From childhood, all she'd ever known was to give in order to feel needed and loved. And yet with every giving, she resented the receiver, herself, the weakness that she saw in their need for her. Her secret shame. Her flawed self.

Flash points of her life appeared before her.

Her parents fed the weakness, as if doing so gave them some sort of strength. She remembered all too well the humiliation, the hurt. She stared out of the kitchen window. The memories rushed by.

"You can do better than this," her father scolded when she'd brought home her sixth-grade report card. She was eleven years old, proud of her accomplishments. But all her father could see was her C in math, her B in science. Not the As in art, music, English, and history.

"Your brother gets all As. Every time," he said, handing the card back as if he might catch her inadequacies like a bad cold.

His brown emotionless eyes rolled up and down her body. She felt ugly and small. "You've put on more weight. You need to stop eating so much junk."

He snapped open the paper. "Don't know why you can't be more like Nathan. Fine student, plenty of friends, plays sports." He shook his head as if the mysteries of his daughter would never be revealed to him.

"I bet Rayne never brings home Cs and Bs. Her folks wouldn't stand for it. That William Mercer is no nonsense." He peered at her over the top of the paper. "Now Rayne is somebody you should try to be more like. She's one special girl."

Gayle looked down at her scuffed black shoes, the frayed edges of her jeans. She felt the thickness of her thighs brush together.

She hated Nathan. She hated Rayne. She

hated herself. But she was better than them both. Better than everybody. She'd prove it.

The kettle emitted a piercing whistle. Gayle jumped at the sound.

The doorbell pealed. She froze. It rang again. More urgent, it seemed, this time.

Gayle turned off the flame. Her heart galloped in time with her footsteps toward the front door. She pulled it open.

Pauline stood in front of her, holding up a half-sleeping Rayne.

"I gave her a mild sedative," Pauline said by way of explanation, seeing the hesitancy on Gayle's face. "Just to relax her for the ride."

Gayle looked at her friend, who stared back at her through glazed eyes, and wondered what it was that Rayne saw. How did she view the world at that moment? And for an instant, she envied her. Envied the fact that she didn't have to deal with reality.

Gayle's cat wound in and out of her legs. She pushed it aside with her foot.

Will you treat me that way, too? Rayne wondered through the haze. *Push me aside? I want to go home. Where is home? I am a wanderer — from place to place. No roots.*

Sleepy. So sleepy. Oh, I forgot my manners. "You mind your manners," she could hear her aunt Mae scold.

"Hi . . . Gayle," Rayne muttered, and tried to smile. *My lips feel stiff, like cardboard.* "Thank . . . you. They . . . want to . . . hurt me . . . Gayle." A tear slid down her cheek. She began to tremble.

"The medication will wear off soon," Pauline said, still standing in the doorway, hoping to jar Gayle into action.

Gayle blinked. Mechanically she stepped aside. "Come in. You can take her upstairs." *Before James comes,* she thought, leading the way to the guest bedroom. The footsteps behind her sounded heavy, like lead boots. *Heavy for women.* Her thoughts twisted. *Before James comes,* she repeated, opening the bedroom door.

She heard the car pull up in the driveway. It wasn't the lead boots she'd heard. It was the pounding in her chest, thundering in her ears.

Her head snapped toward the open bedroom door. Listening. The front door opened.

"Gayle! I'm back." The door closed. "Whose car is that in the driveway?"

"I'll be right down." She turned to Pauline, her eyes pleading.

"I'll get her settled," Pauline said, understanding that Gayle hadn't spoken to her husband and that she was terribly afraid.

Gayle nodded, looked one last time at Rayne, and hurried out, shutting the door firmly behind her. It closed solidly with a bang.

"Hi," Gayle said, finding James in the living room. She nervously twisted her hands in front of her.

"Whose car is that?" James looked around, expecting to see someone.

Gayle cleared her throat. "That's what I want to talk with you about." She watched his jaw flex. Her eyes instinctively looked upward. "While you were gone, Rayne's doctor called."

His jaw flexed again and his body stiffened limb by limb as if being dipped into cement. "What happened now?" He wanted a cigarette even though he'd quit months ago. He fidgeted with the pen in his pants pocket.

Gayle dared to step closer. How could she put this so that he would understand, empathize with the pressure she'd been put under, the responsibility she'd been given?

"She asked me to take Rayne in — for a little while."

"What! Are you out of *your* mind?"

"James. Please listen."

"Listen? Listen to what, Gayle? Did it occur to you to talk to me first? I'm your husband, not the tenant in this damned house."

Gayle straightened, raised her chin in defiance. "They were going to perform electric shock on her, James," she said with a steely calm. "I couldn't let that happen."

James's face contorted in anger and confusion. "There must have been a reason." He strode across the room, then twisted back.

Gayle watched his frenetic procession. "Maybe there is. But her doctor said it would erase parts of her memory, part of who she is — destroying her."

"So what are you, the white knight coming to her rescue? Did you think about what having her in this house is going to do to us — to this marriage? Any minute she could snap!" He popped his fingers. "Do something crazy."

"Keep your voice down, she'll hear you," Gayle hissed.

"I don't give a damn if she hears me. I want to make sure *you* hear me. We have a child to think about, for God's sake."

"I've thought about all that and you."

"Have you, Gayle? Have you really? All

you ever think about is yourself, what will satisfy you." Slowly, he turned around, his arms spread wide. "This house." He pointed toward the door. "The cars." Then he glared at her designer outfit. "Your clothes. Money, money, money. You don't give a damn about anything or anybody other than yourself and what your doing for others will get you. You always have."

Each word was thrown at her like a dagger, stabbing her in all the exposed places on her body. She flinched with each new attack. She wanted to strike back, hurt him like he was hurting her. She wanted to shut the door, bar herself from his assault. But he'd left her with nowhere to run, no way out. She could almost feel her back pressing against the wall.

What are you willing to risk? Pauline's challenge rang in her head. *What are you willing to risk?*

James strode back and forth in front of her, propelled by his own rage. "She's the root of everything that's wrong between us. And you bring her into our house. I won't have it!"

Gayle suddenly saw images of the crazed homeless who lived on the street. The ones she stepped around and avoided as she went to work. That could be Rayne. That could be her friend if she turned her back.

"This is no longer about just us, James," Gayle finally said. "This is about salvation."

"Salvation. This is about bringing a problem we can't handle and shouldn't be expected to solve into our house."

Gayle's voice dropped to a deceptive low. "Do you think I've forgotten?"

"What are you talking about?" The space between his eyes contorted into a tight line.

She didn't want to go there. This road she was on turned her stomach, but he'd left her no choice. She'd fight with whatever ammunition was at her disposal.

"We could have lost everything with what you did."

James took a step back as if pushed.

Gayle pressed forward. "When you used your company money to pay off your gambling debts, and your company was going under, you came to me, James. Me. Did I turn my back on you? I didn't. I, with my money, paid back every dime. Stuck with you when you went through counseling. Sat up nights praying that you weren't in some dive gambling away everything we had. I was there for you. Why can't you do this for me?"

She watched the proud posture of his body deflate before her eyes. Her stomach rose, then fell. She took a step forward, reached out to ease the hurt.

James turned his head. "Don't." His voice was a dull whisper.

"I — I'm sorry."

"No. You said what you've been thinking for a while." His short laugh was resigned. "You'll never let me forget it, will you, Gayle? No matter what I do, how hard I try. That part of our life will always stand between us — what you did for me." He looked at her, this woman he'd loved for so long, and realized he didn't know her at all. "I guess this is my time to pay up."

James turned, walked up the stairs to their bedroom, and shut the door.

Gayle crumbled onto the couch. She'd won, she thought, her eyes trailing toward the stairs. At what cost?

Twenty-one

When Gayle looked up, Pauline was standing in front of her. Without asking, Pauline sat down. Gayle pressed her fist to her mouth, stifling a flow of words.

"Rayne is asleep," Pauline said softly, watching the parade of regret, acceptance, pain, and confusion march across Gayle's face.

Gayle nodded. Her gaze briefly drifted upstairs, then returned to stare into nothingness.

"It was a brave thing you did."

Gayle looked at Pauline. A sudden flash of anger bruised her face. "Oh, really?" she responded.

Pauline felt the sting and assumed her professional pose, leaned back in her seat, and loosely folded her hands.

"Yes. It was brave. I know it couldn't have been easy for you to confront your husband that way. It took a lot of courage."

Gayle's soft brown eyes rose to rest on Pauline's aquiline face. "You have no idea what this has done to my marriage." Her tone was nasty, accusatory.

"What has it done?" Pauline asked calmly, not rising to the bait.

Gayle turned her head. "What do you care? You have what you want. Rayne is here, isn't she?" She covered her face with her hands but they didn't stifle the choked sob that fluttered through her fingers. "I said things I should have never said. Things I promised myself and James we'd never revisit."

"Often, Gayle, we believe we are pressured into doing things we regret. But sometimes the things we believe are at rest, pushed to the back of our minds, are not at rest at all." A sudden flash of a thick thigh spreading her young, thin ones, momentarily clouded Pauline's vision, halting her words. She drew in a breath and fought to clear her head. "They are . . . simply dormant." She swallowed down the fear that crept along her ankles and slid up her legs. "Waiting for an opportunity to be revived. Often those things were never fully dealt with when they happened and it becomes a poker chip, a trump card to be played when all else fails."

"But I humiliated him. I made him think I held that part of his life against him."

Gayle studied Pauline for a moment, tried to gauge the almost vacant look that glazed the doctor's eyes and the flat line of her voice. Gayle waited for a response that did not immediately come. "Are you all right, Dr. Dennis?"

Pauline focused on Gayle's face. "Do you?" she asked, slowly recovering. "Do you hold it against him? That's the real question. Not what he believes, but what your true intentions were by raising it. And now that the question has been raised, you'll both find a way to finally heal the wound between you, not simply cover it up with the Band-Aid of everyday circumstances."

"I — can't make it right. Not after what I did."

"You can." Pauline smoothed a strand of her red hair behind her ear. "If you're willing to try. Willing to truly dig down inside yourself and try. You need to decide how important your marriage is. How much you want it, and what you're willing to do to sustain it."

"You make it sound so damned easy."

"Not at all. Fighting for what you want, what you believe, is never easy." The thought of her own life, and the decisions she'd made to alter it, flashed before her.

Where would she go after this?

Gayle exhaled audibly. "How can I hope to repair what's wrong in my life with Rayne right here in my house? What was I thinking?"

"I thought hard about asking you to do this. I had my doubts."

"And now?"

"I know I've made the right decision. You're what Rayne needs now. And you need her, regardless of what has passed between you. Gayle, just as you opened the floodgates to your marriage, you're going to have to do the same thing with Rayne. This is your chance to move beyond this space in your life — where you've been. I can help you to help Rayne. Only you can help yourself and James."

Upstairs Rayne drifted in and out of the drug-induced sleep. Voices filtered through her dreams. Raised voices, accusing voices. She heard James's words hurled across the room at Gayle, flinched at her pain. Gayle's rebuke punctured James's resistance, leaving him bereft of spirit, broken.

A part of her realized that Gayle had retaliated for her, to help her. But there was more than that. She couldn't grab hold of the elusive reason for the sudden retort.

The words. The words. They ran amok in her mind, tripping over one another, confusing her with their real meaning. And deeper intent.

Wasn't she a connoisseur of words? Didn't she take words and translate them into her own vision?

Maybe that's what was happening now. The words and emotions expressed by them were all in her head. Invisible, but potent.

She turned. The light blanket fell softly to the floor.

Her eyes flew open. Somewhere in the distance the thud of a slamming door vibrated through the sudden silence.

Rayne held her breath and listened. Tried to see the images. She adjusted the lens of her mind. The room, by degrees, came into focus.

Where were the crisscross patterns that danced across the floor? The secret passageways to safety? She looked around the room. It spun. She wasn't home where it was safe. She was in a new place, a strange place. But familiar.

Sluggishly, her mind began to clear. *Gayle's house*. For what? She couldn't seem to remember. *James didn't want her here.* Why? What had she done?

Lethargically, she sat up. Her body felt sandbag heavy. She rubbed her eyes, looked around. Memory jolted through her. *Treatment.* Yes. She remembered now. They were going to fry her brain, make her illness go away. That was why James didn't want her in his house. She was ill. She was a problem. Their problem.

She shook her head, hoping to clear it. Maybe she should leave. But how would she get out if there were no crisscross patterns from which to escape?

Just walk down the stairs and out the front door, the voice instructed. *You don't need to be someplace where you're not wanted.*

"But where will I go?"

Home. Back home.

"Shut up," Rayne spat. "Just shut up. I'm tired of running and hiding. Whatever is down there, out there, I need to face it. I can't escape." She felt the other voice skulk away to the corner of her mind.

Rayne listened intently for the sounds in the house. Only a faint murmur of voices could be heard now. She eased out of the bed, stepped into her shoes, and walked on shaky legs to the door. She held on to the door frame for support as the final milligrams of the sedative chugged through her bloodstream.

⋆ ⋆ ⋆

"How will I care for her? What if something happens?" Gayle asked Pauline, her anxiety level escalating again.

"Rayne is not violent. She's self-sufficient. I've weaned her off her medications and her thinking is clearer, her interaction with others stronger. Her initial episodes that you witnessed have been brought under control and all but ceased. All Rayne needs right now is a friend, a supporter. Someone she can talk with to let her know that she's not alone. But I won't lie to you. Rayne still has issues that run very deep, and now that I believe I know what they are I can treat her properly."

"How are you going to do that with her here?"

"I'll make arrangements to visit her here on a daily basis. Treat her as I would an outpatient. I strongly believe Rayne's progress will improve greatly in a warm and loving environment and around those that she trusts."

"Aren't you afraid she'll . . . wander off? I mean, I have a job and so does my husband. What happens when none of us are around?" Gayle shook her head in frustration. "What the hell was I thinking?"

"Listen." Pauline clasped Gayle's hand. "I'll —"

"I'll be fine if you leave me alone, Gayle," Rayne said, standing on the landing of the stairs.

Gayle turned toward the plaintive tone of Rayne's voice. Her heart lurched in her chest when she saw her standing there, a ghost of the fiery, often sultry woman she'd come to know.

Rayne stepped into the room, a bit unsteady but reluctant to give in to the will of the medication. "I won't be any trouble." She braced her hand against the wall. "I know — I think you're putting a lot on the line for me. I wouldn't do anything to ruin that."

Gayle's eyes filled with tears. Looking at Rayne, she saw the little, lonely fifth-grader who needed a friend, sitting alone in the cafeteria with a peanut butter and jelly sandwich. The girl who needed someone to be there even if there was nothing to say. She cleared her throat.

"I have some time coming to me at work. I think now would be a good time to take it."

Rayne's mouth fluttered as a smile of gratitude moved across it.

Pauline looked from one woman to the

other, felt the tenuous bond that existed between them. Maybe this wasn't the best of situations, she thought, watching Gayle embrace Rayne, but she also knew that as Rayne continued on her quest to recovery, she would take Gayle along with her. Pauline only hoped that they would appreciate the people they would inevitably become at the end of the road. And that she would be satisfied with the Pauline who would face her in the mirror. Her greatest challenge was ahead of her.

Twenty-two

Pauline stood in the doorway, reluctant to leave, but knowing she must so the healing process could begin. Her leaving was made more difficult by the realization that she was responsible for what Gayle would face once she was gone.

"Are you sure you don't want me to talk with your husband?" Pauline asked.

"No. Thanks. This is something James and I need to work out."

Pauline nodded. "If you're sure."

"Yes."

"You have my number. Call me day or night if there's any problem. I'll be here to-morrow about midday."

"Sure."

Pauline touched Gayle's shoulder, glancing over it to see Rayne sitting on the couch. She lowered her voice. "Thank you, Gayle. You won't regret this."

Gayle looked behind her, then back at Pauline. "I don't think so, either."

"Good-bye, Gayle."

As Pauline pulled out of the drive, she visualized the briefcase full of case files, treatments, in her trunk. Those were her trump cards, and if forced, she'd play them. All of them.

Gayle watched Pauline get into her car and pull away before closing the door. Not so much because she wanted to witness Pauline's safe departure, but because she wanted to delay what faced her. If only for a moment. It would not be easy.

She fixed a smile onto her face and returned to the living room.

"Are you hungry?" Gayle asked. She picked up a magazine from the coffee table and put it in the magazine rack next to the couch. "I could whip up something." The plants need watering, she thought. Maybe she should do that now before she forgot. She rubbed her hands together. They were damp.

"Where's Tracy?"

Gayle's breathing sputtered for a moment. "She's staying with James's sister." Maybe she should move the plants out of the window for a while. Too much sun may be what was drying them out.

"Oh. In the middle of the week?" Rayne watched Gayle's gaze avoid her, the unnecessary moving and rearranging of incidental items, until Gayle finally turned her back.

"Tracy was begging to go, and you know how hard it is for me to tell her no." She straightened several framed photographs needlessly on the wall unit.

"Gayle?"

"Hmm?" She moved a photo of James and his sister from one shelf to the other.

"Look at me. Please."

Gayle slowly turned and wondered if her smile looked as uncertain as it felt. She wiped one hand and then the other on the thighs of her jogging pants.

"Is Tracy gone because I'm here?"

The question seemed to suck the air from Gayle's lungs. How much could she reasonably say? What was too much? The slightest thing could turn this whole episode uglier than it already was. Damn, what made her think she could handle this?

She'd never felt this way around Rayne. Never. This was something new. And the idea that her friend's presence made her uneasy, no matter how strained the relationship, left her with an awful sensation of sadness.

"Gayle, be honest with me," Rayne began, a bit unsteady. "I know I seem fragile. But what I did to myself . . ." Her gaze glanced away for a moment. "Had nothing to do with weakness of the mind, but of the spirit. I felt broken inside, worthless, dirty, and ashamed." She brushed her wild hair away from her face.

Gayle's expression went from wary to confused. Those words didn't apply to Rayne Holland. Not the old Rayne she knew. How could they? But *this* Rayne wasn't the person she'd known. So was it Rayne really talking, confessing these weaknesses, or was it all some fabrication of Rayne's mind? A symptom of her illness? She didn't know.

"What are you saying?" Gayle finally asked.

Tell her. Tell her, the voice whispered to Rayne. *She'll understand.*

"I — can't talk about it." Rayne's eyes were wide, luminous. "Please, can you trust me, for a little while? I . . . need time to accept what's happened to me, to find a way to deal with it . . . before I can share it with anyone. Even you."

Gayle pressed her lips together, torn between doubt and a sense of loyalty. "I don't know what it is that you're battling, what hurts you're trying to heal." She blew out a long breath. "But I'm willing to help

321

you as long as you want me to."

Rayne reached out and took Gayle's hand. "Thank you."

"Now, how about something to eat? I'm starved."

Rayne followed Gayle into the kitchen. "Do you still make those great tuna sandwiches?"

"I sure do. And I just happen to have all the *secret* ingredients."

Gayle put two eggs into a pot to boil, emptied a can of white-meat tuna into a plastic mixing bowl, then took condiments from the refrigerator.

Rayne sat at the table, quietly watching Gayle as she meticulously chopped red and green peppers, onions, and celery into hair-thin pieces. Gayle was like that about everything, Rayne thought, orderly and meticulous to a point of obsession. She worked so hard at it — making sure that everything appeared perfect.

In that they were alike, she supposed, looking at the brown of her hands against the white Lucite table. She was fastidious about her work, her films, always striving for perfection. Because in her real life, hers was anything but perfect. It was messy. And she, too, had become a master of disguise. She'd learned early that people believe what they see. Now she'd been unmasked, the rawness beneath the polished image exposed and examined. A turtle without its shell. She would have to work hard to create another image, a protective coating, one that would not crack under the pressure next time.

"I hope Tracy doesn't stay away too long," Rayne said, returning to the dismissed topic. "I'd really like to see her."

Gayle's hand halted for a millisecond before continuing to slice the vegetables. "You will." Gayle chopped a bit quicker, focused and intent. She knew how frantic and unsettled she'd felt when James suddenly took off with Tracy, threatening to take her away permanently. She couldn't begin to imagine what Rayne must have lived through and was still living through after losing Desiree and Paul.

They'd never talked about it — what really happened. After the accident, the doctors kept Rayne pretty much sedated, as much for the mental trauma as for her physical injuries. At the funeral, she was a shadow of her former self, visible in body only. Looking into her eyes then was like peering into a bottomless well. There were no clues to be found there. None.

Shortly after the funeral and her official

release from the hospital, Rayne was sent to complete her recovery at her father's home. A big mistake. Gayle wanted Rayne to stay with her, to give her a chance to get through the first agonizing stages of grief in a friendly environment, but William Mercer was adamantly against it, opposed to the point of complete denial. For him, Rayne was never that sick. He would never listen to any change of address for his only child. She belonged with him and only him.

It was a strange and difficult time. Gayle remembered the numerous calls made to his home and the subsequent failed attempts to talk with Rayne, the visits that were prematurely aborted. The first time she'd seen Rayne since the funeral was when she was finally told that Rayne was admitted to Cedar Grove for attempted suicide. She remembered that first chilling conversation, the underlying tension, and the almost relieved tone of William Mercer's voice despite all that had happened. She'd never forget it.

"Mr. Mercer, this is Gayle. I really want to speak to Rayne. I need to know that she's okay. Please tell her to come to the phone. This has —"

"She ain't here."

"What? Where is she? Did she go back home?"

"Doctors came and took her away three days ago."

A surge of heat rushed up from her stomach. "What's going on? What happened to her?"

"Crazy girl tried to kill herself. Cut her wrists. Edith! That chicken fried yet? Yessir, tried to kill herself," he continued, returning his attention to the phone. "Docs said she may be in there for a while. You know, with her being crazy and all."

Gayle paced back and forth with the cordless phone, her heels clicking against the black-and-white linoleum, listening in disbelief and with total contempt for this man. "Have you been to see her? How is she?"

"Naw. Can't stand to see my only child like that. Locked up like an animal. It's too heartbreaking."

Gayle wanted to vomit. "Something had to happen to make her cut her wrists. Were you or your wife there?" She felt like stretching her hand through the phone, grabbing him around the neck, and shaking some real emotion into him.

His voice dropped to a flat landscape devoid of scenery. "Now how would I know what got into her head? Hmm, smells like my dinner is ready. I'll be going now. And thanks for calling 'bout Rayne."

Gayle stood, transfixed. The dial tone hummed in her ear.

"How small are you going to cut those peppers?" Rayne asked, snapping Gayle back to the present.

Gayle blinked, looked down at her handiwork. "Did your father ever tell you that I called?" she asked, surprising herself with the spontaneity of the question. She braced her hands against the countertop.

Rayne stared at her for a moment, re-living those weeks of loneliness, the sense of abandonment, looking for the lie in Gayle's assertion, some reason why she'd forsaken her. Why should she trust her?

"No," she finally answered.

"Did you know that I'd wanted you to stay with me after . . . the accident?"

Rayne slowly shook her head. "All those weeks I couldn't understand why you hadn't called, come to see me. I felt betrayed. I was so lonely. Very scared."

Gayle briefly shut her eyes, experiencing Rayne's despondency. "I tried everything. But every attempt I made was cut off by your father. Then I was sent out of town on business. When I returned, I called." She stirred the mixture. "That's when your father told me you'd been hospitalized."

Rayne looked down at her folded hands, the scars of her past outlined on her wrists. *He'd wanted to keep me isolated,* she thought, *removed from anything kind. He wanted to control me as he'd always done. The only time I had freedom was with Paul and even that was a different kind of prison.* "I'd spent all those weeks wondering, feeling abandoned and let down. With every passing day, I grew more resentful of you." She laughed harshly, a hollow sound. "I thought — sure, it's always easy to be a friend during the good times. The real test is when trouble comes. I even began to think that maybe you thought you'd catch what I had, so you stayed away."

"Is that why you wouldn't talk to me all those times I came to visit you at the hospital?"

"Partly. At the time I didn't talk to anyone. I didn't want to. Felt it was pointless. So I locked myself up in my head until I couldn't stand my own voice shouting at me to get out." Rayne raised her eyes to rest on Gayle's face. "Sounds crazy, huh?" She flashed a crooked smile.

"Well, word is, you *are* slightly disturbed," Gayle teased with a droll grin.

"Only slightly?" Rayne rejoined.

They both laughed, like old times, the first true feeling shared between them in months. The laughter, the sharing, seemed to cleanse them, crack open the thoughts and feelings that had been sealed shut, keeping them out and apart.

But even with the release of laughter, they both understood that beneath the joyous sound was the debris of all they'd tossed aside, a host of thorny issues neither had been willing to deal with at that moment, but knowing that one day soon they must.

Twenty-three

"Just stay out of his way," Judy Simpson whispered to the night-shift nurse. "Howell is on the warpath." They stepped around a medicine cart and a wheelchair-bound patient who was busy having a conversation with the empty space beside him.

"Is it true that Dr. Dennis took Rayne Holland out of the hospital?" the nurse whispered back, jotting notes onto her clipboard as they made rounds. The sounds of voices coming from the recreation room briefly reached out and touched them as they passed the open door.

The vibration of Judy's stockinged thighs brushing together reminded her of her forgotten diet. "I really wouldn't know," she lied. "But if she did, I'm sure she had a good reason. Dr. Dennis may seem cold but she does care about her patients."

"She should care as much about her career," the nurse mumbled. "By the time Dr. Howell is through with her, it'll be over. I know I would have never done it."

Judy knew it was all too true. She'd seen doctors come and go at Cedar Grove, broken and disenchanted with the profession. Anytime anyone dared to stand up to Dr. Howell, they soon became an afterthought — dismissed without references. What Pauline had done was much worse than simply standing up to him, voicing her opinion. She'd physically removed a patient from the premises, and there would be hell to pay. And what about her own career? If it were ever discovered that she knew what Dr. Dennis planned to do — she didn't want to think about it. She couldn't.

Then, as if the mere utterance of his name was an incantation to raise the devil, Reginald Howell suddenly appeared, bursting through the swinging doors. He stormed down the corridor, growling at everyone in his way.

"Bet you're glad to be going off duty," the nurse said, watching the firestorm he created with his presence.

Men and women buried their faces in previously read paperwork, changed direction when they saw him coming. Lighthearted conversation ceased. Even the patients seemed to sense the undercurrents that threatened to sweep away everything in its path.

" 'Scuse me, ladies."

Judy turned toward the sound of the male voice behind her and her heart stammered in her chest. *Rayne's father.*

"I'm looking for Dr. Howell. Came to see about my daughter, Rayne. She was s'posed to have some new treatment."

The two women quickly glanced at each other.

"I'm going to finish rounds," the nurse said, and hurried away.

William Mercer's bloodshot eyes followed the rhythmic sway of her hips. A leer turned up one corner of his thin mouth.

Judy shivered as a sudden chill wrapped its arms around her.

William returned his gaze to her face. "You were about to tell me where I could find Dr. Howell. Isn't that right."

Judy pulled in a breath. "He's right there at the nurse's station," she said, pointing down the corridor with her chin.

"Thank you kindly." His eyes creased into slits. "I seen you before. You're the nurse that works with my daughter, ain't you."

His questions weren't questions at all, Judy realized abstractly. To him they were statements of fact, cloaked in an apparent query. She cleared her throat. "Yes."

"So how did her treatment go today? Said they were gonna give her shock therapy, get rid of all that craziness in her head."

"I'm really not at liberty to say." She wished she had something to cover herself with. "You should speak with Dr. Howell. If you'll excuse me, I'm off duty now." She turned away, walking down the opposite end of the hall before he had a chance to question her further.

Something ain't right, William thought as he watched Judy practically run away. He looked around. *Too quiet for a loony bin.* He started down the hall, toward the sound of Howell's raised voice as he blasted out a nurse, for what, he didn't know. *That's right,* William thought as he drew closer. *A man gotta run a tight ship, or all the crew will think they can get away with mutiny.* He admired that kind of control in a man. The kind of man he himself was.

"Dr. Howell," William called out.

Reginald turned toward the voice, his pink-and-white face a portrait of fury. His neck was red, and the color appeared to creep up toward his face. The veins across his forehead pulsed wildly.

For a split second, Reginald's blue eyes flashed in shock. He hadn't expected this.

William Mercer showing up was the last thing he needed at the moment. What in heaven's name would he tell this man? A nerve twitched in his cheek. "Shit," he hissed under his breath.

William moved forward. Reginald took his stance.

"Dr. Howell. William Mercer, Rayne's father. We spoke on the phone."

"Yes, of course." Reginald put on his professional smile, extending his hand.

"Came to see how the treatment went. The one we talked about."

Reginald's eyes darted around. Staff in the immediate vicinity were motionless, waiting. "Get to work!" he barked. "I don't pay you all to stand around."

William chuckled. "That's the problem these days," he said. "Folks think all they have to do is show up for work, not doing any." He laughed again. "Gotta stay on 'em all the time. Like kids."

Reginald tugged on the lapels of his lab coat. His cheek twitched again. "Why don't we go in my office and talk?"

William cut his eyes at Reginald. "You can tell me whatever you gotta tell me here. The treatment worked, right? You said it would."

"It's a bit more complicated than that,

Mr. Mercer. If you'll come in my office, I'll explain everything to you." He put his hand on William's shoulder in a show of camaraderie.

"I don't like the feelin' I'm gettin' 'round here, Doc." His gaze ran across the space, took in the cautious expressions of the staff, their inability to meet his eyes. The same tightness in his chest, the familiar cramping sensation in his stomach, was how he felt when he'd come to see Carol in the hospital just before she died. The doctors and nurses looked and acted the same way. Couldn't look him in the eye, wouldn't answer his questions, always wanted to pull him to the side "to talk." It was the same thing all over again. Maybe Rayne was dead, too. "Where's my daughter? I wanna see her. Right now."

Reginald cleared his throat, attempting again to usher William toward his office.

William shook Reginald's hand off his shoulder. "Where is she?"

"Mr. Mercer," Reginald said, his voice low, patronizing. "Let's discuss this in my office. There's no need for *staff* —" he said the word as if it were a disease, "— to be involved in our discussion," he said, playing on William's deep-seated need to control. Whatever was necessary to get this

334

man out of earshot, he would do. He had no intention of allowing this callous miscreant to create a scene in front of his staff. And he knew William Mercer was perfectly capable of making this untenable situation an even bigger disaster.

William hesitated. He glanced around, seeing the wisdom in what the doctor said. Slowly his shoulders relaxed. He gave Reginald a half-smile. "Which way?"

Reginald's chest filled with momentary relief. "Just down the hall and around the corridor. The first door on your left."

Judy went directly to the personnel office instead of her locker. "Hi, Tess," she greeted.

Tess looked up from the computer screen, tucking the sheet of sleek black hair behind her pierced ears. "Just about to close up shop. What can I do for you? Anything but a raise," she added, revealing the deep laugh lines around her mouth.

"I only wish. Umm, I can't find Dr. Dennis's home number. I know she gave it to me. Would you mind looking it up?"

Tess angled her head, looked at Judy from the corner of her eye. "You know I can't give out home numbers."

"You said anything but a raise," Judy

tried to joke. Tess was not moved. Her black eyes remained expressionless. Judy leaned down, lowered her voice. "This is *really* important, Tess. You know I wouldn't ask if it wasn't."

"Why don't you beep her?" She felt trouble poking her in the rib.

"I need to talk with her right away. I can't wait for her to get back to me. Please, Tess."

Tess hesitated, thought of the repercussions while tapping her suntanned fingers on the desktop. She'd known Judy Simpson for almost five years and in all that time Judy had always been as straight as they come. Occasionally, Tess watched her with the patients, the care she took with them. She was a dedicated nurse. Her job was her life. If she was willing to put it on the line, then —. Oh, hell. Tess hit a key on the keyboard. "If anyone ever finds out, that's my ass — and yours," she added.

"Mum's the word."

Tess pulled up Pauline's employee profile on the screen and read the phone number.

"Thank you, Tess. I owe you big time."

"Just remember that," she called out to Judy's retreating form.

★ ★ ★

Judy found an empty phone booth on the ground floor, dropped in the change, and dialed. "Please be home," she chanted.

The phone rang once. Twice. Five times. "Damn."

Just as she was about to hang up, the answering machine clicked on. "This is Pauline, please leave your name, number, and a message. I'll get back to you as quickly as possible. If this is an emergency, please call my pager. Thank you."

"Dr. Dennis, this is Judy Simpson. It's urgent that I speak with you as soon as possible. It's about what happened today. I'm on my way home. Please call me at —"

Pauline snatched up the phone. "Judy? What is it? What's happened?"

"Rayne's father is here, meeting with Dr. Howell. They know she's gone." Judy looked around the glass booth. "I just wanted to warn you."

"It was only a matter of time," Pauline said, accepting the inevitable with a calm she didn't feel. "How was her father?"

"Scary," was the first word that came to Judy's mind. "He gives me the creeps."

"Hmm." An understatement, Pauline thought. "What did he say about Rayne?"

"I don't think he knows. At least not

when I saw him. He said he was coming to see how her treatment went. Dr. Howell hustled him away."

"He would." Pauline blew out a breath, pressed a hand to her head. "Thanks for the call, Judy. But I don't want you to involve yourself anymore. You've done enough and I'm grateful."

Judy wanted to ask about Rayne, find out where she was, how she was doing. But also understood that the less she knew the better. "What will you do now?"

"Deal with the fallout."

"Take care, Dr. Dennis."

"Thanks. You, too."

Slowly Pauline hung up the phone. She could only imagine what William Mercer would do once he was told that his daughter was no longer in the facility. Probably he'd put on a real show, screaming and yelling and worse. But whatever she needed to do to protect her patient, she would. Without a doubt.

William's outrage, disbelief, and underlying fear spilled out and overflowed into the hallways, slipped beneath closed doors, rode up and down elevators, rattling everything in its wake.

"You incompetent son of a bitch! How

could you let something like this happen?" he bellowed, storming down the hallway, knocking a nurse against the wall as he passed.

Reginald was hot on his heels, futilely attempting to get William under control. "Mr. Mercer, we will get her back. I can assure you —"

William spun around, his face contorted in a grotesque façade of pure venom. His wild eyes glowed. His body vibrated with raw energy, appearing to have mushroomed in size — large, threatening, intimidating. "You can't assure me of shit!" Suddenly he grabbed Reginald by the lapels of his lab coat, pulled him up close to his face. "You find her, you hear me," he hissed, his breath hot and stale against Reginald's face. "Get her back and treated. Tie her down if you have to. Or I swear on my dead wife's grave, I'll bury you and your fancy little hospital, too." He tossed Reginald away from him as if he were no more than an annoying mosquito, turned and walked away, kicking over a tray of supplies as he stalked through the door.

Reginald brushed off his jacket. His face burned. His heart thundered. *How dare that imbecilic oaf threaten me.* He spun around, but not before catching the open-mouthed stares of the staff.

"Get back to work!"

He stormed off down the hall and back to his office. He had to think of something and quickly. There was no telling what that man might get into his head to do.

Slamming his office door behind him, he walked straight to the bar and poured himself a tumbler of Scotch, something he never did while on duty. "You'll pay for this, you conniving bitch," he swore, tossing down the drink and pouring another. The smooth liquid burned his throat, settled like a hot bath in his stomach, warming him from the inside out.

He paced back and forth across the floor. "You will pay."

William stomped across the grounds, arms swinging, his body a powder keg ready to explode.

Robert looked up from trimming the hedges, but wasn't quick enough to side-step William who ran right into him, knocking the hedge clippers from his hand. The sound of metal hitting concrete jarred William out of his tunnel vision. His eyes zeroed in on Robert.

"You work here."

It wasn't a question.

Robert bent down to pick up the clippers. Slowly he stood and faced William, standing a full head above him. He glared. "If you want to send your apology for practically knocking me down, my address is on that truck over there." He tipped his head over his right shoulder.

"If you work here, then you know what goes on, what happens to the patients."

Robert's stance shifted. There was something familiar about this man, vague but familiar. He watched his chest heave with the exertion of trying to keep his rage contained.

"You work out here on the grounds. So you must have seen her leave."

"Listen, I don't know what you're talking about and I have work to do." He turned to leave.

"Don't you walk away from me. I asked you a question."

"What? I think you'd better leave, or I'll ask security to have you removed."

"Security! These toy cops. They're half the reason why my daughter is gone now. If they were doing their jobs, she'd be in there where she belongs."

Robert's heart beat faster. *Maybe it was the shape of the face,* he thought. "Like I said, I don't know what you're talking about. You need to take it up with administration if you have a complaint."

"You're all in this together. What has she done to everybody around here — made them just as crazy as she is, with her sweet ways, and that sweet begging voice? She was always like that, ever since she was little," he said, beginning to ramble through his memories, his gaze off in the distance. "Try to trick a man into doing things. Oh, no. I never fell for it, though. I knew her type. Could smell them a mile away."

Whoever this man was, *he* needed to be behind these walls, Robert thought.

William suddenly looked at him. "You know Rayne Holland. I know you do, you just don't want to tell me. But I'll find out. And when I do, I'll see you all rot in hell."

He pushed past Robert and headed for the parking lot.

Robert followed William's departure with a bemused stare, the pieces tumbling together. He looked toward the facility. She was gone. Rayne was gone. How? When? Suddenly, he was that little boy again sitting by the window praying that his father would turn the corner. This time it wasn't his father he hoped he'd see, it was Rayne.

Until that moment, he hadn't realized how important she'd become to him, how much he looked forward to spending those few precious hours with her. He'd foolishly taken for granted that she would always be there. Of course, she couldn't be. A part of him always knew that. He'd seen the slow but steady growth in her. Day by day, she'd begun to open up like the bud of a rose.

He could almost hear her laughter, light and musical, given to him as a gift on those rare occasions that she shared it with him.

He looked at the façade of the facility again, then headed toward his van. They'd begun to play a game those last few times they were together. It was a game his grandmother taught him when he spent his summers with her. For every seed they planted she would set a goal. And every thorn that was cut, or weed that was pulled, she'd find something about herself that she wanted to change — get rid of. She encouraged him to do the same.

They were on their hands and knees one afternoon. Their arms brushed lightly, sweat mingled, as they dug a narrow ditch for planting, Robert recalled, seeing Rayne's face as clearly as if she were beside him. She seemed contented.

Robert guided her hand, showing her how to turn the earth with the small shovel.

"Gently," he said. "It may seem hard on the outside, but underneath it's soft, easily broken."

"Like some people?" she said, halting her work to look at him, seeking the meaning beyond his words.

"Like most people."

"Do you really think so?"

"Yes. Most people go through life wearing invisible armor. The more disappointments they suffer, the more hurt they endure, the thicker the armor becomes until you can't reach them at all."

Rayne looked down at the red and brown earth, let the grains run through her fingers, cake her nails.

"Why do you wear armor?" she asked.

Her intuitiveness stunned him. For a moment he didn't know what to say, but then understood that all he could tell her was the truth.

He sat back on his haunches, brushed the soil from his hands, and tried to form the words that lived in his soul. The secret things he kept locked away inside himself, the things he could never tell anyone; at least that's what he'd thought for years.

"I suppose it's because I'm afraid," he said finally. "Afraid of not being worthy to be cared about. Being abandoned."

He dared to look at her and saw the silhouette of his fears reflected in her eyes. She understood what he felt. Probably the only one to understand what that emptiness felt like, gnawing at him year in, year out.

"Nothing lasts forever," she said softly. "Except memories, and even those we can choose what to keep."

In that place, that moment, it was impossible for him to believe that she needed to be there.

She took her hand and covered his. "You should plant that fear and let it go," she said.

He swallowed down the need to pull her against him. "And what will you get rid of today?"

She released his hand, closed her eyes, and held her face toward the sun. Suddenly she smiled and looked at him. "I need some seeds," she said, holding out her hand.

Robert angled his head and eyed her from the side. He reached into his sack and pulled out a small bag of azalea seeds.

Azaleas were strong, resilient, and beautiful, like her.

Rayne opened the bag and sprinkled the seeds into the ditch. "Today," she said, "I plant the seeds of trust. I want to learn to trust my feelings so that I can confront my past and begin my future." She looked across at him. "Here." She held out her closed hand.

Robert turned up his palm. The remaining seeds fell into his hand.

"What dream do you want to plant today, Robert?"

He squeezed the seeds in his hand. "I plant the seeds of memories, that they will sustain us, remind us of the wonderful times when life overwhelms us."

"What about the bad memories?"

"Even those we can choose which to keep," he said, repeating her words.

A slow smile moved like sunrise across her mouth. She eased toward him. "Thank you," she whispered.

"For what?"

"For helping me to believe that new memories are possible. For being a friend and treating me like a person."

He pushed the day aside, storing the memories for another day. And there would be another day. He turned on the ignition and the engine rumbled to life. He drove away.

William tore through the streets of Savannah. His thoughts circled above him like hungry buzzards. He shouldn't have gotten so upset. He should have tried to think things through. He knew he put the fear of God in that Dr. Howell, though. And that suited him fine. But if that fool doctor decided to bring in the police and Rayne started running her mouth, everything would come apart. He slammed his fist against the steering wheel.

What could he do? He had to think of something and quick.

Damn that Rayne. Damn her to hell. Been nothing but trouble since the day she was born. She wasn't going to ruin his life. That was for sure.

Twenty-four

Pauline stood with folded arms in front of her bedroom window. Her light nightgown clung to her damp body, outlining her sensuous form. From the open window, a molasses-like breeze pushed the sheer curtains aside, attempting to stick to her skin with warm fingers of humidity.

She ran her hands across her face, brushing back her hair's stray red tendrils. What would today bring? Her night had been seemingly endless, interrupted by sudden bouts of wakefulness, hazy dreams, cloying fears. In the midst of it all, she saw Rayne, smiling, sitting in her director's chair, choreographing the dance moves of the dream's numerous cast members: Gayle, James, Dr. Howell, William and Edith, Judy, herself — the list went on.

Inadvertently, Rayne's existence, her illness, her road to recovery was a cyclonic force, swirling and sucking up everything in its wake. Would they all be spat out, ragged and useless, when the whirlwind finally ended?

She rubbed her hands up and down her arms. It had to be worth it, what she'd done. It had to be. Rayne was worth saving and so many others like her who are subjected to radical treatment when some doctors want to take the short, quick route.

Slowly she shook her head and turned away from the window. In front of her was the full-length oak mirror that she'd purchased at an antique auction in Atlanta. Her reflection stared back at her, challenging her to look beyond the glass, the image.

The mirror had been a present to herself, or more of a test, like an alcoholic who keeps a bottle around to test his willpower. The mirror was her litmus test. If ever there were a day that she couldn't face herself in it, couldn't look into her own eyes because of anything she'd knowingly done, then she knew it was time to let go and move on.

She looked into her eyes and turned away.

Downstairs in the kitchen, Pauline poured boiling water over the grains of instant coffee into her favorite blue chipped mug. When it was a reasonable hour, she would call Gayle to check on Rayne, make arrangements to see her later in the day.

The doorbell rang, once, twice, persistent.

Her eyes rose to the clock above the refrigerator. 8:30 a.m. She didn't want to think about who it could be at this time of day.

She pushed herself up from her seat with a groan.

The bell rang again.

She pulled the belt tighter around her robe, walked to the door, and peered through the peephole. The muscles in her throat constricted. What was he doing here? What did he want? She twisted the locks, took a deep breath, and opened the door. Reginald Howell stood before her.

"I realize that my unannounced visit . . . is inappropriate." He paused and cleared his throat, looking decidedly uncomfortable, Pauline quickly assessed. "However, we need to talk and it won't wait until you return to work."

Caught off guard by the sudden appearance of her supervisor at her door, Pauline simply stood in the doorway, speechless for a few seconds.

"May I come in, Dr. Dennis?"

Commanding. Direct. Not that it was a tone that was foreign to her. He often talked to her like an owner speaking to a pet.

"Yes . . . come in." She stepped aside to let him pass. In all the years she'd worked at Cedar Grove, she'd never once seen Dr. Howell outside of the hospital grounds, away from his domain. Suddenly it was as if she couldn't quite place him — a familiar face, but from where? She shut the door and he turned toward her, apparently waiting for some directive from her. That, too, was disconcerting. It was always Dr. Howell who played the lead actor, the star, the conductor of the orchestra.

Pauline straightened her shoulders and extended her arm toward the living room. "We can talk in here," she said. She led the way and took a seat on the overstuffed easy chair. He sat across from her on the sofa.

Reginald looked around. "You have a nice home, Dr. Dennis."

"Thank you." She waited for something more, and when nothing came she asked if she could get him something to drink.

"No. Thank you. Let me get to the point of my visit."

She pulled her robe tighter around her

body and pressed her knees together.

"Rayne Holland's father came to the hospital yesterday." His mouth was a taut red line.

Pauline's eyes rested on his tense expression. "What happened?"

"He's a very interesting and deeply disturbed man." He clasped his hands together on his knees. He detailed his encounter, the verbal sparring match, the insults, everything right up to William Mercer leaving the grounds.

Pauline sat perfectly still for a moment taking in what had been said. "Do you fully agree with my evaluation now, Dr. Howell?" she finally asked, hoping that this would turn into a meeting of the minds and not a duel of adversaries.

Slowly he rose, turned away from her before pacing across the short space that separated them. He paused at the mantel, grimaced for a moment, then faced her. "It isn't often that we agree on much, Dr. Dennis, but in this instance . . ." His words drifted off as if he couldn't bring himself to say anything further. "I listened to the tapes of your sessions," he said, steering the conversation away from himself. "There's much more there than what appears in your case notes."

"Of course, the tapes are more detailed," she responded defensively. "I couldn't begin to duplicate the sessions verbatim on paper."

"That's not what I mean." He stroked his chin in thought, then began his strategic assault. "Doctor, you've lost your objectivity when it comes to this patient. Your tone with her becomes pampering and cajoling as if you're attempting to make her your friend. This is not professional. She doesn't need you as her friend. She needs you as her doctor. You discovered the fracture in her personality weeks ago and yet you've done nothing concrete to address it, not even telling the patient."

"I am being her doctor. I concluded that my approach was what she needed."

"What she needed or what you needed? You needed to share your own trauma with her, someone who would understand. Isn't that true, Dr. Dennis?"

Pauline jumped up from her seat. "You don't know what you're talking about."

"Don't I?" he asked calmly, watching the array of emotions race across her face. He was right. He knew he was right. All the indicators were there. He could kick himself for not seeing it sooner. Her overidentification with Rayne Holland, the increase in the one-on-one sessions, case notes that barely scratched the surface of what was really going on. She'd over-stepped the boundary between practitioner and patient. She'd lost all objectivity. A classic case of counter-transference — the therapist's overarching response to the patient as a result of *her own similar trauma.* "I listened to the tapes, Pauline," he said, using her first name as if they were actually friends. "I listened to one tape in particular." He reached into his jacket pocket and pulled out a microrecorder.

Pauline's expression froze into one of curiosity mixed with fear.

"I don't think you were aware that the tape was still running, which makes it all the more revealing." He pressed the play button and Pauline's troubled voice joined them in the room. Her own words pushed her back into her seat.

"I know exactly the terror you felt, Rayne. How dirty and unworthy you felt. How many nights did I lie awake in bed listening for the footsteps at my door, waiting for my uncle Thomas to appear, whisper things to me that no man should whisper to a child? I know the helplessness. Who could I tell? No one would believe me. They would all say it was my fault, that I brought it on myself. But you

would understand. You would know that I didn't like it, I didn't want it. But I couldn't stop it. I couldn't." Sounds of shuffling papers and soft sobs followed.

Dr. Howell pressed the stop button.

Pauline raised her head from the cradle of her hands and looked at him with cold distant eyes, seeing a past that had been resurrected and put on display for all to see. Her dark secret. Now he was the transgressor, taunting her with her own pain, showing no regard for the risk she'd taken in desperation to reach her patient. That was all there was to it. She took that path to reach Rayne before it was too late. Maybe it was the wrong thing to do but it seemed the right choice at the time.

"You can't help your patient if you can't help yourself," he began, his voice condescending. "You can never let your neurosis enter into your work with a patient. You know that, Doctor. It's too dangerous. The consequences for both the practitioner and the patient could be dire. You know that, don't you?"

She didn't want to hear him chiding her like an unruly child. "I thought I could handle it. I thought I'd put it all behind me. But the more we talked, and the better she felt, the worse it got for me. I was back there again . . . in that room." Tears rolled down her cheeks. Why was she telling him this? He was the enemy. But it was as if she needed to purge herself, to say the words aloud.

He stood over her, looking down at her, as if she'd committed a cardinal sin. His whole being seemed to pass judgment on her, his failed employee, his discredited healer who had forgotten her professional ethics. For several seconds, he glared at her in utter disgust, angered that even momentarily he'd expected more of her. But, after all, she was only a woman.

Suddenly she felt regret at not standing up for herself. There was no reason for her to endure this kind of treatment from anybody, especially not from him. He was her boss, not her father. "How dare you lecture me on ethics and morality? You of all people. Get out of my house."

For an instant, he was taken aback by her sudden vehemence, but more so that she had the gall to direct her tantrum at him. Who the hell did she think she was? Ungrateful bitch! His eyes were wild and menacing. "You've gone too far this time. Where is she?"

She didn't reply, ignoring his tirade. This was her house, after all.

Reginald walked away from her, determined to conduct his search until he'd located the missing patient. It was time to take action. No more talk. "Where is she?" he demanded, stalking toward the stairs.

"Get out, you self-serving sonafabitch!" She jumped up and crossed the room to block his path. No way. He was not going to rummage through her house, acting like he was a cop. If she must, they would really tangle. Her arms were outstretched as if they were barricades of flesh, blocking him from further access.

He was stunned momentarily but he would not be stopped. "You have no idea what you've done," he said, his voice deep and threatening. "You are the one in the wrong here. I'll have your license revoked. Do you hear me? You'll never practice again. I'll ruin you. Now where the hell is she?"

"I don't know what you're talking about." Her voice was defiant. She was not giving ground on this even if it meant her job. There would be no repeat of the Cole case.

"I'll not ask you again," he said. "Bring the woman to me. I know she's here."

His entire being, his overbearing presence, infuriated her. She stepped back and put her clenched hands in front of her, her physical stance declaring to him that this situation could get ugly . . . fast. "I want you to leave now. Damn it! Get out of my house right now!"

This startled him. Being on the defense was not his usual posture. He couldn't believe this woman had the audacity to order him around. He didn't give a damn if it was her house. *His* career was on line.

"Don't play games with me, Dr. Dennis," Reginald growled, taking an exaggerated step as if he were going to push past her. A thread of sweat rimmed his hairline. His top lip trembled. "Rayne Holland is missing from the hospital. Taken without the proper discharge evaluation or committee consultation. She was your patient."

"That's right. She is my patient, doctor." Her brow creased. "A patient who would have been subjected to radical and unnecessary treatment that would do her more harm than good. I was never consulted about this. It was your idea. We both know electroshock is a last resort. You never even thought enough of me as a professional to discuss this with me."

"So you *did* take her out of the hospital," Reginald shot back. "I wanted to give you the benefit of the doubt. But I should have known. What you did was unlawful, illegal. It was criminal and you know that. Still you pull a stunt like this. You took her from the hospital without first consulting *me*. Admit it!"

"What if I did?" she challenged. "Maybe this will finally put a stop to the unnecessary treatments that go on at Cedar Brook and the tyrannical hold you have on the staff. Everyone is too afraid to speak up. But not anymore."

Reginald took a threatening step closer. "What are you saying?"

"I'm a doctor, but I'm also a human being. There was a time in my career when I didn't trust my instincts, my skills. I let others make my medical decisions for me, even though in my heart, I knew the decision was wrong. Very wrong. I must live with what I *didn't* do for the rest of my life."

She walked around him, forcing him to turn, to follow her with his eyes as she moved toward the phone. "Rayne Holland is broken. But she can be whole again. *I* know she can. I won't sit back and let you destroy her. Or anyone else again." She took a steadying breath. "As a human being, Doctor, I will fight you and anyone like you with the last breath I have. Her father stole her youth, innocence, and her womanhood. I won't let you steal the rest of her life."

"You won't let me?" Reginald sputtered. "You have no idea what you've done, Dr. Dennis. None. Your career will be over. I'll see to that." He shook his finger at her, but really wanting to grab her by the throat, squeeze the smug life out of her. "You won't get away with this."

Pauline stared at him and raised her chin while lifting the phone from its cradle, her finger poised near the buttons. "Can the hospital handle a scandal like this?" she asked, knowing she held the trump card. "Can you imagine if all the families started coming forward, filing complaints about the vile treatment of their loved ones? What if they go to the press? Suppose the state investigators get involved in the whole business? What would happen to your precious hospital then? Are you prepared to deal with that?"

Reginald glared at her, his mouth agape. "Are you threatening me?"

"Look at it any way you want, Dr. Howell," she snapped.

"You won't get away with this." He was

back on his heels, reeling from her verbal blow.

"What is it that you're really so pissed off about, Dr. Howell — the fact that Rayne is no longer a paying customer, or that one of your orders was overruled?" she taunted, the phone remaining in her hand.

His broad body visibly shook with barely contained rage. "Where are your files?" His fingers curled into fists. "I checked your office. They're gone."

She smiled, enjoying his feeble attempt to make her submit to his commands. "They're my files, my patients. They're my property, not the hospital's or yours."

He paced back and forth in front of her, his mind whirling with a summary of what retaliatory actions were available to him. He could lose everything because of this insolent, arrogant bitch. "This is bigger than you or me, Doctor. We're talking about an institution, a place of healing, the practice of medicine," he bellowed. "Stop thinking with your bleeding heart. I thought you had what it took. What kind of doctor can you ever hope to be if you can't make the hard decisions?"

"A human one." She put down the phone. Victory was hers. It was in the tone of his voice, his defeated demeanor. She smiled at the man, walked toward the door, and opened it. "Good-bye, Doctor."

"You haven't heard the last of this, by any means." Knowing it was time to retreat and regroup, he didn't resist and headed out, but not before tossing off one last threat. "Your troubles have only begun," he said harshly, through bared teeth. "I only hope you can sleep at night with your decision. And God help you if you're wrong."

Pauline showed no emotion, choosing to wait before taking a shuddering breath only after slowly closing the door behind him. She rested her forehead against the cool wood surface.

"I'm not wrong. I can't be," she whispered. "I can't be."

Twenty-five

"So you're planning on putting your whole life on hold so you can babysit. Is that the deal?" James challenged, tugging his tie around his white shirt collar. He studied Gayle through her reflection in the mirror.

Last night they'd slept in separate beds for the second time in their marriage. But this time was different. This wasn't about anger. It was about feelings of betrayal and mistrust.

"It's not that simple, James. I think you know that."

"I don't know anything anymore, Gayle. I thought I did."

His voice sounded so empty, Gayle thought, as if all the energy that made James the vibrant man that he was had been suctioned from him. She'd done that. She was responsible. Somehow she had to make it right.

"James, what I said last night was wrong. I broke a promise to you and to myself." She twisted a thread on her robe between her fingers. "I can never apologize enough for that."

He turned to her, his wide eyes heavy with sadness. "You're right, you can't."

Her breath came faster. "I still love you, James."

He looked down at the carpeted floor. "Do you, really?"

Gayle got up from the edge of the bed and crossed the room to stand in front of him. She reached out and cupped his cheek in her hand. "We've been an 'us' since senior year in high school —"

"Maybe we've outgrown each other, Gayle. It happens."

"I don't think so. We simply haven't grown into the people we've become."

James turned away, putting some distance between them. He didn't want her to see the need in his eyes, the loss of his self-esteem, his pain. He'd loved Gayle for as long as he could remember. And a part of him still did. But he no longer believed that his love was enough to hold them together.

"When did it all start unraveling, Gayle? When you fell in love with Paul?"

With his back turned to her, she could hide the truth that hovered in her eyes. "It wasn't what I felt for Paul that changed things between us. Not really. I never loved him. Not like that. Paul was only an easy substitute for what I thought I needed."

James slid his hands into the pockets of his navy pants. With head lowered, he turned toward her. "What did you need, Gayle?" His gaze rose to meet hers. "Have I ever fulfilled your needs — ever?"

She couldn't hide behind a broad back, a turned cheek. There was nowhere to run except straight ahead.

"There wasn't anything you didn't do, James. What happened between us wasn't only your fault. It was mine, too. My own perception of who I was, and wasn't. I tried to find ways to fill up all the holes in my sense of self."

"But you turned to everyone else to fill them except me. Why, Gayle? Just tell me — why?"

She'd run from this piece of her reality for nearly ten years. The simplicity of it. If there were ever any hope of salvaging what was left of her marriage she needed to do what she should have done a long time ago — accept it for what it was.

"You were . . . easy, accessible."

The muscles in his face fluttered like butterfly wings. Funny she would notice something so infinitesimal at that particular moment.

He suddenly tossed his head back and laughed, a delirious sound. "Shit. You're telling me that because I tried to treat you decent, like a lady, wanted to make a life for you and with you, you couldn't deal with that? You went after another woman's husband, let all kinds of bull get in between us — your job, your friend, your want for things? Is that what you're telling me?"

He made her sound so empty, shallow, as if she had no substance. It wasn't like that. She wasn't like that.

"I never felt as if you needed me, James. Not really. You were always so self-sufficient, self-contained. You always had everything under control." She paced the floor, her bare feet sinking into the thick carpet. "There was never a mystery or a challenge to what you would do. You would do the right thing. Every time." She lowered her head, tugged on her bottom lip with her teeth. "I could always count on that."

"But I did need you, Gayle. I needed you to give me the will to keep getting out there every day, waking up in the morning. I didn't have all the answers. That's why I wanted you at my side — to share my life."

She stopped her pacing. Her voice was faint. "I never felt that way."

"How could you not?" he asked in disbelief.

How could she explain what was so complex in her mind, twisted in her heart? There were parts of her she didn't understand, was only slowly coming to grips with. She sighed heavily before trying to form the words.

"By the time you came to me with anything, you *did* have the answers, had worked out the details — from when we would get married, where we would live, how much money to put aside, vacation time, everything. I never felt I was part of anything that had to do with us — the making of us. So I started building my own life." She turned her head, her eyes filling. "The only time you needed me was when your business was falling apart and your gambling debts were on the verge of collapsing everything we had."

"And the first opportunity you had you threw it in my face." He shrugged into his jacket. "Is that how it goes?"

"I only did it because —"

"Because what? You wanted to hurt me."

"No. Not to hurt you. Just to stop you and make you listen. Not just with your ears but with your heart. You of all people know what it's like to have nowhere to run, nowhere you can turn, when everything is stacked against you." She pressed her hand to her chest. "That's where Rayne is now, James. We — you and I can't turn our backs on her and live with ourselves. I know I couldn't. And neither could the man I married."

She walked up to him. They were a breath apart. She could see the faint shadow of where his beard would be. James glimpsed the first strand of gray in her hair, and suddenly couldn't imagine being old and alone — without Gayle.

"What are we going to do, baby?" he asked, brushing her bangs away from her eyes.

She pressed her head against his chest, listening to the steady beat of his heart. That was James Davis — steady, dependable. Her husband.

"Work at what we have. One day at a time," she said. "Find our way back into each other's lives."

"I don't know which path to take with you, Gayle."

"I'll help you, if you help me." She looked up at him, needing him more than she ever thought possible. "I'm asking you to try. Please."

"I . . . need some time, Gayle. I've been thinking that maybe we need some space, to clear our heads."

Her heart escalated its beat. "W-what are you saying?"

"I'm going to stay with my brother for a while until I can find a place."

The sensation of descending from the apex of a roller coaster swept through her. Slowly, she backed away. Disbelief weakening her legs. "You've already decided," she uttered, her voice shaky. She shook her head as she spoke. "Why are you doing this? How can we expect to work things out if we're apart?"

"All I know is that right now, Gayle, I can't be with you. I need time to think about where I want to be with this marriage. Who we are in it. I can't do that here, not clearly."

Tears spilled down her cheeks. She wouldn't beg him. She wouldn't. "If that's what you want to do . . ." She brushed the tears away. Her nostrils flared as she sucked in air. "What about Tracy? I want her home."

He buttoned his jacket. "I don't think she should be here with Rayne."

"Rayne would never do anything to hurt Tracy. You know that."

He released a breath. "Maybe in her right mind she wouldn't. I don't know what Rayne is capable of now."

"I'll be here every day. Nothing will happen."

"Gayle —"

"Don't do this, James. Bring Tracy home. Please."

He walked to the closet and took out his briefcase. He kept his back to her, thinking of how easy it would be to use Tracy to get what he wanted. He knew Gayle would bend even if she seemed to care about everything in the world except her family. He knew she loved her daughter. And he couldn't think of what it would do to his life if Gayle had threatened to take her away. That wasn't the kind of man he wanted to be.

"I'll bring her home tonight — when I come to pick up some of my things."

Gayle stood alone in the silence that surrounded her; the only sound was the dull drumbeat of her heart. She pressed her hand to her mouth to stifle the sob that bubbled up from her throat.

She spun around, her arm wrapping her waist. Her reflection stopped her. She was a little girl again, left out, forgotten, wanting to be wanted.

She stepped closer to the mirror.

Her reflection became clearer. She wasn't a little girl. She was a grown woman with a child and a husband, a career, a future. She wasn't ready to let any of them go.

James would come back when he was ready. And when he did they'd work out what was wrong between them. Whatever that meant. It would take time and she knew it would hurt like hell. But she would deal with it. They would deal with it.

One day at a time. She had to believe that.

Twenty-six

Sitting on the banquette in her temporary bedroom with Dr. Dennis, Rayne was drawn to the squeals of laughter that floated up to her window. Gayle and Tracy were playing in the yard below. As Gayle pushed Tracy higher in the swing, the child's shouts of joy grew in volume. It made Rayne smile and at the same time left her with a feeling of incompleteness.

In the three weeks that she'd been in residence she'd been an unassuming witness to Gayle's transformation from the efficient, no-nonsense businesswoman and militaristic housekeeper to a gentle, fun-loving woman who doted on her daughter.

Although Rayne's presence in their home had sparked a series of revelations and upheavals, in one regard it was helpful. A mother found her daughter. Rayne thought of Desiree. Her image, the scent and touch of her were suddenly as real as the breath she drew through her lungs. Desiree had loved and relied on her, too.

Just as Tracy relied on Gayle. Desiree's love was unconditional and freely given. Her presence in Rayne's life gave her a sense of worth. Each time she looked into her daughter's eyes or stood over her as she slept, she could, for a moment, believe that life was worth living, that she was blessed in the midst of all the dark shadows and fears.

"Stop! Stop!" Tracy giggled, barely able to catch her breath, her ponytails whipping around her cherubic face.

Gayle stopped the swing, scooped Tracy out, and hugged her tight before Tracy tagged her mother as "it" and darted around the yard with Gayle hot on her heels.

Rayne smiled, not so much with happiness but with wistfulness.

"Tell me what made you smile, Rayne," Dr. Dennis asked.

Rayne sighed and momentarily lowered her head. "I'd been that way with Desiree, so close, so loving. It's still too painful to think about — her loss, what my life is like without her in it. A void." She focused again on the activity in the yard below. "We'd shared special times, too, times just for us. I remember taking Desi to the studio and was amazed at her acute eye for detail and uncanny memory . . ."

"Mommy, wasn't the lady sitting in the other chair?" she asked as Rayne was peering through the camera to set up the next shot.

Rayne mumbled something about being happy with the framed shot.

"Huh, Mommy?"

"What is it, sweetheart?"

"That lady's in the wrong seat, Mommy."

Rayne moved from behind the camera and viewed the staging to her left. A smile of incredulity tilted her mouth.

"You know something, sugar, you're absolutely right. I think I'll have to hire you."

"Desiree was like that about everything, from the outfits she wore to the way she took care of her toys. Gayle used to say she was a little girl in an old soul. She loved being at the shoots. The crew treated her like a little princess, and Desiree sucked it up and tugged their heartstrings for more. She invariably brought home a shopping bag full of gifts and snacks after each visit."

Rayne smiled at the recollection.

"The attention showered on Desiree may have made some children unbearable to live with. Not Desi. If anything, she seemed to grow more loving and giving, and she shared all her treasures with Tracy."

"May I have two, please?" she would routinely ask. *"One for me and one for my best friend in the whole world."* Rayne swallowed hard.

"From what Gayle has told me, for weeks after the accident Tracy became totally withdrawn. A half of the whole without Desiree. Gayle insisted that Tracy was too young to be told about death, especially Desiree's death. And I was so trapped in my own grief that I couldn't begin to help Tracy adjust. I believe James is right. They should tell Tracy the truth."

She looked across the short space into Pauline's green eyes.

"It's very difficult for me, Dr. Dennis," she continued. "I've always been so close to Tracy. She's like my own child. It's killing me to keep lying to her, pretending that . . . Desi has just . . . gone away for a while."

"What does the lying do to you? How does it make you feel?"

"Every time I lie, I lose another piece of myself, another memory of Desi. I can't keep this up, but I can't go against Gayle, either."

"Death is a very difficult subject for everyone. Unfortunately, in our adult role as protectors, we often protect too much, thinking we're doing the right thing. In the end it only hurts the child. They're a lot more resilient than we give them credit for. As long as the love and support is present, the difficulties can be overcome."

Rayne nodded.

"It's the not knowing, Rayne, the uncertainty, that's so frightening," Pauline said, easing into the direction she wanted Rayne to head. "That's part of the difficulty of your getting well, Rayne, coming to grips with the uncertainty."

"I am getting well," Rayne insisted.

"Yes, you are. But there are still basic truths you have to deal with if you ever hope to put the past behind you for good. Truths that you've buried inside of yourself, pretended that they weren't there in order to get through your days. Lying to yourself, Rayne."

Rayne turned away. She knew what Pauline was saying, what she was trying to get her to do. *Confront my past, my fears, the shadows — my father — the root of it all.* She wasn't ready. Not yet. She knew those weeds still needed to be pulled.

Pauline was right, of course. She knew that, even as she watched Gayle and Tracy below. The rest of her life was shrouded in a misty haze of doubt.

Because of those weeds, those thorns, she lived her life unsure of who she was as a woman, a wife, a friend, and a mother. Maybe facing it all would help and she could begin to build a life for herself.

But maybe it wouldn't.

It was the unknown factor that halted her. Perhaps the rest of her life would only be a reflection of what it had always been.

The sound of a ball slapping against the pavement drew Rayne's attention back to the activity below.

Her chest felt tight as she watched the scene play out. *Mother and daughter.* The pain, the emptiness, was so acute at that moment. This is what she was missing, would always miss. All that was left were the memories. At that moment she wanted to be back in the garden with Robert, planting the seeds of her life with Desiree. Sharing those memories with him and building new ones.

She felt the wet, salty drops caress her lips. She blinked them away as she watched James walk across the back lawn and sneak up on Tracy, who giggled in delight. Even though he hadn't moved back home, he came to see Tracy every day, and usually stayed for dinner and put her to bed.

"Gayle and James may have their difficulties, but their common goal is to ensure Tracy's happiness," Rayne said thoughtfully.

"What do you think held you and Paul together?"

"I suppose it was the same for Paul and me. Beneath the hurt, the unkind words, the confusion of what went wrong between us, we wanted Desi's happiness. She was the factor that kept us human, allowed us to remember that there was still goodness in the world. And if there was still goodness in the world, then it was in us, because Desi was a part of who we were." She paused for a moment.

"But even knowing that, you both understood it would take more than loving your daughter to make what was wrong between you right. It's the same with Gayle and James. Whatever wall they'd erected could only be dismantled by them. Choices," Pauline added. "To choose what is easy and safe, or choose to face the demons that haunt us." Images of Linda Cole's vacant eyes merged with the feel of thick hands on her young body. The urge to share her experience with Rayne, let her know she understood her anxiety, became so overpowering that the words rose to her lips and only Rayne's voice beat them back down.

"The choices I'd made over the years had been the easy ones, the choices of least resistance," Rayne admitted. "I chose to keep silent all those years ago about what terrified me in the night. My silence allowed it to continue. I chose to keep it a secret from the one person who would have understood — Gayle — and it caused a rift between us that widened through the years."

Pauline fought against the rapid beating of her heart, her sense of drifting away, and forced herself to concentrate on her patient and not her own personal trauma.

"I chose to marry Paul," Rayne was saying, "because it was easy to care for someone who adored me and expected so little in return. I had nothing to give."

"You also chose to work in a profession where fantasy becomes reality, because it allowed you to escape from the real world, your world," Pauline said, knowing that she'd done the same. By engaging in a profession where she explored the minds of others, she could keep her own thoughts at bay. Until Rayne. "And you also chose to take your own life because it was easier than living with yourself and what you allowed to happen to you," Pauline said a bit too harshly, suddenly needing to distance herself from this woman who was a reflection of herself. *She* had not tried to take her life. *She* was strong, stronger than Rayne. They were different . . . not the same. She must remind herself of that or be drawn into the abyss that threatened to engulf her.

Rayne flinched at the attack, turned away from her attacker, and seemed to withdraw. Pauline slowly regained her sense of balance.

Rayne glanced around the room, took stock of where she was and why she was there. *Don't let where you are define who you are,* she could hear Robert say.

She had to admit, even if it was only to her inner self, that both Gayle and Pauline had decided to take control of their lives, go against the obstacles and to hell with the consequences. They took risks. They'd done it for her, sacrificed all of what they'd worked for because of her, Gayle her marriage and security and Pauline her career. What sacrifice was *she* willing to make?

Tell her, the voice whispered in her ear. *Tell her!*

"My . . . father . . . hurt me," she said in a whisper, then stronger, more assured. "My father hurt me?" She looked into

Pauline's eyes, searching for affirmation and consolation.

"Yes, Rayne, he did. Your father, the man who should have loved and protected you, hurt you. And saying the words out loud, owning them, is a giant step toward acknowledging what happened to you was real and not your imagination, some nightmare." Pauline paused, allowing Rayne's admission to sink in, become more than mere words. "Tell me what you remember. Close your eyes and tell me how you know it was your father."

Rayne shut her eyes, let her mind run backward, the images flashing like quick snapshots, here and then gone.

"I think a part of me always knew," she said slowly, the idea of what had been done to her taking shape, taking a physical form. "The fear and anxiety I always felt in my father's presence. The scent of him that assaulted me any time a man tried to become intimate with me."

"Even Paul?"

Rayne nodded. "Yes."

"Why can you finally say the words, say that it was your father? Do you know?"

"Seeing Gayle and Tracy, knowing the damage that lies can cause, what that does to you day in and day out, until it gets to a

381

point that you can't distinguish fact from fantasy." She looked at Pauline, her eyes pleading for understanding. "I don't want to lie anymore, especially to myself. I want to be free. I don't want to be a victim anymore." Tears of pent-up release flowed freely. She wrapped her arms around her body, suddenly needing to be held or perhaps to hold back the deluge of emotions that roared through her: anger, shame, resentment, the sensation of being dirty and sinful.

"You are not a victim, Rayne. You are a survivor. You lived through it and you will be well. Tell yourself that. Say the words. Own them."

"I . . . am not a victim."

"Say it."

"I'm a survivor."

"Say it again."

"I am not a victim. I am a survivor."

"I will be well," Pauline said, as much for herself as for Rayne.

"I will be well."

"Everything that has happened to you in all of your relationships is a result of what your father did to you. How you react, how you feel about yourself, the choices that you make."

"But why would he do that to me?"

Rayne asked, her voice breaking with the pain. "What did I do to make him want to hurt me?"

"It was not your fault. You did nothing wrong. You must understand that. You were a child. You had no power over him."

Pauline suddenly saw her uncle Thomas standing over her, felt the fear that his presence evoked, and the helplessness that left her immobilized. *"Just hush now,"* he whispered. *"It will be over before you know it. Come on and treat your uncle nice . . ."* Sweat trickled down her back. She blinked away the vision.

"Many . . . women believe that they somehow brought it on themselves, that they somehow deserved what they got."

"Please don't hurt me," she'd begged.

She swallowed, tried to concentrate.

"No one deserves that. No one deserves to be abused," she said faintly, then focused on Rayne. "Now you have the power."

"Me?" Confusion clouded Rayne's expression.

"Yes. You have the power of knowledge. And as you get better and grow stronger you will understand how to use that knowledge, one step at a time." Pauline leaned back and took a cleansing breath. "I think this is enough for today."

The door to Rayne's past had finally been pushed open. All that was left was for her to finally have the inner strength to step across the threshold. Perhaps they would cross it together.

Pauline stood. "I want you to remember what we talked about today. Don't be afraid of what you feel or think. It's all part of the healing process. Let the images come. They can't hurt you anymore."

Rayne nodded. "I'll . . . try, Doctor."

"Good. Then I will see you in a couple of days." She patted Rayne's shoulder as she gathered her things. The sudden connection, the feeling of kinship, was so potent it nearly stopped her cold. With great effort she walked toward the door, shutting it, but not her swirling emotions, behind her.

She didn't know how long she sat staring out of the window, going over her conversation with Dr. Dennis, but the one thought kept resurfacing: *What sacrifice are you willing to make?*

Turning from the window, she left the bedroom and walked down the hallway. Picking up the phone from the table, she called Cedar Grove and asked to speak with Robert. It had to begin somewhere. Robert would understand.

There was a small diner called the Arch because of its horseshoe shape, located about ten minutes away from Gayle's house. The Arch had character: a jukebox that sometimes could only be played by kicking it at just the right spot, sundaes to die for, the odors of grilled burgers and onion rings, all added to the ambience. You could almost see the girls in their bobby socks, pressed hair, and plaid skirts, getting kisses stolen from them by the captain of the basketball team.

She and Gayle had spent many an afternoon tucked away in the red plastic booths, sipping Cokes and swapping gossip.

As the cab pulled up in front of the rundown structure, she wondered how Gayle would respond to the note she'd left. She hoped Gayle would know that this was something she needed to do.

"That's five-fifty, ma'am," the driver said.

Rayne dug in her purse and pulled out a crumbled ten-dollar bill and smiled. The simple act of paying for a cab ride made her feel like a giddy little girl doing something grown-up for the first time. For her it was an act of absolution, a step toward washing away the past, a move toward independence.

Nearing the entrance, a wave of nervousness accelerated the beat of her heart. Would Robert be waiting? What if he didn't come?

Until that moment, standing on the threshold of a new beginning, she did not fully understand how important seeing Robert was, how important he'd become to her.

In the weeks that they'd traversed from silent partners, tentative friends, to something undefined, he had been a constant source of affirmation, nurturing her back toward wellness. He allowed her to believe that the elusive thing called emotion could be trusted, if given to the right person.

Robert made her feel like a woman, someone of value, and for no other reason than simply being herself; not a filmmaker, a wife, friend, lover, or a mother. Just herself, Rayne Holland, whatever that self was and could become. Even Dr. Dennis, in all her wisdom, had been unable to give her that part of herself.

She stood in the open doorway and looked down the narrow aisle, the worn red-and-yellow linoleum telling the tales of the many who'd left their marks. Then her lungs seemed to cease delivering oxygen.

His back was turned toward her. Still she could tell it was him. She knew by the set of his shoulders, that slight angle of his head, as if he were listening to an internal melody.

As always, he sensed her presence before seeing her. Just like those times when she stood silently in the doorway of his father's hospital room. Would she run if he turned around? He dared to find out.

She could have been an apparition but she wasn't. He could tell as he felt the warmth of her, her womanness, as she came closer.

He stood.

"I wasn't sure you would come," she said, holding him with her eyes.

He smiled halfway. "I thought the same thing about you." He extended his hand toward the seat opposite him. "Please sit. Can I order something for you?"

"No. Thanks. This water is fine."

His voice intimately lowered, drawing her closer. "Can you tell me what happened?"

Rayne pushed her purse to the far side of the table. She looked around, half expecting hospital security to tell her it was time to go back inside, or Gayle to ask if she was hungry, needed something.

This was her first taste of freedom in months. Curious that it should begin with Robert. But of course it could be no other way.

"Before you say anything," Robert said, leaning forward, "tell me how you are. Really."

Tentatively she placed her hand atop his and floated into the depths of his eyes. "Better," she said softly. "Day by day."

She took a long breath and reached for the glass of water. "I needed to let you know that I was all right," she began. "One of the doctors was planning to use . . . shock treatment on me."

Robert saw her shiver. He cupped her hand. "I know. I heard. Where are you staying?"

Rayne told him how Pauline had managed to get her out of the facility, and her subsequent stay with Gayle and all that entailed.

Robert slowly shook his head in wonder. "You mean a lot to them, both of them," he said. "I'm just glad to know you're all right."

Someone dropped a quarter into the jukebox and "Ain't No Mountain High Enough" began to play.

Rayne glanced down at her hands wrapped around the glass. "I . . . still have a way to go, Robert, before I'm . . . really well . . . able to . . . be with someone." She looked into his eyes, searching for the understanding she'd always found there. "I know that now. There are things, people in my life, that I have to face, exorcise. I'm almost ready . . . and that's partly because of you."

He frowned in confusion. "Me?"

"I want to thank you for everything. For helping me to remember that I was a person, worthwhile, that the future wasn't just more of yesterday." She smiled, the edges of her mouth trembling. "That I could plant my new dreams and make them grow."

He reached across the table and with the pad of his thumb tenderly brushed away the tear that slid down her cheek. "What is your dream today, Rayne? Tell me."

She closed her eyes and breathed in deeply, the words coming from a place deep inside her. "I dream that both of us will get beyond the pain of our pasts. Find the strength to wrestle free, taking on each day, and not be held in place by what could have been."

As he listened, he shuddered to imagine

what must have happened to her at the hands of her father. His own brief meeting with William Mercer had left him deeply disturbed, mystified that such a man could have fathered Rayne, a topic he chose not to discuss with her. It would serve no purpose to tell her of his troubling meeting with her father.

Watching her now with her eyes closed and listening to the one dream she longed for made him fully understand how special she really was, and what she was willing to face in order to be whole.

Could he do any less?

"Will I see you again?" Robert asked as they faced each other outside the diner.

"One day, I'm sure. I'd like that."

"How will I find you, know where you are?"

She took his hand. "I'll call you." She smiled, looked toward the diner. "Meet here again, sometime. Make new memories." Her eyes sparkled with the play of the afternoon sunshine.

"At least let me drive you back to Gayle's house."

Without warning she wrapped her arms around him, holding him close before she brushed his cheek with a kiss. "I'd like to take a cab. It's something I need to do."

As he watched the cab pull away, a sense of everything being possible replaced the feeling of loss. He would see her again and when he did, they would both be better.

Twenty-seven

The old man's eyes were closed when Robert entered the room. The rhythmic rise and fall of the sterile white sheets was the only sign of life from the once strapping man in the bed.

Robert started to turn away when his father's reed-thin voice reached out to him. "Bobby . . . don't leave, son. Just restin' these old eyes."

Robert smiled weakly and stepped into the room. He took his customary seat beside the railed bed. "How are you today?" He straightened the sheet over the frail body.

"As well as can be expected, I guess." He turned his narrow head toward his son. His brows drew together in a thin black line. "You married, son? Got a family? Can't seem to remember today."

"No, Dad. I'm not married. No family."

Frank nodded his head as if it was all suddenly clear. "You're right. I remember now. Havin' a family is a big responsibility, son. Big responsibility. Don't ever forget that."

"I won't."

"That's why I worked so hard to take care of mine. That's what a man does. A real man." He took a breath of conviction. "What you do for a livin', son? Can't remember." He blinked as if trying to clear the blur in his vision.

"I'm a landscaper."

"Hmm. Work with your hands, with the soil. That's good. No shame in that. Your grandfather worked the land — all his life. Made his livin' like that down in Mississippi." His mouth curved in a smile. "You remind me of him, big, strapping."

"I never knew him."

"Dead before you was old enough to remember." He unearthed some more memories. "Daddy used to get up 'fore the sun to tend to the fields, then he'd go off to work on the white folks' land 'til long after dark. Sometimes he'd come home so tired he couldn't sit down to eat. Just drag himself to bed for a few hours' rest before starting all over again." His gaze drifted away.

" 'Why Papa always so tired, Mama?' I asked my mama one night.

"She pulled my ragged plaid blanket up

to my chin and patted my chest. It smelled like brown soap," Frank said, the memory washing over him.

" ' 'Cause he's workin' so we can eat and pay to stay in this house, baby,' she said."

Frank turned toward his son. "House wasn't no more than a few beaver boards slapped together with cutouts for windows. We used old newspaper to cover them at night," he said, caught up in the hardship of his boyhood. "My mama cooked everything in a huge black pot that sat on some bricks. My room, which wasn't no more than a mat and a box for my few things, was separated from my folks with a curtain made out of a sheet. Didn't have doors or nothin'."

Frank closed his eyes, and Robert thought he'd fallen asleep. A wave of disappointment, a feeling of being cheated, suffused him. This was a snapshot of his father he'd never seen. He wanted more. He wanted to shake him, force him to finish the trip Frank had taken him on when he began to speak.

"I watched what my father endured to take care of us," he said, his voice cracking like old, yellowed paper. "Having to bow and scrape to get a few pennies for his work. But he kept doing it.

" 'I can help you, Daddy,' I told him one day when he actually sat down to eat. He looked so old. His skin was hard and slick as leather from the hours of baking in the Mississippi Delta sun. His fingers curled almost like claws from pulling wheat, corn, cotton. He'd never be able to stand up straight again from those seventy-pound bags he carried on his back. But there was still a pride about him, even though his back was bent.

" 'I want to help take care of things, too,' I told him. 'I can get a job that will pay me some real money.'

" 'Ain't no jobs for black men 'cept what I do.'

" 'But you work hard and don't get nothin' for it. Why can't we live like white folks in a real house with real food? If you was a real man —'

"My mother jumped up from the table and slapped me so hard she knocked me outta my seat onto the floor. She stood over me while I held my burning cheek. I could feel the water filling my eyes.

" 'As long as you live, you will respect your father.'

"Her voice sounded like thunder, deep and booming. I'd never heard her sound like that before. It seemed to reach down into my belly and shake it.

" 'The measure of a man ain't how much money he makes, but what he does to earn it.'

"My father stood and looked down at me. Even with all the agony his body and soul had gone through, I'd never seen such pain in his eyes before. It was the first time I ever saw him look like he would cry.

" 'Every sunrise and set I take this old body of mine out to those fields. I work until my hands bleed.' He held up his curled fingers, stared at them. 'And my limbs burn with weariness. Maybe we don't live like the white folks and never will, but I do what I have to 'cause I am a man. A man provides for his family, whatever that takes. When he stops, he's no longer a man. You wanna live like white folks? They done took everything from us. Our language, our home, our families, our lives. All we got left is our pride, our manhood. And I'd rather be dead than be less of a man.'

"He turned and walked away, leaving me there on the floor."

Frank opened his eyes and looked across at his son. "I never forgot that. I never forgot the pain on his face or the shame I felt for putting it there. I made a vow then and there that I'd make it up to him, make him proud. That's why I worked so hard to take care of my family and myself. Couldn't stand it, son." He slowly shook his head. "Just couldn't. Reason why I had to leave."

Robert's heart thudded. He pressed forward and the door to understanding slowly opened, beckoning to him. "What — do you mean that's why you left?"

"Lost my job. Couldn't find work. Held on as long as I could, pretendin' and all. I knew I wouldn't be able to look at myself in the mirror or look at you, your mama, and sister in the eye. I didn't have a choice. I didn't have any real skills, eighth-grade education. All I knew how to do was work. Drive a truck. When they started cutting back, the black men were the first to be let go. Every day that I was outta work, I'd lose a piece of myself. I walked around for months lookin', having doors closed in my face." Water seeped from beneath his closed lids. Silent. Powerful. Steady.

For several moments, Robert was without words, taking in the enormity of what his father revealed. All these years, all this time, he'd hated his father for abandoning them, for what he believed was without reason. In truth, it was for the greatest of reasons. Conviction and sacrifice. His father had been willing to sacrifice a life he'd built because he believed deep in his soul that he was no longer able to give them what he'd vowed he would.

Robert reached out and stroked his father's paper-thin cheek. For so long he'd believed his father had felt nothing, lost nothing. His father had suffered, too. Suffered the loss of everything that was important to him. He suffered the loss of himself.

He lowered his head, pressing it against his father's chest, reaching out to him for the first time in more years than he could count. He finally understood that a real man had to stand for something no matter what the cost. He must have a bedrock of belief.

Frank reached out and stroked his son's head. "I never stopped loving you all. Never. Wrote to your mother, tried to explain."

Robert raised his head. "She knew?"

Frank nodded. "Told her it would be easier on the whole family if there was one less mouth to feed. She could get government help if I wasn't around." He turned away. "Then my letters started coming back, 'addressee unknown.' Lost track of you all."

Robert's mind raced backward. He remembered the day they'd moved.

"The rent's cheaper," his mother had said.

"But how will Daddy find us?" Nicole asked.

"He won't," Lena answered.

"Your mama still hasn't come to see me," Frank mumbled, his brief interlude with lucidity slowly easing away.

"Dad. Don't go. Not yet." Robert squeezed his father's hand. His throat tightened.

Frank smiled wanly. "Got to get some rest. Got a big day tomorrow. Long drive. You need to get some rest too, son. Get ready for school. Where's your sister?"

"I love you, Dad."

Frank nodded and drifted to sleep.

As Robert walked out of the hospital room, the sounds and smells melding into a potent assault on the senses, he finally understood the true measure of a man. A man stood for something. His beliefs were his foundation, who he was, the base upon which he built his life. If he didn't have that, he had nothing.

He'd built his life on resentment, anger, and pain. Those were his beliefs. They had kept him stagnant, incapable of being whole.

Robert turned the corridor and approached the sealed doors. His reflection wavered in the glass, growing larger. It became clear. Solid.

Finally he understood who *he* was. He'd come from a line of strong, black men. A peace settled in his center. He could only hope that he would one day be the man his father was. The doors slid open. What sacrifice would he be called upon to make? Would he be ready?

Twenty-eight

Pauline was on her way to Gayle's house for her session with Rayne. In the weeks since Rayne had been removed from Cedar, she'd adjusted well and was responsive to therapy. Rayne's brief rendezvous with Robert wasn't the obstacle Pauline thought it would become. The last thing Rayne needed in her life was a romantic distraction.

But it was something beyond attraction between Rayne and Robert Parrish. Something much more substantial. Somehow they'd become important to each other. There was a level of trust, an openness between them that can't be bought or gained by sitting in a room asking questions, as Pauline did. In a way she envied Robert's influence on Rayne, and at the same time she had to applaud it.

Just as Robert was a positive influence on Rayne, oddly enough, so was she for him. When Gayle told her that Rayne had left the house to meet him, Pauline immediately sought him out.

They met at the very same diner where he and Rayne had met only hours earlier.

"I can't begin to tell you how disturbed I am about what went on between you and Rayne," Pauline began, gripping her glass in an effort to control her outrage. "But as much as it disturbs me, I have to admit that it hasn't adversely affected Rayne."

Robert remained quiet, watching her. Although he knew in Pauline's current situation with the hospital, she'd be the last person to turn him in. But he couldn't be sure.

"There's something between the two of you." She frowned a moment. "What is it?"

"Not what you think," he said simply.

"What is it that I think?"

"That there's some sexual thing going on. There isn't. Never was. Am I attracted to her? Yes. Do I have feelings for her? Yes. Would I act on them? No. It's not what she needs from me." He took a long breath and leaned back against the worn red leather seat. "In so many ways she reminded me of my sister, Nicole. Rayne is like an untended bed of flowers, Dr. Dennis. All around her there's nothing but weeds strangling the life out of her. All I tried to do was take the weeds away. Let her know she was worthy of being cared for. Treat her like a person and not an object." He stared directly into her eyes. "Or a subject to be studied."

Pauline took the barb in stride. She brought the glass of water to her lips.

"Her will to survive," he continued, "her natural insights helped me, too."

"How?" she asked, genuinely curious.

He looked away as he thought about their times together, saw them walking on the grounds, working in unison, talking together and sometimes not at all.

"This may sound strange, but in her I was able to see myself. My own weaknesses. With all that she'd endured, she hadn't let it make her bitter inside." He paused, then his voice took on an urgency as if everything depended on making Pauline understand. "Day after day she found a reason to survive. The will to try one more time. I'd let my life cripple me, rule how I felt, what I thought. As I watched her struggle toward the surface, I realized that I could, too. I could swim beyond the hurt, if I was willing to let go of the anchor that held me in place."

He told her about his father, the whole story from the day Frank left his family and what it had done to his family and to him. The telling was a catharsis for him. The final cleansing.

As Pauline listened, she saw herself through his eyes. Each of them had been challenged by a lie, a misconception. Rayne had lived with what her father had done to her, ultimately creating a world and a self where that part of her didn't exist. Robert believed, for the better part of his life, that his father had abandoned them, and it molded the man he had become. Who he was had been created by the lack of truth.

Her own silence, her lack of inner strength because of the secret *she'd* harbored for so many years, had allowed a young woman's life to be erased, altered forever. For years she'd lied to herself, believing that if she pushed away the ugliness, kept it from the world, it would forever remain hidden. In truth, it was a lie. What is done in the dark will one day see the light.

And what of Gayle? She, too, was one of the fractured souls, trapped in a myth of misconceptions and hidden truths — her silent guilt about her marriage, her relationship with Rayne, and her feelings for Rayne's husband. The quietness, the turning away, had caused a snowball effect, which was now barreling down on her.

At the epicenter of them all was Rayne Holland. It was through her shattered image that they had been compelled to see themselves and all their frailties. As she'd traveled along the road to recovery, so did they all.

"I understand it all now," Robert had said, cutting into her thoughts. "And hopefully in the time I have left with my father I'll find a way to build a strong bridge between us."

As she drew closer to her destination, she had a very strong feeling that Robert would bridge that gap between him and his father and be a better man for it. Her remaining concern was Rayne's other self. She hadn't made an appearance since that episode with her father, and Rayne seemed to have no recollection of the incident. But if Rayne were to ever be well, complete, the two would have to merge. The key was to find the trigger to make the transition. When that happened, she knew her job would be done, and her new life, somewhere, would have to begin.

As she pulled onto Gayle's lush tree-lined block, the solitude and comfort of the old neighborhood surrounded her. Cars were parked neatly in the driveways. Lawns were manicured. Several newspapers still lay untouched on porches. A group of three or four children were spraying one another with hoses to cool themselves from the blistering August heat. Their giggles and squeals of delight echoed up and down the block. Yet in all the sameness, she sensed that today would be the turning point. She wasn't sure how, or why she knew, she just did. For as much as Rayne had journeyed on her own, Pauline knew that she must help her across those last dangerous miles, for everyone's sake.

"She's out in the yard," Gayle said, drying her hands on a black-and-white dish towel, as she led Pauline through the house. "We just finished lunch. Can I get you something?"

"No, I'm fine, thanks. How is she today?"

Gayle slowed her step, then stopped and turned. She leaned for a moment against the island kitchen counter, angled her head a bit to the right.

"She's . . . herself, but different." She shook her head, knowing she wasn't making sense. "How can I explain it? We talk, you know. I mean really talk. Not just me running my mouth and Rayne going along. She finally talked to me about Paul and why she married him. At least one of the reasons."

"Did she?"

Gayle nodded.

"What did she tell you?"

Gayle took a breath. "She thought he could protect her. Make her feel safe."

"From what?"

"I don't know. That she wouldn't tell me."

A flash of William Mercer flared before Pauline's eyes. "Did Rayne live at home until she married Paul?"

"No. We went away to college right after graduation. When we came back to Georgia, we both got our own places."

"Did she talk to you about the accident at all, anything that happened that day?" Pauline asked, wanting to know if Rayne had spoken to Gayle about the note she'd found in Paul's pocket.

"No. That's still a very painful subject. Anytime I'd bring it up, she'd shut down."

"Hmm. Have you noticed anything . . . different about Rayne since she's been here?"

"Like what?"

"Any odd or out-of-character mannerisms, changes in her personality?" She really wanted to determine if Rayne's other self had made her presence known to Gayle.

Gayle's nose crinkled. "No," she said, drawing out the word. "Nothing that I can think of. Why?"

"Just wondering. Sometimes that happens during treatment," she said, giving her a pat response. "Speaking of which, I'd better get started."

"Did you want to use the living room?"

"Actually, I think we'll talk outside today."

"Sure." Gayle folded the towel and hung it neatly on the rack by the window. "I have some errands to run. Tracy is at the park with my neighbors, and James —" Her voice drifted away.

"How are things between you? Better?"

Gayle emitted a weak chuckle. "Let's put it this way, they're not worse. We still have some things to work out. But I believe we will."

"I think it's worth the effort."

"So do I," Gayle said, and knew that she really meant it. "See you in about an hour." She started to leave when Pauline's statement stopped her.

"A great deal of what will help it to work is being honest with yourself, each other, and your daughter. I'm telling you this as a doctor and a friend of sorts. Your daughter won't benefit from silence or keeping her in a world of fantasy. If you want to be a family, Gayle, then make every member a part of it. Tracy is much more resilient than you think."

Pauline walked through the back door of the kitchen out into the yard, leaving Gayle with her conscience. She found Rayne stretched out on a green-striped lounge chair, reading Fitzgerald's *Tender Is the Night*.

"Interesting choice," Pauline commented as she approached, thinking of how the main character's madness had driven the man who loved her mad as well.

Rayne looked up, shielding her eyes with the cup of her hand. She smiled. "He's one of my favorites." She closed the book, letting it rest on her stomach. "I read every chance I got when I was little. I always felt it was the best free vacation you could get."

They both laughed.

Pauline sat down opposite her.

"It's true," Rayne said. "Sometimes, I could actually see the moors that Heathcliff rode across in *Wuthering Heights*, or feel the passion and pain in the prose of Ralph Ellison's *Invisible Man*." She sighed.

"I suppose that's why it was so easy for me to get involved in filmmaking. It was a way to get my vision across, to create images and ideas."

"Do you also think that maybe it was something you could control?" Pauline asked.

Rayne hesitated. "In a way."

"Do you feel you had control over your life, Rayne?"

Rayne looked away. Her slender bronze fingers gripped the edge of the book. "No. Not really. Maybe not ever."

"Why?"

"I . . . just didn't."

"You must feel there's a reason."

"I don't know."

"If you didn't have control over your life, then who did?"

Rayne didn't answer.

"Was it your father?"

She flinched.

"Paul?"

She gripped the book tighter and crossed her outstretched legs.

"Who, Rayne?"

"I — I don't want to talk about this today."

"We need to talk about this. It's time we thought about getting you back out into the world. The real world. On your own. You can't stay here forever. You know that."

Rayne turned her head away. It was safe here. Safer than the hospital. Since she'd been here the shadows had stayed away. The terror of finding someone in her room had disappeared. What would happen if she left, went back home? What if it came? It said it would.

"You must face your fears, or they will always haunt you. You have to find a way to deal with them in order to conquer them and be whole. You . . ."

Slowly Rayne turned toward Pauline, her gaze flat and smooth like a polished stone.

"She's scared, Doc," the other self said in that edgy, almost barroom voice. "Don't know why you keep pushin' her like that. You know she can't take it." She grasped her hair in both hands and pulled it behind her head. Then looked curiously at the book on her lap before placing it on the ground beside the chair. "Always reading. Never anything I like, though," she mumbled.

Pauline felt the hair on her arms begin to tingle.

"Is that why you're here, now, to protect Rayne from being hurt — scared?" Pauline asked, studying the subtle transformation. There was a streetwise assurance, a sassiness about this one that was lacking in the Rayne she'd come to know.

"Of course. She can't handle it. Never could."

"Do you remember when you first had to . . . protect her?"

She pursed her lips. "Sure. When that rat bastard father of hers raped us." She sucked her teeth. "I told her she should tell somebody, but she was too scared."

"Why didn't you tell?"

The other self frowned. "Not really sure. I guess it's because I really can't do what she doesn't want."

"But you just told me."

She smiled like a surprised child. "You're right. I did, didn't I?"

"Why do you think that happened?"

She shrugged. "She must have wanted me to tell you, I guess." She frowned, confused.

"Have you ever shown yourself to anyone beside me?"

"Sure. Plenty of times. Like in math class. If you ask her, she can't do decimals. Rayne hates math. Used to go into a panic at test time." She laughed. "I took the math classes for her. I'm a whiz at math."

Her mouth twisted to the side in thought. "Most people just look at me funny and say, 'This doesn't seem like you, Rayne,' or 'You sure aren't yourself today,'" she singsonged, then broke out laughing, slapping her thigh.

Pauline smiled indulgently. "Can you tell me about any of those times?"

"Hmm. Let me think." Her brows drew together in a line of concentration. "Oh, yeah! When I told Gayle I wasn't going to college in Atlanta, that I was going to New York to study film." She grinned. "You should have seen her face. She thought I was crazy." Her expression sobered and her voice dropped to a monotone. "I had to leave. We had to get away."

"From Rayne's father?"

"Yeah. I wasn't going to let him hurt us again." Her features hardened by degrees.

"Does Rayne remember any of the rapes?"

The other self shook her head, looked off beyond Pauline. "No. Not really. She only remembers the fear, the shadows, the notion of someone coming. She's not sure what. I try to protect her from that, you know." She bit off the tip of her nail on her index finger and spit it onto the grass. "Oh, yeah, and the time I scared the hell

413

outta Paul and told him he wasn't gettin' any. That was funny. Stopped him right in his tracks. And the time I jumped up and knocked that son-of-a-bitch father on the floor to keep him off her. That was just before that crazy girl cut her wrists. Damn near killed us both."

Her throat worked up and down. "She . . . she wanted to end things. But I —" She poked herself in the chest. "I feel the pain, take the abuse. And I remember every fuckin' thing." Her eyes suddenly filled. "Oh, shit. I can't be crying. That's not me." She swiped the tears away.

"It's okay to cry," Pauline said gently. "It's okay to be afraid. We all have those feelings."

She blinked repeatedly as if the action would make sense of what Pauline said.

"Not me, I'm not afraid of anything. She's the one who cries all the time. It's annoying. Shows your weakness and then people take advantage of you. Like Paul."

Pauline sat up a bit straighter. "Tell me about Rayne and Paul. Can you?"

"Well . . ." She shook her head in doubt. "That's kind of personal, Doc. They were married."

"But you were there. You said you know

414

everything." Pauline leaned back. "Maybe you don't."

The other self angled her head and grinned, then wagged her finger at Pauline. "Got me on that one. Well, I suppose I could tell you." She thought a moment, then lowered her voice just above a whisper. "I don't want her to hear this," she said.

Pauline nodded in agreement and fascination.

"She always thought if she whined and cried it would stop him."

"Paul?"

"Yeah, that's who we're talking about, right?"

"Yes. I'm sorry. Go on."

"But it only made him angry. He thought she was a tease. Paul was a decent guy. He just didn't understand her. He really did love her, but because it was so hard for her to have normal sex —" she whispered the words, "— it used to make him crazy."

"What do you mean?"

"She didn't understand his tenderness, couldn't accept it. Not really. Sex to her meant being taken advantage of, being hurt, humiliated. So she would enrage him on purpose. Even though she wanted

415

something else, something sweet."

"And you would step in to help her through it when he became . . . aggressive?"

"Absolutely. I'd stand right up to him so he couldn't hurt her. See, she doesn't really accept our body, that it's beautiful and can get pleasure as well as give it."

"But you do."

She grinned wickedly. "Of course. Who do you think was always unbuttoning the blouse? Her?" She tossed her head back and roared with laughter. "I'm the one who loves that clingy peach dress." She sucked her teeth again. "Only decent thing she has," she mumbled. "I'm the one who used to stand outside Robert's father's hospital room, waiting for him to look at us. Then she'd get all scared and run. He's a cutie. She likes him, too, but she's too scared to admit it." The other self began to tap her foot to some unheard beat.

"I think that if it weren't for you, Rayne would have never survived," Pauline said with caution. "You're obviously the stronger one."

She eyed Pauline with skepticism. "You really think so?" she asked.

"Yes. I do." The more she'd listened to this "other Rayne," the more she realized that she was in actuality a rebellious child, the one Rayne had never been allowed to become. She was the one who stomped her foot and said no, had the tantrums, the spontaneity, and the provocativeness. And because the aspects of adolescence and all that went with it had been fractured at such an early age, the two parts that would have made the whole had grown up as separate individuals, appearing and disappearing as the need arose.

"Rayne? Can I call you Rayne?"

She shrugged. "Sure. I guess. Everybody else does." She smiled.

Pauline watched her push up the sleeves of her white Oxford shirt, exposing her arms, something *her* Rayne would never do. Pauline began slowly and deliberately, watching for any change in demeanor. She didn't want to lose her. Not yet.

"I was thinking — Rayne — that since you are the stronger one, you could convince her to confront her father with what he'd done to her — to both of you."

She flashed Pauline a dark look. Her eyes narrowed. "She'd never do it. Too scared."

"But *you* could."

"Why should I? That bastard doesn't care what he's done. I'm just going to make sure he doesn't touch us again." She turned up her palms and stared at the scars on her wrists. "Look at what he made her do. I tried to stop her, but that time she just wouldn't listen. It was weird. It was like she was suddenly stronger than me." She turned wide-eyed on Pauline. "But how could that be?"

"Rayne is strong, too. In her own way, she's strong. She's the one who goes on day to day. She's the one who lives with this unnamed, unseen fear she can't quite remember because you won't tell her. She's the one struggling to be well, really well and whole. But to do that she truly needs your help this time. More than ever. She'll never get better, be stronger, because you won't let her. Maybe you're the one who's really scared."

"Shut up. I told you I wasn't scared of nothing," she said, with a bit less conviction.

Pauline pressed forward and took her hands. "Just think how strong the two of you would be if you came together, worked and thought together as one individual. One strong, beautiful, talented woman with a promising future ahead of her."

The other Rayne's eyes danced across Pauline's face. She heard the words, understood them. "I-I always wanted to know what it would be like to have a real life, a full life. Not this half-existence, like a ghost floating in and out." Sometimes, though, she felt real, and she couldn't tell the doctor this, but it did scare her sometimes. "I felt pain. I felt joy. But it's only sometimes. Other times it's as if I'm looking at the world through a one-way mirror. I can see and hear everything but I'm never a part of it."

"But you can be a part of it. A complete part of it. If you're not afraid."

"How?" she finally asked.

Pauline's heart raced. If what she believed succeeded, she knew this would be the turning point for all of them. "You must convince her to face her father. If Rayne can do that, she can make the leap toward being well and whole. Only you can do it. She can't do it alone. In order for you both to heal it is important that you face the person who hurt you. Confront him with what he's done. You have a choice. You can forgive him or not. It is your decision. And only yours. But I think it's time you finally faced your demon."

She slowly shook her head. "I don't know, Doc."

"I'll go with you. I'll take you there."

"What if she doesn't want to go?"

Pauline straightened and gave her a smile of challenge. "You're the stronger one. Make her go."

Twenty-nine

The car slowed to a stop at the curb. The pink tissue that Rayne held in her hand had been twisted until it lay like pink sprinkles on her lap.

She turned to look at the green-and-white clapboard house. To the passerby it appeared as innocuous as all the others, set back from the street, nestled among the hanging trees that shaded the front porch. No one would ever guess what had taken place behind those doors.

Apprehension, like dew, damp and heavy, clung to her skin. It crept up and down the column of her back, accelerated her heart. Now she wished she'd agreed to let Dr. Dennis come along. In a moment of bravado she'd said she could do this alone. Must do this alone. But she no longer believed she could.

"Of course you can, girl," the other Rayne whispered in her ear. *"I'm right here with you."*

Rayne slowly began to relax. The bizarre

comfort of knowing that she wasn't alone fortified her. She almost smiled. If she'd told anyone that, they would think she was crazy. Just as she'd done when Pauline dropped her bombshell.

Pauline had talked to her at length about the discovery of her other self. The self also named Rayne.

"She is the part of you who witnessed what happened between you and your father. You and Paul," Pauline said. "She said she comes out when you're afraid. She protects you from hurt. The assaults happen to her. That's why you can't remember."

Rayne sat on the couch, stunned, staring at Pauline in disbelief. "You — you're trying to tell me I have some — some spilt personality?" Her voice rose. "Are you?"

"Yes. There are two of you sharing one body, with separate personalities and experiences."

Rayne stood and began to pace the floor in front of Pauline. "So . . . I *am* crazy." Her voice trembled. "Just like Dr. Howell said."

"No. That's not true." Pauline clasped Rayne's shoulders. "Listen to me. You are not crazy," she said, carving out each word. "You've been deeply hurt, to a point that your mind couldn't handle the pain. So it shut down. And your other self was there to absorb the trauma."

Rayne fell back against the couch. For several moments she said nothing but simply stared at a place Pauline could not see.

"Rayne?" Pauline called gently.

Rayne blinked, bringing the room and the present back into focus.

"It . . . would explain so many things," she said, her voice hollow and distant, faint like an echo.

"Tell me what it would explain."

Rayne placed her hands on her lap, linking and unlinking her fingers.

"I don't really remember what my father did to me. But there always was a part of me that believed I knew — something. It was like a dream that you barely re-member, fading as you wake." She paused, gathering the moss of her thoughts. "What stays with me is the fear. Fear of something dark and smothering. Heavy and pressing. A shadow that lurks just beyond my line of vision."

Pauline slowly nodded her head as Rayne's gaze met hers, searching for un-derstanding.

"You need to finally deal with this,

Rayne. If you ever hope to put your life together, have a real loving relationship with a man, accept your body, yourself, you must confront the one person who changed it all. Your father."

Rayne lowered her head, then slowly shook it. "I . . . I don't know if I can."

"I know you can." Pauline leaned forward and took the busy hands in hers, stilling the fingers. "I can help you. The strength to deal with this is right inside of you."

"How?"

"I want to bring her out. Let you hear her tell *your* story. I want to put you under hypnosis."

Pauline had taped the session and for the first time Rayne had full knowledge of what had been inflicted upon her. Knowledge about whole areas of her life she'd been unable to remember clearly.

Rayne stared at the house again. Her hands gripped the steering wheel. She saw herself in the room, listening to the tape, experiencing the eerie feeling of hearing a voice that sounded so much like hers, but different. It was the voice she'd often heard in her head. The one that would tell her everything would be all right.

The retelling was graphic, from the first assault after her mother's death to the last, just before she was sent away to live with her aunt Mae. The voice was full of pain. But beneath it was a fierce determination. A will to survive and win.

There *was* strength in her. She wasn't weak and defenseless as she'd always believed. Had she been, she would have never arrived at this place. She had fought back, in the only way she could.

Rayne turned off the engine and unlocked the doors, just as Edith stepped out onto the porch.

Hearing a car door slam shut, Edith turned toward the approaching figure. She shielded her eyes from the glare of the sun and felt her insides tighten as recognition took hold.

For a moment, she panicked. William's loud threats and rantings about Rayne reverberated in her head. What if he came home and found her? She didn't know if she had the strength to protect her again. But a part of her always knew Rayne would come. She'd both waited for and dreaded this moment.

She looked so fragile, Edith thought, her heart constricting with emotion. Yet there was a purpose in her dark eyes, an assurance in her step. This was not the deranged daughter that William spoke about after his last visit. This was not the same broken woman she'd found crouched on the bathroom floor covered in glass and blood, her eyes glazed, her hair wild. She was not the budding teen who slept with the night-light and hid herself beneath oversized clothing to camouflage her womanness, as if that would somehow neutralize the attraction men had for her. Nor was she the little girl who shrank from being held when she cried herself to sleep at night, unable or unwilling to say what was wrong.

There was something beneath the surface of Rayne. Something beyond the natural beauty and the soft voice. Everyone who came into contact with her seemed compelled by forces stronger than their wills to reach under the cool exterior, to touch her, thaw her.

What could she say to her now? More important, what had Rayne come to say?

Edith's nervous fingers fluttered to her hair, smoothing the gray strands. As Rayne drew nearer, Edith slid her hands into the oversized patch pockets of her faded yellow house coat. She pulled in a deep breath and tried to smile. The edges of her mouth fluttered like the wings of a bird.

Rayne stood on the step below her. Edith wanted to hold her. Tell her how sorry she was. But she didn't.

"Hello, Edith."

She was too thin, Edith thought absently. "How are you, Rayne? You should have called . . ."

Rayne looked at the woman who'd tried to be a mother, but never could, not really. The woman who'd stood silently by while her father, *her* husband, raped her. How many years had she hated the woman in front of her, hated her for not protecting her as a mother should?

Rayne flinched as the thoughts, the images took hold, clawing her throat, cutting off her air. She felt herself being sucked into the abyss of the past, visions flashing before her, on either side of her, reaching out to grab her, make her a part of what was.

". . . I would have prepared something," Edith was saying.

Rayne's descent jerked to a violent halt, the echo of voices and screams bouncing around in her head. Rayne blinked slowly as if arising from a deep sleep. This thing, these spells, had begun shortly after the session of revelations with Dr. Dennis.

In the past week, they'd increased in intensity and frequency. Directly after one of them, she'd feel momentarily weak, disoriented. But soon after the spells departed, she felt stronger, as if a missing brick of who she was had been replaced, fortifying the structure, building the whole.

Rayne suddenly focused on Edith's weary face and for the first time recognized the same pain in Edith's eyes that she'd seen reflected in her own. The realization startled her.

Edith's expression softened. "It's . . . good to see you." A light breeze ruffled the gray hair. She glanced over Rayne's shoulder. "Where are your things? In the car?" She started down the steps. "I'll —"

Rayne clasped her arm. "I don't have any bags. I'm not staying."

The two women faced each other in an instant of revelation.

"I never thanked you —"

"I did what I had to do. I should have done more. I —"

"He hurt you, too, didn't he?"

Edith's eyes darted around the yard, down the path to the street. Her bottom lip trembled.

"Why did you stay? Why didn't you leave him?"

"I guess . . . I thought, prayed, that one day he'd stop seeing Carol's face, your mama. Stop . . . seeing her . . . in you, and finally see me." Edith pressed her lips together, ashamed, yet relieved to have at last said the words.

Rayne's temples began to pound. Her vision grew hazy as if looking through smudged lenses . . .

She was in her room, upstairs. Her suitcase was open on the bed, filled to bursting. She was a week from her sixteenth birthday and she was being sent away. Torn away from everything that was familiar: Gayle, school, the community she'd grown up in. She should be sad. A part of her was afraid of starting over. Even as frightened as she was at times, there was a macabre sense of the familiar. She had no idea what any other type of life would be like. This was all she knew. And because of that, she had no clear understanding of why she was being sent away. The only thing she was certain of was that Edith was the force behind her exile.

"You'll like it at your aunt Mae's house," Edith said from the doorway of Rayne's room.

Rayne turned. A single line ran between

her brows. Something inside her shifted. "How would you know?" She stuffed a pair of jeans into the suitcase and squeezed it shut.

"Your aunt Mae is a real sweet woman. She'll look after you. She always wanted to have kids."

"So you got tired of having me around and figured you'd pass me off on my aunt," Rayne spouted, the unusual nasty tone surprising Edith. Rayne tried not to cry. "I can take care of myself. I don't need somebody to take care of me."

"That's not true, Rayne," Edith said, twisting her hands in front of her. "You do need somebody." She stepped into the room. "You'll —" She looked over her shoulder. "You'll be safe there." She walked closer.

Edith looked as if she wanted to embrace her, Rayne thought, and for an instant wished that she would. But she didn't.

Edith's voice lowered. "Things will be better for you. It's the best I can —"

"What the hell's going on up there?" William yelled from the bottom of the stairs. "Mae's down here waitin'. She ain't got all day."

Rayne snatched her suitcase from the bed, brushed by Edith, and never looked back.

★ ★ ★

She remembered that day. Clearly. For the first time, she remembered. Edith had been the one who'd sent her away. But not for the reasons she'd always believed. She understood that now as she looked upon the weathered face, the sadness in the soft brown eyes that had seen too much.

Rayne reached out to touch her cheek. "Edith, I —"

"What are you doing here, girl?"

Edith shrunk back as Rayne turned toward the all-too-familiar drawl.

William strode toward the two women, his broad figure at once intimidating. And for a moment she was that frightened young girl who feared the sound of nightfall. She wanted to run. She wanted to curl up in a ball so he couldn't touch her. Wouldn't hurt her. And as he drew closer, the two Raynes battled, one needing to bury the memories forever, the other demanding to resurrect them. In the end they stood side by side.

He looked Rayne up and down. "You done turned that hospital on its ear, runnin' off like that." He wiped his brow with the back of his hand. "I had a good mind to sue that place and everybody in it," he bellowed, waving his hands in the air.

431

He squinted at Rayne. "You on any kind of medication, girl?" He wiped his head again, then his top lip.

"No. I'm not."

"Hmm. Dinner ready, Edith?"

"Uh, almost. I was just talking to Rayne here, and —"

"Is that right. Now did I ask you all that?"

"No, but I was —"

"You was what? Runnin' off at the mouth instead of seein' to dinner."

"Leave her alone."

William jerked as if he'd been slapped. His eyes narrowed. "What did you say?"

"I said: leave her alone." Each word was sharp, meant to make her point.

William chuckled, a nervous edge that made it wobble. "You *are* crazy." He tried to walk past her. "I'm gonna call that hospital right now, and have 'em come get you. Right now."

"I know what you did."

The air around them ceased to move. Conversation between the nested birds came to an abrupt halt.

William stopped short.

Edith's hand flew to her mouth.

He spun around, his features pinched. He tilted his head to the side. "Go in the house, Edith," he said under his breath.

Edith snatched a look at Rayne, then hurried in the house.

William's shoulders inched up toward his ears, his back curved slightly like a boxer preparing to defend his title. He swiped at his brow.

"Yeah. I put you in a place so you could get better. Get some help. Damn near scared me to death when you tried to kill yourself, baby girl."

"I know what you did to me after Mama died," Rayne said. Her voice was a flat, hard line.

The corners of his mouth quivered. "All I did was take care of you."

"You raped me, Dad-dy," she slung at him. "Over and over again."

"You crazy, girl. I ain't never touch you." Sweat trickled down his cheek.

"You tried again the day I cut my wrists. That's why I did it. I didn't want you touching me ever again."

His face reddened in fury. "I'm callin' the hospital —"

"I'm not the only one who knows. Not anymore."

William's chest heaved in and out. "Nobody would believe that kind of foolishness," he said, losing his bravado by degrees.

"But they do believe me."

William stood in front of her, frozen.

"Why, Daddy? Why? I trusted you. I needed you. I lost Mama, too."

"You don't know nothing about loss. I lost my wife!" He banged on his chest. "My Carol. The only person who ever loved *me*." He shook his head in denial. "I would never hurt you. Never."

"You did. You ruined my life. What you did to me made everything I touched dirty. *I* was dirty."

"I never touched you," he insisted.

"You — raped — me," she said, giving each word its due.

"No." He shook his head, pointing an accusing finger at her. "That's all in your mind. The doctors said —"

"I lost my life. You stole it from me and I can never get it back. Just like you can never get Mama back. I'm never going to be Mama, Daddy. Never. And neither is Edith. Mama's not coming back. And it's not our fault."

Rayne watched his jaw work, but no words would come.

"Do you know what it's like to be violated, to be afraid to touch yourself, to be touched, to look at yourself? That's what you've done to me. Every time you crept into my room at night, you took another piece of me away." Her voice started to break, but she pressed on, the call of freedom pushing the words forward. "You've made me afraid of who I am, and took away who I could become. Oh, yes, Daddy, I know what loss is. Maybe one day you'll be able to look at yourself in the mirror, Daddy, and see what you've done. Who you are."

She walked past him and up the steps. "I'm leaving now. I'm not coming back, and I'm taking Edith with me."

His body seemed to deflate, like air let out of a tire. He simply stood there. Accused.

Upstairs, in the bedroom, the two women faced each other. One on either side of the bed.

"It's over, Edith," Rayne said calmly. "He can't hurt me anymore, and he can't hurt you, unless you let him."

Edith shook her head. "I don't know what you want from me. I told you I did what I could."

"I want you to be the woman you showed me you were all those years ago when you sent me away — to protect me. You stood up to him, maybe for the first time in your life. I don't know what you said or how you did it, but you did. You won. Now it's your turn. Come with me. Let me protect you."

"I . . . I can't leave him. He's my husband. I love him."

"But he doesn't love you."

Edith reeled back as if slapped.

"He forgot how to love when he lost Mama. And there will never be anything you can do about that. It's not your fault. Love is not pain. Love is not anger. Love is a mutual caring for each other, wanting the best for each other. Together."

"But all these years . . ."

"All these years have been a lie, a hiding from the truth of what it really was. You have a choice now. You can either continue to live the lie or begin to really live the life deserving of you . . . Mama."

When Rayne finally emerged from the house with Edith, she saw her father's figure outlined against the tree, his head pressed against its trunk, silhouetted against the backdrop of the orange sky. Alone. His body shuddered as the muffled sobs floated along the stillness of the impending evening. And suddenly he wasn't this threatening dark monster that came in the night. He was just a man. A broken man.

She wanted to reach out to him, find a place in her heart to forgive him. But she couldn't. Still, she couldn't completely harden her heart to him.

"I loved you, Daddy," she whispered, just as she closed the door to the car and pulled away.

Thirty

Gayle flung open the door at the sound of a car pulling into the driveway. The last thing she expected to see was Rayne ushering Edith Mercer into her home.

Edith's eyes were empty as if someone had gone in and turned out the light, cut away the soul, Gayle thought, alarm growing with each footfall.

"Rayne, what happened?"

"Can I take her upstairs?" Rayne asked, her own eyes red and swollen.

"Uh, of course. Sure." Gayle stepped aside to let them pass, her thoughts running out of control. "Are you all right?"

Rayne didn't answer, but continued down the hall and up the stairs to her bedroom.

Gayle pressed her palm to her forehead, watching the stoic procession. First Rayne, now her stepmother. How much more was she expected to deal with? This was stretching the limits of friendship to the breaking point. What could possibly be on

Rayne's mind? Rayne knew she had no love for Edith.

Gayle eased to the foot of the stairs. Muffled voices and muted sobs could be heard from above.

What in heaven's name could have happened over there? When Rayne told her earlier that afternoon that she was going to her parents' home, Gayle had been insistent that she rethink it. Her biggest fear was that William would have Rayne taken back to Cedar Grove.

"Your father wants you back in the hospital, Rayne," Gayle had said, pacing back and forth across the black-and-white kitchen tiles. "And you know what's waiting for you there."

"I have to go, Gayle."

Gayle stopped short her pacing. "Why? Just explain to me why. You're getting better, stronger, every day. I don't want to see anything happen to you. Not after all this."

"If I don't go, I'll never get better."

"Rayne, for God's sake, look at what everyone has put on the line for you." Her voice escalated to that edgy pitch. "I put my marriage on the auction block. Dr. Dennis has lost her job and possibly her career. And all because we want to help you! This is our thanks? You're going to throw it all back in our faces?"

"Gayle, you have no idea what's really at stake here. Do you think I don't realize what everyone has done for me? Of course I do. Maybe this may sound selfish, but this is my life I'm fighting for."

Gayle stared at Rayne for a moment. "It's always been about you, hasn't it, Rayne? Everything you've ever wanted, you got. For as long as I can remember, people have gone out of their way to please you, give you what you needed. Do you ever think about anyone other than yourself? What about me, Rayne? What about me?"

Rayne felt her eyes burn and her throat knot. A part of her wanted to crawl into a tight ball, shield herself from the angry words, the accusation in Gayle's eyes. She wanted to hide away in her bedroom until all the ugliness that was rearing up between her and Gayle had passed. But the other Rayne wouldn't let her. Not this time. She felt the strength, the determination. And she knew she couldn't back down. If she did, she would be lost forever.

Her head began to pound and the shadows ran loose in her mind, waiting to swallow her if she didn't hurry.

Gayle snatched the keys from the hook above the sink, turned, and tossed them on the table.

"Take them. And I hope to hell you know what you're doing." Gayle spun away and stormed out into the backyard where Tracy was on the swing, slamming the screen door behind her.

Gayle thought about that now as she heard the bedroom door above softly close. She quickly moved away from the stairs and into the living room as Rayne came down.

"Thank you," Rayne said to Gayle's back.

"I'm not too sure I want to be thanked," Gayle responded, refusing to face her friend.

Gayle walked toward the compact bar and poured herself a tumbler of rum and Coke. Drinking was something she rarely did, but she felt as if she needed one now. She turned the glass in her hands, listening to the sound of the ice tinkling against the sides.

"I'm going to start dinner. Should I fix enough for — Edith?"

"Gayle, please, look at me."

Gayle slanted her eyes in Rayne's direction, but refused to turn around.

"Fine, don't. Then just listen."

Rayne folded her arms beneath her breasts and slowly crossed the expanse of the living room. Intermittently, she fingered a photograph here, touched a sculpture there, as she tried to sort through her thoughts, find a way to explain the lie she'd lived most of her life.

"The things you said to me earlier," she began, slow and deliberate, "finally forced me to see myself as you saw me, and maybe everyone else. But they don't matter, Gayle. You do."

Gayle briefly lowered her head, then took a sip of her drink.

"I never took our friendship for granted. Never. I know I may have seemed distant, or only thinking of myself. A part of me was, for my survival. I lived in fear, Gayle, every day of my life. Fear that it would happen again. Fear that someone would find out and realize that I wasn't Miss Perfect, but a soiled, dirty little girl, a used teenager, an unworthy woman. That somehow they would believe I let it happen, wanted it to happen."

Gayle's heart began to pound. Suddenly she felt warm with the slick heat of apprehension, as the unthinkable crept beneath her skin, raising the hair. Slowly she turned toward Rayne.

"What are you telling me?" she asked, her words dropped like stones, one at a time.

Rayne pressed her lips together, briefly looked away, gathering her courage to speak the words.

"My father — raped me." Her nostrils flared as she sucked in air. "It started when I was six years old."

Gayle felt the air leave her body, as her stomach rolled, concaving her chest as if she'd been hit. Her eyes widened as she tried to find words, but none would come.

Rayne lowered her gaze and turned partially away, unwilling to face whatever was in Gayle's eyes.

"It went on until I was sent away to live with my aunt Mae," she continued, taking Gayle along the road of shame and horror. "Edith didn't send me away to get rid of me. She sent me away to save me from my father. And all these years . . ." She shook her head.

Rayne told Gayle of her fear of closeness, her inability to show deep emotion, to allow anyone to truly care for her.

"I know it was hard on Paul," Rayne said, her voice far away and filled with regret. "He did the best he could, but he didn't understand what was wrong with me, why I couldn't be a real wife to him. And I was unable to help him. I didn't understand either."

Gayle remembered the abbreviated conversations she'd had with Paul, the many times he'd eluded to something being wrong between him and Rayne. Now she understood why. God, how could she not have known that something was deeply wrong with Rayne? Why didn't she see that things weren't right in the Mercer household? She'd been so preoccupied with her own petty jealousies and insecurities that it was easier to lay blame at Rayne's feet. How could she have called herself a *friend?*

"I don't blame you for loving Paul, Gayle." She looked Gayle in the eyes, her mouth in a tight smile. "I also know that you would never betray our friendship because of that love."

Gayle tugged on her bottom lip with her teeth. Her eyes filled. "Rayne — I —"

"It's all right. I found the letter. I found it the night of the accident."

Gayle slowly sat down on the loveseat, covering her face with her hands.

"I told him I found it," Rayne said. "I

told him in the car, on our way home from the awards."

Gayle looked up, the rims of her eyes streaked with mascara.

"I told him I understood how easy it was for him to turn to you. You were the closest person to me." She took a long breath. "During my time at Cedar Grove, my thoughts, my memory, and emotions were so twisted by despair that I believed you'd slept with Paul. I almost wanted to believe it so I could somehow justify shutting down, shutting you out. Yet there was a part of me that struggled against that, knew better. It just wasn't strong enough until I was ready to let it go."

Rayne caressed a framed picture of herself, Paul, Gayle and James, Desi and Tracy on their annual picnic. Images of better days flashed across her mind, jostled her heart. She adjusted the picture on the mantel. "I'd buried Paul's and my last conversation. I suppose the whole trauma of his and . . . Desi's death made it almost necessary to forget because the pain —" her voice caught, "— of losing them was so unbelievably hard. He . . . told me everything . . ."

"Nothing ever happened between us, Rayne. I swear it," Paul said, tearing out of the

445

parking lot and onto the wet highway. The rain was coming down in blinding sheets. He was driving so fast. I asked him to slow down. He wouldn't.

"If it had, I don't know if I could blame you. I haven't been much of a wife to you, Paul. I realize that. At least in the physical sense. And it's destroying our marriage. It's turning you into someone else, someone mean and cruel, not the man I married. It's making me feel less and less worthy as a person every day."

"Rayne —"

"I want to change things, Paul. I want our marriage to work. I want to be well. But I don't know where to begin, what to do." He hit the curve on two wheels.

"Baby, I'll help you. Whatever it takes. We'll do it together. I promise you that."

"Paul, I'm so sorry. For everything."

"I love you, Rayne. That's all that matters. We'll get through —"

"Those were the last words I heard him say. The next thing I remember was blinding headlights ahead of us, the sound of tires squealing, trying to gain traction on the wet road.

"Paul instinctively grabbed my hand. I turned to look behind me at Desiree.

446

There was a sound like an explosion and then nothing. The next thing I remember was waking up in the hospital."

Gayle cried openly now, pushing the tears aside with swipes of her hands, only for them to be immediately replaced.

"How can . . . you . . . ever forgive me?" Gayle asked, her words hinging in her throat. "I blamed you, envied you, wanted to be you for as long as I can remember." She sniffed. "I always had this picture of Rayne Mercer's wonderful life and wondered how come I couldn't have it, too. How come I wasn't as smart, as tall, as pretty, as talented?"

She looked across the room at Rayne. "I wanted to just out and out hate you, Rayne. Hate you for having it all. Hate you for acting like you didn't give a damn. But I couldn't because you never treated me any different or any less, and that made me hate myself for the pettiness I felt. I spent most of my life trying to find ways to be a better version of you, believing your life was so much better than mine." Slowly she shook her head and wiped her eyes.

"Why, Rayne? Why couldn't you tell me? I would have helped you," she choked. "You could have come to me. God, how could you have lived with that all those years — alone? That bastard!"

"Until recently, I didn't remember. All I knew was that I was always scared that I was somehow different from everyone else."

Gayle frowned in confusion. "What do you mean you didn't remember?"

Rayne languidly crossed the room and sat next to Gayle. She folded her hands on her thighs.

"A couple of weeks ago," she began, measuring her words along with Gayle's reaction, "Dr. Dennis . . . helped me to remember . . ."

All Gayle could do was stare in wide-eyed astonishment at what Rayne revealed. *Two people sharing one body.* That only happened in the movies, to someone else's friend. She wasn't sure what she was feeling when Rayne concluded — disbelief, awe, or apprehension.

"I guess I really don't know you at all," Gayle was finally able to mumble, still trying to assemble the pieces of this bizarre puzzle.

"I'm learning who I am day by day, too, Gayle." Rayne angled her body in the seat and took Gayle's hands. "And I'm still afraid. Not of what's hiding in the dark, but what's in the light — right in front of me. I don't know what it's like to share myself with someone. I'm just beginning to learn." She smiled, thinking of Robert and their garden at Cedar Grove. "But I want to have a friend along the way to make sure I do it right."

Gayle's bottom lip trembled. "I haven't been a friend," she said, her voice shaking. "Not the kind you needed, when it mattered the most."

Rayne squeezed Gayle's hands. "Who else but a friend would have stuck with me all these years, and in her own way loved me unconditionally, even when I didn't give it back? Who else but a friend would have taken me into her home at the risk of her own marriage?"

She released Gayle's hands and stroked her cheek. "If that's not a friend, then none of us knows what one is. I can only pray I'll be that kind of friend to you one day."

Sitting there, facing the one person whom she thought she knew better than anyone, Gayle realized that it wasn't Rayne who she didn't know, it was herself. She'd built and lived her life based on false impressions, hidden truths, unstable foundations. As a result she'd created a person whose inner self was simply a fabrication.

If she stripped away the jealousies, the half-truths, the envy, and feelings of competitiveness, who would she find? And when she did, because she knew she must, would this Rayne who sat before her still be willing to call her *friend?* Would she be able to look in the mirror and finally feel good about the person reflected there, the person she would need to become? If Rayne could, after all she'd endured, find the will to face the unbelievable challenges ahead of her, how could she do any less?

A slow smile of acceptance eased across Gayle's mouth. "You know I've always been a sucker for a sob story," she said, sniffing away the remainder of her tears.

Rayne laughed, truly laughed, feeling the weight lift from her heart and spirit. She opened her arms to her friend and their laughter mixed with tears, and a joy filled her as she saw them reflected in the mirror that hung on the wall.

Suddenly a crack appeared in its center and spread like a spider's web until it crumbled and fell at her feet in her father's bathroom, hairbrush in hand. Her reflection taunted her with countless broken shards. It was her, fractured pieces of a whole, unable to be put together. Broken.

Before her eyes flashed images of the

past, the abuse, the torment she'd suffered, the losses, the challenges she'd faced. She saw the garden, where the healing began, and Robert, who told her it was possible. There were Paul and Desiree, playing in the yard. She saw Gayle who'd always held out her hand, and Pauline who risked so much. And she saw her father, a tortured, troubled, and lonely man.

And with each image she saw herself. She had managed to survive even at her weakest point. She was here. She was alive. She *was* strong.

Finally, believing that, accepting that — like watching a movie in reverse — one by one the cracks began to seal. The fallen pieces of her life were filled until the mirror reflected what was truly before it. One piece. One reflection.

The final break was mended.

"Thank you, Gayle," she whispered.

Epilogue

Six Months Later

This was the most difficult thing she'd ever have to do. For weeks she'd battled against making the call, coming to this place, exposing herself. She stood in front of the closed door. The sound of muffled voices could be heard from the other side. She reached for the knob, turned it, and stepped inside, unsure of what she would find.

Smiles greeted her, welcomed her with their eyes.

"Come in. Have a seat and join us. We were just getting started."

She took a seat on one of the floor pillows that circled the room.

"Why don't we start over here," the group leader said. "Tell us your name and why you are here."

One by one the women gave their names and told their stories, stories so much like her own. Sooner than she would have liked it was her turn. All eyes looked in her direction, not with curiosity or condemnation but with compassion.

She pulled in a deep breath, looked at all the waiting faces. "My name is . . . Pauline Dennis and my uncle raped me when I was nine years old . . ."

Rayne sat on her porch, swinging on the white wood bench, writing in her journal. It was a lovely day in Savannah. Not too hot, just enough puff in the air for a breeze, and a sweet bed of sunshine that was cozy enough to relax against. Yes, a new day. Rayne looked across the green grass and saw all the hope waiting out there for her, just beyond that ridge. Soon. She felt it. It was coming. She returned to her writing.

Still it is strange and sometimes painful to be back in the home that I shared with Paul and Desiree. But it's becoming easier. Rather than let the memories overwhelm me, I embrace them, allow them to comfort me.

I received a letter from Dr. Dennis, and her lawsuit against Cedar Grove for questionable practices is currently in litigation. She's since moved to New York and is thinking of starting a practice there after she deals with some of her own issues, she wrote. "We have much more in common than you think, Rayne," she'd said in her letter. I wonder what that means?

Edith called this morning and she sounds really good. Moving to Louisiana with her sister was the best thing for her. I'm going to try to get down to see her for Christmas.

My father — well, who knows? I haven't seen or spoken to him since that day in the yard. Every night before I go to bed I pray for the compassion to forgive him. I'm getting there. Day by day.

Even as I make these entries, Gayle and James are on their second honeymoon and she's talking about having another baby. I'm really happy for them. Who would have thought that Gayle would risk losing her figure again? Changes.

The sound of a car moving into the drive pulled Rayne away from her notes. She closed her journal and stood, shielding her eyes against the glare.

The car door opened and Robert stepped out.

Warmth and a sense of ease gradually flowed through her as he drew closer. How did he know where to find her? she wondered. His familiar smile greeted her.

"You're just as I remember," he said, stopping on the opposite side of the porch. He glanced briefly around. "This is the perfect setting for you, Rayne. Beautiful and tranquil."

Rayne pulled in a breath. "I'm finally beginning to think so. I even started my own garden out back, just like you taught me."

She rested her hands on the railing and Robert covered them with his. "Gayle told me you'd come home. I wanted to visit before now to see how you were, but I wasn't sure if I should."

"I'm glad you did." She hesitated, uncertain of where they were going. "How's your father?"

"Some days are better than others. But I've made my peace, with him and myself."

"We've all made a peace of sorts over these past months."

"That's what I came to tell you." He looked away, briefly, then back at her. "Meeting you changed me somehow, Rayne. Talking with you and watching you

battle the ghosts inside you showed me I
had to face mine as well." His hands tightened around hers. "You'll never know how
much those days in the gardens meant to
me. How they helped to heal me."

"They did for me, too."

"I think I knew that, hoped that." He
looked into her eyes, the softness there, the
pain. But he also saw something else: a
strength and determination that had been
missing at Cedar Grove. The wariness was
gone, the uncertainty. This was a different
woman, a richer one. It was both disconcerting and challenging. "I'm leaving for
California in the morning," he finally said.

"Oh."

"I've tracked down my sister, Nicole, to
Vallejo, just outside of San Francisco. I want
to tell her about our father, what really happened. Maybe she'll even come back and
see him — make her peace."

"All you can do is plant the seed," she
said with a wise smile. "It's up to her if she
wants to see it grow."

He smiled and shook his head in
wonder. "Yes, it is, isn't it? Well — I'd
better go. I still have to pack."

"I hope everything works out for you,
Robert. I really do."

"I'd like to tell you about it when I get

back. Maybe you could meet Nicole."

"I'd like that."

He looked at her a moment, then brought her hands to his lips, dropping a light kiss there. "Take care of yourself, Rayne." He released her.

"You do the same."

He paused a moment, then turned and headed for his car.

Rayne watched him until the car was out of sight. She turned and picked up the journal, holding it to her chest.

The sun was beginning to set. The sky was aglow with the waning orange beacons of light. Rayne inhaled deeply of the scents, letting them fill her.

Walking around to the back of the house, she looked out at her blooming garden, the riot of color, the feeling that all was possible.

"I hope he does come back," she said. "He's a special man."

She waited for the answering voice that had always dwelled in the recesses of her mind. Hearing nothing, she smiled.

She was alone. One with herself. At last.

References

Countertransference in Psychotherapy with Incest Survivors: When the Therapist Is a Survivor of Child Abuse: Karen W. Saakvitne, Ph.D., Traumatic Stress Institute, South Windsor, Conn. Paper presented at the 99th Annual Convention of the American Psychological Association, San Francisco, Cal. 1991.

The Courage to Heal: A Guide for Women Survivors of Child Sexual Abuse: Ellen Bass and Laura Davis.

The Art of Psycho-therapy: Anthony Storr.

The Logic of Forgetting Childhood Abuse: Betrayal Trauma: Jennifer J. Freyd.

Transference Neurosis and Psychoanalytic Experience: Perspective on Contemporary Clinical Practice: Gail S. Reed, Ph.D.

24 Stages of Growth for Survivors of Incest: Developed by Karen Uson, M.A. Based on the work of John Dean, Ph.D. "Outcome Milestones for Treatment Evaluations," copyright 1980.

About the Author

Donna Hill has eighteen published novels to her credit. She is a public relations associate for the Queens Borough Public Library system and runs a promotions and management company, ImageNouveau. She is also a writing instructor at the Frederick Douglass Creative Art Center in New York. Donna lives with her family in Brooklyn, New York. You may visit her at www.donnahill.com.

Reader's Guide available at www.stmartins.com.